Trace of Evil

MARGO CAREY

CHAMPAGNE BOOK GROUP

Trace of Evil

This is a work of fiction. The characters, incidents and dialogues in this book are of the author's imagination and are not to be construed as real. Any resemblance to actual events or persons, living or dead, is completely coincidental.

Published by Champagne Book Group
712 SE Winchell Drive, Depoe Bay OR 97341 U.S.A.

~~~

First Edition 2022

pISBN: 978-1-957228-52-5

Cover Art by Melody Pond

www.champagnebooks.com

Version_1
~~~

To my two Pauls: my husband for his patience and belief in me, and my son for our late-night brainstorming sessions.

Dear Reader:

Salem, Massachusetts is the perfect setting for a romance plagued by witches and ghosts. You can find any number of ghostly events around the city or consult a witch or two about your future. I based the idea for this book on a city that caters to the supernatural, my love of gothic mysteries, and my belief that psychic energy is all around us. I hope you enjoy reading it.

Prologue

Salem, MA, 1698

Her agonized screams echoed through his mind. Elias Gale leaned forward, every muscle taut, and dug his heels into his steed.

At the crest of the hill overlooking her cottage, he halted. *Too late.* His breath deserted him. Where Rebecca's home had stood, a pile of black rubble smoldered. Pain, sharp as a dagger, pierced his chest. He no longer sensed Rebecca's terror. Her essence was gone.

Spying an old man by the side of the road, Elias leaped off his horse, rushed over, and demanded, "What occurred yonder?"

"It were awful," he said. His shoulders trembled, and he dropped his gaze to the ground. "I heered her screams all the way to my place." He shook his head. "She were trapped. She ne'er made it out."

Elias gripped the horse's reins to keep from strangling the spineless fool. His voice an agonized growl, he said, "Did no one seek to save her?"

The terrified fellow made a hasty step backward. "I-I can tell no more."

When Elias sneered, the simpleton gasped and scuttled off before Elias's final pronouncement. "Do not fear, Rebecca, my love. I shall ne'er forget."

Chapter One

My mother always told me tripping up the stairs was good luck. If so, this must be the lucky apartment. I pitched forward, but my friend Eddie caught me before I hit the floor. “Sorry, Dani. I should have warned you about that step.”

“No problem.” I inspected my surroundings. “Nice.” I’d fallen into a good-size kitchen. Plenty of oak cabinets and room for a small table.

“Everything you need, right down to the microwave and coffee pot,” he said.

“Great.”

I’d been living with my boyfriend and needed lots of the kitchen essentials people take for granted. I didn’t care, though. I’d be happy to replenish whatever I needed if it meant I never had to see Tom Westin again. I inspected the front door. A heavy-duty lock. Good.

The window above the sink framed a pigeon as it burst from the leaves of a large maple tree. I grinned as I ran my hands along the smooth countertop. Hope fluttered. This rental was much nicer than the others we’d visited today. It might be the one. At a sudden tingling in my neck, I glanced behind me and blinked. Did I just miss something? A trick of the light, no doubt. The empty room unnerved me, and I hurried to catch Eddie.

An archway in the kitchen led to a small, comfortable living area. Three windows channeled the late afternoon sun, adding to the warmth of an already-hot August day. My clammy tank top clung to me. Even my hair was heavy. When I reached to lift the mop off my shoulders, Eddie stared and adjusted his glasses.

“It’s a little stuffy in here.” He grabbed the neck of his polo shirt and tugged the fabric away from his skin. “The apartment’s been vacant for a few months. If you lower the shades and open the windows, the cooler air should make you more comfortable.”

I checked out the clean white walls and hardwood floor. "Good." The small bookcase built into the wall on my right made me smile. Oh, yeah. I could picture myself there, cuddled on the sofa lost in the pages of a good mystery.

I pointed to a door at the other end of the room. "What's out there?"

He gave me a big grin. "Your private yard."

"Seriously?" I scooted over and peeked out. Sure enough, there was a small, fenced-in plot of grass. I nodded in approval. Private and secure. I swung back. "It's perfect!"

My enthusiasm might ruin any attempt to negotiate, but I didn't care. Besides, Eddie was a friend. We worked for the same management company, and he owned a few buildings in Salem. That's how I'd found this place.

Unable to resist this incredible perk, I opened the door. Eddie took my arm for the two steps down. I chuckled. My hero, with his serious attitude and the lock of brown hair tumbling over one eye.

Out there, the tall fence had a sturdy gate to provide privacy and protection. I squealed when I recognized the green leaves of forsythia bushes along the back. When I was a child, their bright-yellow flowers protected my favorite hiding spot.

"This apartment is perfect for you. That's why I saved it for last."

Excitement coursed through me. This one might work out, and Tom would never expect me to move to Salem.

"I have another surprise for you. The bedroom's unique. You won't find its equal anywhere." Eddie pointed to the L-shaped structure protruding into the yard. "The back of the original cottage. The owners kept the small home and connected it to the main house."

He must have caught my open-mouthed confusion, because he laughed. "Come on. I can't wait for you to see it."

Back inside, I shot an approving glance at the handy rear exit. We crossed the kitchen to the bedroom and paused at the threshold. I stared in amazement. This large room belonged to an earlier era. A huge fireplace, the kind people used for cooking, took up a chunk of the opposite wall. The wide floorboards would have rung to the tune of colonial boots. A loft with a tiny window cut off the high beamed ceiling on the right. No doubt, the last vestige of a second story, and a spiral staircase, the single concession to the present era, provided access to the platform.

Eddie's voice reverberated through the space. "This room was the home of a seventeenth-century ship's captain. According to all accounts, he lost his love and, heartbroken, set out to sea in a violent storm, never to return."

I laughed. "A little dramatic?"

"What?" He frowned then broke into a grin. "You have to admit it's a great story."

Although the rest of the apartment could pass for a sauna, I shivered. Did the fireplace make the difference? The cold, gray stones gave me a chill.

"Why don't you inspect the loft?" Eddie said.

I scurried up the stairs, eager to examine the bonus area, but paused at the top and ducked. Slanted eaves created the illusion of a dark cave. Dim light emanated from a smudged window. The floor was about fifteen feet square. Because of the roof pitch, though, I'd have trouble standing everywhere. I wasn't thrilled.

"Turn on the light," he called.

A string hung from the ceiling. One tug transformed the spot. I didn't need to duck. There was a good eight feet of room to stand. As I faced the metal railing and surveyed the bedroom, my whole perspective changed. I liked the space and had to admit the loft was a nice extra I hadn't expected.

"If you like the apartment, you can move in next week. I'll have it cleaned."

I did a quick survey. The room was odd. Not quite my style, yet the rest of the place was perfect. It checked all my boxes. I wondered why such a great apartment had been vacant for so long, but then Eddie quoted the rent.

Yikes! For that price I could handle lots of weird. "Okay, Eddie. I'll take it."

We headed back to the kitchen, *my kitchen*, I realized with a thrill. A curious scent tickled my nose. I sniffed. Tobacco? I glanced at the loft. Was that smoke? I paused and squinted in the dim light. Nope. Nothing. Nothing but shadows.

~ * ~

After I'd moved out of Tom's place in Boston, I stayed with my sister and her family in Gloucester. One benefit of my stay at Kirsten's house was Isobel, my six-year-old niece. I loved her despite her guileless intentions. Every morning, she'd taken it upon herself to awaken me with a very distinctive approach. First, she'd place her pudgy little finger on my eyelid, then lift it and use her loud voice. "Wake up, Auntie Dani. It's morning time."

Last night, I'd set my alarm. I shouldn't have bothered. Izzy's eye-poking finger beat the musical alert by half an hour. She was a small clone of her mother. Their hair reminded me of puffy dandelions, and they had the same pixie-like features. I take after my mom—high cheekbones and dark hair, but not her height. At five feet, six inches, I tower above both mother and sister. Any time I stand near them, I tend to slouch.

Izzy looked adorable perched at the kitchen table in her pink PJs. While she talked to me, she shoveled Fruit Loops into her mouth, and spit milk and cereal in my direction.

I chuckled. I'd miss this time with my cute niece. "Wait till you finish chewing."

She made a concerted effort to finish the mouthful. After the final swallow, she grinned. "Want to play dolls?"

"I'd love to, honey, but the movers will be here today."

My sister arrived, stretched and yawned. "What are you up to at this hour?"

I gave her a cheeky grin. "Are you serious?" She'd enjoyed extra sleep time since her daughter found a new playmate.

Kirsten sat down with a cup of coffee and a scowl. "I'm happy you found a great apartment, but are you sure Tom can't find you at this place?"

Izzy perked up and said, "Are you playing hide-and-seek?"

"Sort of." I glowered at Kirsten. "We've already gone over this. I'll be careful." When I noticed Izzy's wide-eyed concern, I smiled and lightened my tone. "If I have any problems, I'll call the authorities." I didn't want to use a scary word like "police."

At her daughter's intense stare, Kirsten bent and kissed the top of her head. "Izzy, honey, give Auntie Dani a hug and go play in your room."

She leaned in for a big squeeze before she scampered off with her doll. I sighed as she disappeared into her room. My sweet little niece made me want a family of my own.

Kirsten touched my arm. "You have to be careful. He's liable to appear anywhere." She huffed out a breath. "What if he comes back to your office?"

"Don't worry. My built-in bodyguard took care of him." A few weeks ago, our muscular maintenance man ushered him outside and made it clear Tom would live longer if he never returned. He hadn't been around since.

"He'd better not. If he touches you again, I'll kill him."

"Atta girl!" I blew her a kiss and escaped to get dressed.

The minute I left the shower, tiny flutters tickled my chest. I'd be on my own tonight, all by myself. For twenty-four years, I'd lived with someone else—my parents, roommates, and Tom. I took a deep breath and squashed down the bout of nerves. Today was the beginning of a new adventure, and I was up for the challenge.

Before I headed to my car, I checked the front window. All clear. "I'll call you later, Kir." I gave her a hug, straightened my shoulders, and strode outside.

I wanted to believe my problems with Tom were over, that he was history. Just in case, though, I made sure to check around me. I didn't want him to find out where I lived.

At one point, a black car like Tom's pulled out behind me. I tried to identify the driver and had to stomp on my brakes to avoid rear-ending the car in front of me. When tires screeched in my wake, I checked the mirror. Narrowed eyes, busy lip movements, and interesting hand gestures greeted me. At least the driver wasn't Tom.

Once I regained my composure, I frowned. I'd played my part in the failed relationship when I accepted his control, but that didn't absolve his behavior. Whatever the cause, the man I'd cared for had changed.

My hands shook as I remembered his twisted sneer and final words. "Tears won't cut it, sweetheart. Don't ever piss me off again."

In the three weeks since I'd left, I'd been on alert. Tom didn't like to lose what he considered his.

Chapter Two

I spent the rest of the ride flipping my gaze back and forth from the road to the mirrors, to make sure no black cars followed me. Still, I circled the block twice. The Salem streets were quiet on this Saturday morning. I scored a parking space in front of my new home. The white clapboard colonial had a side lane leading to my entrance.

The sweet scent of roses greeted me when I stepped out of the car. For a minute, I paused to savor the neighborhood. Different house styles with picket fences and stone walls showcased colorful gardens. The day promised to be a scorcher, but right now, close to the water, the air remained cool. In the last moments of morning calm, car engines, barking dogs, and the intermittent sound of voices heralded the street coming to life. My shoulders relaxed, and some of the tightness left my stomach.

"Hi. You the new lady moving in?"

Startled, I spun around to face a tall man somewhere in his forties.

He stuck out his hand, and we shook. "I'm Jimbo Dugan. I live down the street with my sister. I took care of Rose's place."

Who was Rose? "Dani Trent. Nice to meet you."

While we spoke, the movers arrived. The same crew who'd helped pack my stuff last night spilled out.

I checked my phone. "Right on time. I'll unlock the door."

The driver leaned his ample butt against the truck and rubbed his beard. "No hurry. We'll wait for you."

I hurried, though. I couldn't help myself. As I sprinted along the side of the house, I wondered again what mind conceived this weird architectural integration. I climbed the steps to the back hall that led to my apartment.

The key I held symbolized a fresh start. At last, I was in control. When a tiny shadow of doubt snuck in, I pushed it aside and flung open the door of my new home. For the next few hours, I rested against the counter in the kitchen, gesturing like a traffic cop to send boxes to their proper destinations.

"Where do you want this desk?"

"The bedroom loft."

They shuffled in, and one of them yelled. "Hey, lady, you got a spiral staircase."

I peeked around the door. "Too tough?"

A burly guy with numerous tattoos on his arms frowned and looked away. "Nah." He gave the complainer a hard punch.

Minutes later, at the sound of a loud crash and an "Oh, shit," I ran in and skidded to a halt. A sea of glass glittered across the pine floor. A lump wedged in my chest. "Please tell me those fragments aren't all that's left of my grandmother's vase."

The tall one next to me adjusted his wire-rimmed spectacles and lifted his head with a sorrowful stare. "I guess they are."

I tried not to scream at the loss. Grams always helped me cut flowers from her garden and arrange them in that beautiful crystal container. I glared at the men. "What happened?"

The tattooed bruiser piped up. "I can't figure how the carton slipped. I put that box square on top of the other one. It shouldn'ta moved." He scratched his head. "I can't understand how the hell the vase slid out of its paper."

Amid assurances of company reimbursement, a couple of the guys gave nervous glances around the room. I didn't buy their innocent act. Damn, with my luck, small shards of Gram's treasure would lie in wait between the floorboards, ready to attack my feet. The day's excitement dampened, and I headed off to find the broom, rubbing my arms against a sudden chill.

When the movers left, I worked in the kitchen. My meager supplies didn't make a dent in the roomy cabinets. I'd enjoy poking through the nearby shops to fill the empty spaces. The final touch was placing my shiny, new red teapot on top of the stove.

I stepped back to survey my kingdom, pleased at what I'd accomplished. I no longer needed someone else to take care of me; I'd handled the move to my apartment on my own. New furniture perked up the bedroom. I spun up and around the spiral staircase to the office loft where my desk sat snug against the rail overlooking what had been a seventeenth-century home. I jumped when a waft of air slid past my neck, then laughed. In a place this old, I'd have to expect drafts.

Music kept me company as I hit a groove with the rest of my unpacking. Time flew by. A little before noon I decided to take a break.

The results so far pleased me. The new sofa bed sported colorful throw pillows to match the rug, and I'd hung two small watercolors above shelves full of my favorite books. The perfect finish would have been a bright spray of flowers in Grandma's vase.

I groaned as I leaned back and raised my arms in a long stretch. A knock on the door startled me. I froze. I hadn't told anyone other than Kirsten and my parents about the move, and they wouldn't be here until next week. "Who's there?"

A female voice answered, "Your neighbor."

I eased the door open to discover a petite blonde with blue eyes and a ponytail. Her neon-orange top enhanced her lush figure, quite different from mine. I caught the sweet smell of chocolate as she spoke. "Hi. I'm Heather Somers. Welcome."

"Dani Trent."

Her grin broadened as she handed me a small dish of brownies. *Ooh, still warm.* My kind of neighbor. I clutched the chocolaty concoction and invited her in. "These will go great with coffee."

Another sign of my good fortune, my amiable visitor was also my age. The best part was I didn't have to entertain her—she loved to talk. "You're going to love living here," she said. "It's just you, me, and the Formans upstairs." She brushed her fingers across the table tiles. "Good choice." Her gaze moved to the living room, and she pointed to a framed photograph. "Who's in the picture?"

"My niece Izzy and my sister Kirsten."

"How come you two don't look alike?" She walked over for a closer peek.

The question didn't surprise me; people always asked. I gave the stock answer. "My father's ancestors lived in Sweden, and my mother is a French-Irish blend."

"Cool." She sat down again. "I'm thrilled someone under eighty moved in. The one before you was a little old lady. Don't get me wrong. Rose was nice but boring. Toward the end, she wigged out. They took her to a home. Poor dear."

Without pause for an extra breath, Heather launched into a tale of her first week here. "Rose, the former tenant, asked me in for tea. It was sad. She'd misplace her possessions then insist someone had come in and moved them." Heather tightened her lips and sighed. "When she started to see things, her niece put her in a home."

"What a shame." I glanced at the clock above the table. "Hey, since it's lunchtime, why don't we go out to eat? You can show me around if you have time."

"A great idea. Let's go."

We didn't get far before a loud "yoo-hoo!" from across the way claimed our attention. Heather, who'd been extolling the advantages of Salem, stopped in mid-speech and grasped my arm. "Come on. You've got to meet Mrs. Wallace." She leaned in to whisper, "I call her Mrs. W. She's a trip."

Across the street, Mrs. Wallace held court in a chair on her front porch. Arms crossed, she leaned on top of the railing. A heavy gray-haired woman whose dour expression didn't bode well, but her eyes sparked with interest. "You must be the young lady who's moved into the old Gale house."

Our place had a name?

Heather jumped in. "Mrs. Wallace, meet Dani Trent."

The woman directed her sharp gaze at me. "Where do you come from?"

I hadn't finished my answer when she said, "Are you married?"

"No, I'm—"

"Boyfriend?" I twisted my head back and forth. No sense trying to speak. Curiosity gleamed in her eyes. "No? Well, you're certainly old enough. Don't you like boys?"

I opened my mouth in disbelief.

Heather interrupted, "Sorry, Mrs. Wallace. I'm starving. We'll see you later."

Before I could follow Heather, the woman sat back, a smug grin on her face as she resettled her glasses on her nose. "How do you like the bedroom?"

Oh rats. She'd honed in in on my least favorite room. I managed a semi-sincere smile. "I find the whole apartment charming."

I blinked at her sharp laugh. There wasn't anything funny about what I'd said. I hurried to catch Heather. "She's kind of rude."

That brought a snicker from my neighbor. "She's wicked nosy. Doesn't miss anything that happens on the street. Be careful, our place is right in her sights."

No slouch herself in the gossip department, she proceeded to give me the lowdown on the rest of the neighborhood. Whenever she talked—and that was most of the time—her swinging ponytail kept the beat.

We passed a house with a colorful garden. "Jimbo's house," she said. "The guy's a super gardener, although he's a little slow. More like a big kid than a man, but he's good people."

I didn't have time to comment before she nodded toward a rundown place across the street. She lowered her voice. "The Creightons. I like her. She's a nice woman," Heather wrinkled her forehead and pursed her lips, "but the husband's nasty when he drinks."

I made a mental note to stay far away from there. I'd had enough of that with Tom.

We strolled along in the afternoon sun. I was glad I'd changed into a sleeveless top. Heather began the tour on Derby Street. We stopped at an impressive two-story, redbrick building whose stairs led to a palatial, columned entrance.

"The Custom House," she said. "Nathaniel Hawthorne worked there for a few years."

I recognized the name from *The Scarlett Letter* in high school.

Heather leaned in as if to pass on a juicy bit of gossip. "He was fired because he kept seeing ghosts in the corridors. You should take the tour."

I crossed the Custom House off my mental list of Salem attractions. You wouldn't catch me in one of these haunted buildings.

A constant flow of people streamed around us. "Derby Street is a great tourist attraction." Heather pivoted toward a three-masted ship across the way. "The *Friendship*. Visitors claim footsteps follow them and cold tickles their necks."

Though I chuckled at her dramatics, a chill swept through me. I'd forgotten how much Salem relied on its supernatural reputation.

"Over there is Pickering Wharf. We'll have to go sometime. The shops are great and the restaurants are fantastic."

A couple of streets later, we encountered an old cemetery. Heather's mood shifted, and her voice dropped to a whisper. "Players from the Salem witch trials are buried here—judges and accusers. Not the victims, though. Those poor things were hidden in family graves."

The dismal stones gave off unhappy vibes. Even the trees were creepy. Their horizontal branches seemed ready and waiting for the hanging rope. A quiver of unease shook me. Around the corner she showed me a memorial.

"These names represent the twenty people killed during the witch trials," she said. "Nineteen hanged, and one pressed to death. That doesn't count the poor souls who died in prison."

I'd listened to the stories since my childhood. They were horrible, a sad reminder of cruelty in the guise of faith and justice. I was relieved when we left.

We turned onto a cobblestone street, and Heather indicated a maroon-colored colonial house. "Here we are. Red's. Hope you're hungry."

"It doesn't look like a restaurant." If not for the sign in the window, I'd have gone right by.

"The best breakfast in town and dynamite lunches. The place has been here since the eighteenth century, when the restaurant was some kind of coffee house."

An image popped into my head of staid men in puritan garb sipping from metal cups. I smiled. History was coming alive for me in Salem.

The tables and counter were filled. Our waitress led us into a repurposed eighteenth-century living room, complete with the original ceiling, wainscoting, and multi-paned windows. My stomach grumbled as the aroma of good food swirled around us.

Ensconced in a booth, we initiated the friendship dance. Bit by bit, we divulged information. When she stopped to munch a chip, I dove in for a question. "What about you? Do you have a boyfriend?"

The query made her pause and concentrate on the glass in her hand. "Not right now. I date, but there's no one special." She took a sip of her soda. "I moved here with a dude. It didn't work out." She paused for a moment then her expression tightened. "We came home one night from a party. I was pissed because he'd been flirting with some chick. I told him I didn't like it and, bam, he hit me. Just like that. No warning. Bam."

I flinched at her tone. "How awful. I'm sorry."

She flipped her hand in the air. "Oh, don't be. He was cute, but no way would I stick around for that kind of abuse. I dumped his ass."

"Wow, good for you."

A guilty twinge inspired me to reward her honesty with some of my own. In a hurry to explain the Tom debacle before I changed my mind, I blurted out, "Me too. I mean, I left a relationship."

Heather waited for me to continue. Did I want to dredge up that pain now? Why not? Didn't she deserve the same honesty she'd given me? Besides, maybe I could enlist her as a lookout for Tom.

I gave her the short version. "We lived together for six months in his Boston apartment. Talk about Jekyll and Hyde. At first he was funny and charming. Later he began with the control—what to wear and how to act. Once I dared to oppose him, I glimpsed his rage.

"After a night out and quite a few drinks, he slammed me against the wall. Instead of apologizing, he laughed and threatened me. His bouts of anger had become more frequent, and I was unhappy, but his physical abuse terrified me. I snuck out while he slept. I'm grateful I left when I did. Salem is a new start." I rubbed my arms. "I hope he never finds me."

When I leaned back with a sigh. she pursed her lips and narrowed her eyes. "What a jerk. Good for you. No woman deserves that kind of treatment."

Her words brought me to the edge of tears. "I'm glad you're my neighbor."

With an impish grin, she said, "You'll appreciate me more after you meet the couple upstairs."

"Why?"

"They're, like, weird. The good news? They don't like to hang out. He's way creepy—silent stares, and she's like an evil Internet address."

She'd lost me. "Huh?"

The satisfied grin should have warned me. She lifted both hands palm up and said, "Www? Wicked Witch of the West?"

I laughed. "Oh boy. I'll be careful when I meet her. Should I keep water handy in case I have to shrink her?"

"Beware. That's all I'm saying."

"Speaking of strange, what's the deal with Mrs. Wallace? How come she called our place the Gale house?"

"That's what everyone calls it. Around here the houses are named after the original owners. The old geezer who built the first cottage, your bedroom, was Elias Gale."

"Oh, yeah. Eddie mentioned him—a ship's captain."

"Some people say he was a pirate." She tossed a chip into her mouth.

"A pirate? You mean like Johnny Depp?"

She snorted and a piece of chip flew onto the table. "You wish." We veered off on a discussion about the handsome movie star.

In a flurry of giggles, we both agreed we'd accept a little booty from Johnny's Captain Sparrow.

Before we left, I asked one more question. "Why did Mrs. Wallace ask about my bedroom?"

"Gossip. I told you about Rose. She talked about strange noises in there. I'm sure the sounds were her imagination. Don't pay too much attention to what Mrs. W says. When I first moved here, she said the place was unlucky." She lifted one shoulder. "I've never noticed any problem. She sometimes comes off gruff, but don't let her bother you."

I rubbed the goosebumps on my arms. "Sheesh. Sounds like she's a weirdo who enjoys terrorizing people." I took a sip of my coffee. Too cold. "The apartment is odd, though. My bedroom must have been the captain's house."

"Yeah." Heather frowned. "Rose gave me the tour. Creepy. I'd never be able to sleep in there."

"Thanks a lot. Way to ruin my rest."

“Oh, sorry. I’m not into ‘old.’”

I bit my lip. No way could I afford to move again. Despite my misgivings, I’d better ignore the gossip and get used to my *unique* apartment.

Chapter Three

A delicious warmth stole through me. I lifted my lips for his kiss. Moments from sweet fulfillment, the dream changed.

My lover's face transformed into an ominous pulsing light. I snapped open my eyes. Inches from my face loomed the invasive strobe-light monster—my alarm clock. The electricity must have gone off.

Rats! The best dream I'd had in months. I rubbed my face and reached for the bedside lamp. When I clicked the button, a huge spark flashed. I jerked my hand back. The *zzzt* sound it made didn't bode well. Damn! The clock was off now. I shivered. Man, cold had seeped in. Creepy!

I'd get my flashlight from the kitchen. No sense in wasting my phone battery. When I swung my legs to the floor, the sound of light scratches made me snatch them back. Yikes, I swiveled my head toward the chimney, worried some critter had snuck in. Bats loved the night.

I ducked my head and aimed my cellphone toward the ceiling, looking for tiny creatures with beady eyes, pointy wings, and sharp teeth. Nothing. I exhaled in relief until a movie image of blood-tipped fangs in a pasty face flashed through my mind. My nerve endings tingled. *Stop it!* I took a deep breath, then I chuckled. I lived in Salem, Massachusetts. If there was anything to be concerned about, it would be witches, not vampires.

With a nervous giggle, I headed to the kitchen, surprised to find the stove clock worked—2:55 AM. I checked the living room and the locks on both doors. The electricity worked everywhere but the bedroom. Weird!

Flashlight in hand, I crept back to my bed. A noise like a sigh slid over me. I jerked my head up. The metal staircase coiled like a giant, writhing snake. Had it hissed?

I prayed not. I lifted my gaze to the loft and wished I hadn't. A filmy mist drifted above my desk. Fiery pinpricks erupted along my skin.

I stopped breathing. The clamor of my banging heart reverberated in my head, and I was afraid I might wet myself.

I stared at the foggy cloud. A twisting smoky essence that faded in and out as if straining to evolve. The back of my neck tingled, and my chest tightened. I was unable to tear my gaze away from the writhing vapor. Strength drained from my body. My limbs became paralyzed. Reason deserted me.

After a few seconds, survival mode kicked in. *It isn't real. It isn't real.* My fingers clenched around the flashlight, and I shot the beam toward the loft.

Poof! Whatever I'd imagined had disappeared.

My pent-up breath surged through my lips. I swung the beam around the room. Cleansing light cleared away the rest of the shadows.

Dope. Why do you do that to yourself? No more horror movies for me.

I shook off the fear as I ticked off a list of excuses—new apartment, no lights, my tendency toward the dramatic, and, oh yes, let's not forget Mrs. W. There hadn't been a monster in the loft. The smoky vision was all in my mind, nothing but a stray draft that snuck in through the old boards in the house and agitated a layer of dust. For a minute though…

~ * ~

Morning arrived bright and unwelcome. I rubbed my eyes, trying to wake up, and cursed the sun's glare. Seconds later, memories from last night blindsided me. Flashbacks of the blurry vision in the loft fought with my intellect. I reassured myself ghosts didn't exist. The electricity fizzled out and I'd imagined the whole spooky incident. In the light of day, my concerns from last night faded. I'd have to get used to my new solo living status and not jump at every little noise.

I wriggled in my comfortable new mattress and inspected the room. Even in the light of day, the room exuded a bleak vibe. To make the place cheerier, I'd added a colorful array of African violets, philodendron, and a spider plant in the window. The rug added soothing earth tones to complement the old pine boards.

My attention veered to the bright, flowered cushion on my new rocking chair. Its cheery oasis in the otherwise dreary room called to me. Soothed by the comfortable back-and-forth rhythm and the warm sun in my face, I closed my eyes.

After a minute, I stopped, crinkled my nose, and sniffed. Smoke? I leaned forward to smell the fireplace. No, not from a wood fire. I sniffed again. More like cigarettes. One of the men from the moving crew must have sneaked a butt in here yesterday. First

Grandma's vase. Now the reek of tobacco. I wouldn't give a recommendation for those guys any time soon.

A loud gurgle in my stomach reminded me I needed breakfast. Time to christen my new kitchen. When the aroma of hot coffee tickled my nose, I poured a cup and sat at my new table to phone Eddie about the electricity. I still marveled this place was available and move-in ready. Finding decent, affordable apartments in Salem wasn't easy. Eddie had come through big time.

"Hi, Eddie. It's Dani. I have a little problem."

After I described the outage, he apologized. "I'll call Gregory Electric. Everything else okay?"

"Perfect." Unless you counted last night's hallucination.

I ended the call, pleased at his response on a Sunday morning. I got dressed, poured myself a second cup of coffee, and slathered butter on my bagel. As I bit into the greasy concoction, I mentally thumbed my nose at Tom Westin. No way would he ever again tell me what to eat. He was history. Thank God I hadn't married him.

I decided to finish breakfast outside on the back stairs. When a warm breeze teased my face, I inhaled the light flowery scent mixed with tantalizing hints of seaweed. I breathed out a satisfied hum, grateful my apartment was so close to the harbor. Sipping my coffee, I chuckled at the antics of a few busy squirrels. Everything was perfect. Even better, I had the freedom to enjoy my new home on my own—no expectations, no criticisms.

Later today I planned to go shopping for the things I'd forgotten in the rush of the move. Right now, all I wanted to do was chill. Leaning back, I relished the wind against my skin and the soft cooing of mourning doves.

Just when I was relaxed to an almost trance-like state, a noise from inside startled me. The sound came again, knocking. I scrambled up and hurried inside but stopped when another loud knock echoed. I leaned toward the door. "Who is it?"

"The electrician." A man's voice.

On a Sunday? I kept the chain on to peek out at my visitor. Once I opened the door, a pleasant surprise greeted me. A man I'd describe as "hot" towered above me. For a second, I stared. The strand of unruly dark hair across his forehead accentuated his cool aqua eyes.

"Hi. Sam Gregory. I'm sorry. Am I too early? Eddie asked me to check on the problem right away."

My heart raced, until I remembered Eddie's words this morning—*'Gregory Electric.'*

As I matched the names in my head, the guy gave a rueful grin.

"I'm the electrician?"

I needed to get my nerves under control. Eddie would never have sent someone he didn't trust.

My gaze traveled to the tool belt slung over those slim hips. Mmm. Nice. I snapped my attention back to his face. "I didn't expect you this soon."

A devastating dimple appeared when he smiled. "I had time this morning, and Eddie's a good customer. We aim to please."

We were still in the doorway. Sam's head tilted as if to say, "What next?"

Oh damn. My manners. I reached out my hand. "Thanks for the quick response. Dani Trent. Please come in."

I'd forgotten my appearance. Damn it. I looked terrible. To combat the heat, I'd thrown on an old T-shirt and shorts and whipped my hair into a ponytail. Perspiration ran down my neck, cementing my shirt to my body. After he moved past me, I pulled the shirt away from my chest. It didn't help. I quit worrying about my appearance and ushered him into the bedroom, explained what had happened, and left him to play with the wires.

While I cleaned the kitchen, my musings veered toward the man in my bedroom. Though I'd been single less than a month, any attraction to Tom had died a long time before, and Sam was handsome. I stopped when I remembered that's what had attracted me to Tom. He'd been sweet when I met him. One of my mother's mottos popped into my head, "Never judge a book by its cover." Oh, well, no sense in daydreaming. No doubt some woman had him wrapped around her little finger.

A while later, the object of my fantasies strolled into the room. "I have some bad news."

"Oh, no."

"You've got a major problem. I told Eddie the system was bound to crash. The wiring in the bedroom has to be replaced. I'll have to take it off the old fuse box and tie it into the rest of the apartment. Changing the circuitry is a big job. I called him, and he okayed the plan. Now I have to find the time to do the job. I'm hoping to get it done next weekend."

"Next weekend?" My face must have mirrored my disappointment.

"Yeah. I'd like to get here faster. As it is, I'll have to shuffle a couple of jobs to fit you in."

His answer disappointed me. I twisted my mouth into a pout, but I didn't care. "Oh, great. Right after I move in, the electricity tanks. What am I supposed to do?"

"I can fix a temporary plug in the bedroom to hold you until Saturday. I'm sorry this happened to you."

The outage wasn't his fault, and I'd forgotten I was trying to impress him. I put on my brightest smile. "Thanks for your concern." I switched to the role of brave little trooper. "I'm sure I can work around the electrical problem this week."

My helpless woman act didn't faze him. He sauntered off to the bedroom. "I'll install the plug."

I followed him in and offered a cup of coffee. I pictured us getting better acquainted over caffeine. When he wasn't interested, I shrugged. I'd tried.

Sam took longer than I expected. He showed me the outlet and handed me his card. "If you have any problems, give me a call. If there's an emergency, my service will page me."

He put two fingers to his forehead in a sexy kind of salute before he left. I closed the door humming one of my favorite songs, "Another One Bites the Dust."

Chapter Four

In the face of a beautiful Monday morning with the sun sparkling across the water on both sides of the Beverly Bridge, all concerns about my Saturday middle-of-the-night disturbance melted away. Like Heather, I didn't appreciate the antique aspect of my apartment. Add to that my overactive imagination, and I wasn't surprised I'd envisioned phantoms. I'd have to learn to live with my miniature museum or drive myself crazy. Maybe, if I did a little research on Captain Elias Gale, I'd learn to appreciate the room's historical significance.

I pulled into the parking lot at Beach Street Apartments and chuckled. Better if I didn't mention my aversion to "old." Not the best philosophy for an apartment manager at a complex for seniors.

Before I opened my office door, Mrs. Craigie caught me. Always some complaint. "Good morning, Mrs. Craigie."

"Hmpf." Her wrinkled face twisted into a grimace. "It would have been good if Edith hadn't banged on my door at 4:00 AM and asked if she could hide in my apartment because her husband threatened to kill her. For heaven's sake, he's been dead for ten years."

Oh, hell. I'd always liked Edith. Everyone did. In the past few weeks, though, I'd gotten complaints. She had a form of dementia, rapidly deteriorating. I'd already spoken to her daughter. "I'm sorry you had to go through that. I'll speak to her."

"Won't do any good." She tapped her temple. "Nobody's home there anymore." She left with a disgusted look on her face.

In my work with the senior population, I had to acknowledge life's natural progression. Physical disabilities played a constant role in the lives of people in this age group. Activities weakened, and morale deteriorated. For me, the diseases that attacked the mind were the most alarming and difficult to accept.

After lunch, my favorite resident, Mary Tucker, brought me a plate of chocolate chip cookies right from the oven. The aroma was pure heaven. Her soft white hair, plump cheeks, and sweet smile screamed "perfect grandmother." I liked to pretend she was mine.

One of her greatest gifts was her sympathetic smile. Today, she wanted to reassure me about Edith. "There's nothing to be done for her, but I figured you might need a pick-me-up."

"You're a love. Thank you. These will help smooth over a bad day."

Homemade cookies were my secret passion. Maybe, not so mysterious. I tended to make a spectacle of myself in their presence, scooping, scarfing, and making satisfied noises. I licked my lips and made a note to buy cookie ingredients on the way home.

Mary perched on the chair. "Poor Edith. She always kept the rest of us in line." She stared down at her hands. "Looks like we'll have to find someone else to plan our bus trips now."

"I wish she didn't have to leave."

She patted my knee. "The change is best for Edith, dear. What she needs is supervision."

After she left, I made a call to Edith's daughter.

If no problems side-tracked me at the office, my workday ended at 4:30 PM. At 4:25 PM, Stephen Fischer, my boss and sadistic tormentor, arrived.

He'd been on my case since the day I'd seen him in a compromising situation with a married colleague. I didn't care, but everything changed after that.

"What's going on there?" he said. "Any problems?"

"No. Everything's good." No sense telling him about Edith until I had a solution.

"The newsletter's due on my desk Friday morning."

I used to enjoy the creation of an interesting bulletin for my tenants, but Fischer went out of his way to denigrate my effort—the articles, the layout, and my writing style.

"Okay, you'll have it."

"Make sure I do."

He left. No goodbye.

The man made my stomach hurt.

~ * ~

Later that night, the dreaded newsletter topped my priority list. I tucked my laptop under my arm and brought my files into the living room, unwilling to give Fischer any ammunition against me. Lulled by the fading sun streaming in the windows, I closed my eyes for a minute. The sharp ring of the phone jerked me awake. I blinked in the darkness.

Damn, I'd fallen asleep. I groped around for my cell. "Hello?"

"Hey." Heather's voice. "Am I disturbing you?"

"Oh, no. I'm glad you called. I fell asleep in the middle of arranging the newsletter for work. What time is it?"

"A little after 8:30 PM."

"Rats, I've got to get this done. His Highness, my manager, bugged me about it today. If the finished product isn't perfect—even if it is—he'll rip the whole thing apart."

"Poor baby. I'm lucky to have such a great boss. That's why I'm calling. He gave me a couple of tickets to a charity event at the yacht club in Marblehead for a week from Friday. They'll have a super band, great food, and a chance for you to meet a bunch of awesome people. You game?"

"Uh..."

"Come on. We'll have fun. What else have you got to do?"

Jeez, I'd known her for two days and she already had me pegged.

Right on target. I didn't have anything else to do, but a fancy charity function? "Formal?"

"No. Styles run from casual to dressy. I'm wearing a sundress. We'll have a wicked good time. If you hate it, we can always leave. What do you say?"

What the heck? I did need to get out, and Heather was fun. She'd make a terrific date. "Okay, why not? My wardrobe sucks, though. Wanna help me choose a new dress?"

"Yeah, cool. We can get an outfit this weekend."

After we settled on Saturday, I headed toward the bedroom. I took the heavy, square flashlight I'd purchased yesterday and placed it next to the bed with a flourish. A great light for the room, and, if necessary, it could also double as a weapon.

Sam's plug enabled me to pull together an outfit for the next day. I fixed myself a cup of tea, snuggled in bed with my laptop, and let my creative juices flow. Every manager was required to submit a newsletter each month. Mine was called *Beach Street Buzz*.

I wanted the piece to be informative and to capture the residents' interest. I planned to include a few funny cartoons. I'd be furious if Fischer decided to delete them. There was data I needed in the loft, but with no light in there, I could wait until tomorrow to retrieve it. Two cups of tea later, I quit.

I inhaled the cool air in the bedroom. Though perplexed by the temperature change, I enjoyed it. No matter the reason, the refreshing atmosphere made for a comfortable rest on warm summer nights.

After my earlier nap, I'd never fall asleep right away. I lay back on my pillow and contemplated Heather's invitation. The wardrobe possibilities intrigued me. I might follow her lead and get a sundress, something in dark green to match my eyes. Why not splurge and get a pair of strappy sandals to complete the ensemble? I have nice legs. I hadn't been out for a fun evening in a long time.

I grinned. If I put my hair up and let a couple of auburn curls hang loose, those big earrings, the dangling kind Tom hated, would be perfect. I was sure I'd find some cool sailor-type at the yacht club who'd love them.

My mind drifted into fantasyland conjuring Mr. Tall, Dark, and Sensitive. A deepening chill made me tuck the covers around my neck. I closed my eyes and floated into slumber.

I found myself in a large room full of tables covered in clean, white linens. Outside sounds of seagulls and intermittent splashes played on the periphery of my mind. I rubbed my arms to combat the chill in the air and gazed around the room, empty except for a tall man in a well-cut suit. He stood with his back to me. I enjoyed the sight of his broad shoulders and wavy black hair and longed to see his face. In dream-like slow motion, he turned toward me. I choked.

Jumping backward, I slammed into the table, trapping myself. Nothing about this man came anywhere near sensitive. He loomed above me. His dark eyes burned into mine. I gaped at his thin-lipped grin and the ragged scar slicing his cheek.

When he opened his mouth, the words came out in a low growl. "Good evening. I believe it's time we met."

Chapter Five

Hot water beat against me in the shower the next morning, cleansing my skin, but nothing could wash away the brutish face from last night's dream. The same queasy sense of revulsion I'd experienced while I slept seized me. Naked and vulnerable, I shut off the water to peek through the curtain.

The sight of the empty room should have eased my tension, but I couldn't shake the perception of being watched. I recalled my vision and remembered another detail—smoke swirled upward from his pipe. I fancied I smelled tobacco now.

I rubbed at the goosebumps on my skin and struggled to breathe. The fear was unreasonable. I'd had a bad dream; that was it. Nevertheless, the man's black eyes and chilling words undermined my sanity. As cool air played against my dripping body, I shivered and hugged myself.

For a minute more, I stood there then remembered work. I didn't have time to worry about a stupid nightmare. I had to get to the office. I hopped out of the tub, grabbed my towel, and finished dressing in record time.

The drive to work took twenty-five minutes. I arrived at 8:30 AM. Thank God I had my own parking space. I hurried inside, a few minutes late, and released a thankful breath for the empty hall. No complainants waited to ambush me.

I relaxed and ambled into my office. When I checked the calendar, however, I swore. A mere seven days remained in August. I needed to dive into the end-of-the-month paperwork.

A few minutes before lunch, I received a text from Kirsten. "Hey, sis. Hope you're settled in. Wish I'd been there to help. Be there Sat for lunch. Luv, Kir."

Typical. No "How are you?" or "How do you like the apartment?" Instead, she dictates when and what we'll do this weekend.

For once I'd like to be able to say, "No. That doesn't work for me." I'm sure she'd find a way to change my mind. I smiled. Despite my big sister's high-handed ways, I loved her.

During lunch, my office phone rang. *I'll bet it's Kirsten.* I snagged the receiver.

"Hi, honey. How are you?"

My gut clenched. After more than three weeks, the sound of Tom's voice rattled me. "What do you want?"

"We need to talk. When I called your sister a couple of weeks ago to apologize, she wouldn't let me speak to you. She's never liked me. I wouldn't have to call you at work, if you hadn't changed your phone number."

I almost apologized before I caught myself. I wasn't in the wrong. I'd changed my number to keep him from contacting me. I bit my tongue and kept quiet.

With a whine in his voice, he said, "You have to forgive me. I promise it'll never happen again."

Always the well-timed "I'm sorry." He believed those two words would fix everything. Not today. There was nothing left to fix.

I took a deep breath to steady myself. "Listen to me. There's nothing more to say. We're over."

Before I could finish, he rushed on, "Come on. You still love me. Meet me for coffee after you get off work. I'll wait at the diner around the corner."

"No." Whoa, way too loud. If I didn't tone my voice down, I'd alert the building's gossip brigade.

My lunch soured in my stomach as I tried for a more reasonable tone. "I don't want to see you or talk to you. Please don't call me at work again. Goodbye." Then reason deserted me. I slammed the phone into its cradle.

My hands shook so much I clenched them together. Once I took a couple of deep breaths, my anger quieted, and I experienced a sense of relief. I'd put an end to Tom. I was free. Time to get my life in gear. The party at the yacht club popped into my head. *Perfect.* A *new beginning.*

Five minutes later, my boss marched in. Was the universe punishing me? Fischer's smirk made me feel like a mouse cornered by a cat. Twice in two days? He'd never shown up that much in two weeks. "Why didn't you let me know about the trouble with Edith Wade?"

I wanted to ask him what he could have done. Instead, I said, "Her daughter is going to pick her up tomorrow."

"You should have taken care of the problem weeks ago." Before I could say anything, he strode out the door.

I hated that man. The biggest downside of my current home was that he lived in the same city not too far from me. I hoped I never ran into him. If I hadn't spent most of my savings on the new apartment, I might tell him to stuff this job.

On the way home, I amused myself devising fitting murder scenarios for Fischer. I pictured his demise at my hands. Although pounding him with my fists would be the most satisfying, I figured poison would be easier. By the time I arrived home, I'd decided to hide the body in the bowels of Beach Street Apartments, where no one would ever find him. Once I'd taken care of my nemesis, my mood brightened.

When I arrived home, I was startled by a man's backside sticking out of the bushes. After he crawled out, however, I recognized Jimbo, my neighbor. Concerned he was in our bushes, I backed away, but relaxed when I noticed a trowel, pruners, and a rake on the ground.

He grinned. "Hi Ms. Trent."

"Hey, Jimbo. You take care of this property?"

"Yeah." He tossed some leaves onto a pile. "I do the flowers, cut the grass, and get rid of the weeds."

"You do a great job."

He gazed at his feet. Most of his face was hidden, but the curl of his grin peeked out. "Thanks." He brushed off the knees of his pants and walked over to me. "Maybe you'd like me to do work for you? Put some pretty flowers in your backyard?" His face changed from eager to serious. "Everyone says I do a real good job."

Though Heather mentioned Jimbo was slow, she liked him. 'He's a great guy, and Eddie trusts him.' I figured hiring Jimbo would be a smart move.

When I hesitated, he puffed up his chest. "I get the flowers at a discount because I buy so much, and I'm a whole lot cheaper than the landscape guys." He continued on to describe how many plants and what kind would work for me. His estimate sounded fair. Jimbo was a good businessman.

What the heck? This was my new home. A riot of color outside my kitchen window would brighten the dreary chore of doing dishes. "You make an excellent presentation. I'm sold. When can you start?"

He pulled in his chin to squelch a smile. His eyes shone with pride. When he received praise, the little boy in him appeared.

"I can get started tomorrow." He ducked his head. "If...if that's okay?"

I told him his suggestions would be fine and headed to my apartment. Despite the turmoil of my life, the move, personal demons, and aggravations at work, I'd done pretty well. I found it hard to believe

I'd been there less than a week. Not bad for, what did Tom call me that last night, an ungrateful, needy little bitch?

~ * ~

The next day kept me busy. Edith's daughter arrived in the midst of grumpy tenant concerns and painters refurbishing apartments. I was grateful to get home and crash in my living room. Too bad the house didn't run itself. I'd purchased food at the local market. Now I needed clean clothes. The washer and dryer were downstairs. The natural home of vermin, creepy crawlies, and, according to the movies, lurking serial killers, cellars were to be avoided whenever possible. Nevertheless, I had no choice. Tonight, laundry called.

Eddie had given me a tour of the facilities my first day. I'd cringed when I followed him into the dark entrance across from Heather's apartment and held my breath as we descended through the shadowy, and, I worried, spider-infested stairwell. When we reached the bottom, I exhaled in surprise. The room opened to a large, airy space. Huge windows let in plenty of light.

Tonight, armed with detergent and a basket full of dirty clothes, I braved the claustrophobic stairway. To bolster my spirits, I serenaded any lurking bugs with a litany of upbeat songs and loaded the washer.

A couple of hours later, bent over the washing machine to transfer the wet clothes to the dryer, I spun around at a noise behind me. My abrupt move caused the woman who stood there to jerk backward. Irritation filled her chubby face.

Eyes narrowed, she said, "You must be the new tenant." Neither her expression nor her voice oozed "warm and cozy."

I offered my hand. "Dani Trent. You must be Marie from upstairs."

"Right." Ignoring my gesture, she leaned her hip against the table. With an eyebrow raised, she pursed her lips. "How do you like your apartment so far?"

Her grating tone bordered on sarcastic. In an effort to elevate the quality of the conversation, I said, "It's great."

She frowned. "I'm surprised Eddie was able to rent the place again after what happened to Rose."

My faltering smile disappeared. "What do you mean?"

"Oh, Eddie said she was losing it, but Rose was fine when I spoke to her." Marie's words became a reprimand. "All the weird incidents in there had her scared to death. She couldn't wait to move. I don't blame her. What do you make of that crazy room?"

After she clipped out those words, her stance became more aggressive. Marie annoyed me more than her superstitious nonsense about the room. No way did I want to discuss any of this with her. In my best "give me a break" voice, I said, "Don't be ridiculous. The apartment's fine. Rose must have had an overactive imagination."

Marie had been leaning forward; now she stepped back, an angry scowl on her face. "We'll see if your attitude changes after you've been there a while."

She stomped off, not bothering to do her laundry. I didn't envision a happy future for us.

While I waited for my clothes to dry, I took out my annoyance on the apartment floors with a sponge mop. By the time I returned to get my clothes, the sun had set. I switched on the lights and surveyed the cellar. Piles of unused furniture filled the corners. I poked around and found an interesting old armoire.

Lost in my inspection of the wardrobe, I got the familiar uncomfortable sensation I'd experienced in the shower, as if someone was looking at me. I swiveled my head around toward the laundry and inhaled. With the descent of night, all those great big windows I'd admired earlier formed an impenetrable dark barrier. I was no longer able to see out, but anyone could look in.

I dragged my laundry from the dryer and beat a hasty retreat up the murky staircase, vivid memories of Saturday night's disturbing illusion chasing me. With the recent emergence of my eerie mental gymnastics, I could moonlight as a horror writer.

Since I found it impossible to banish the icy tingles biting my skin, I decided to work on the newsletter in the living room. I'd left the laptop on the coffee table last night but couldn't find it now. Not on the chair or sofa either. Then I spotted it on the floor. Oh, no. It had fallen off the table.

I grasped the computer, uttered a silent prayer, and turned it on. Yes! The familiar tone of my operating system greeted me. I set it back on the table and noticed a scratch on the cover. When did that happen?

After I finished the newsletter, I brought my wounded laptop into the bedroom, unable to understand how it had fallen. That made two victims since Saturday—the computer and Grandma's vase. The movers swore no one had been near the crystal when it slid to the floor, and no one other than me had been in my apartment.

Were we having mini earthquakes? Was the house settling? Then, like an invasive worm, Marie's words came back to me—*"All the weird incidents in that apartment had her scared to death."*

Chapter Six

On Thursday, I agonized over the finishing touches for the *Beach Street Buzz* before I dropped the newsletter off to Fischer's secretary. Relief I didn't have to worry about him bugging me for another month carried me through the rest of the day.

On Friday, however, the emotional and physical strain of the week caught up with me. My rear end dragged. By three thirty, I found it difficult to keep my eyes open. When the phone rang, I glared at it.

My frown evaporated when I recognized Heather's perky voice on the other end. "Hey, I'm almost ready to go home, change into my bathing suit, and head to the beach. They've got a terrific restaurant there. Interested?"

I perked up, forgetting my lethargy. "Sounds like heaven. Count me in. I can leave in a half an hour." Fischer left after lunch most Fridays, so I shouldn't have any trouble.

I looked at the clock—a few minutes before 4 PM. I shut off my computer. When the phone rang, I prayed it wouldn't be Fischer. I grimaced. The name glaring up at me wasn't my boss, but my other nemesis, Tom. Why would he call again?

I glared at the phone for a few seconds. My hand was halfway toward the receiver before I caught myself. No. I wouldn't answer. I'd told him not to call here. I'd wait him out. Every ring was like a jab to my insides.

I sat there, back rigid. When the shrill bursts stopped, I relaxed and flopped back in my chair.

Damn! I'd been excited about the idea of hitting the beach. Now Tom's shadow dampened my enthusiasm.

On the way home, as usual, I checked behind me for his car. I'd taken to turning up the street before mine to check the cars behind me. His phone call had brought back the ache in my chest.

Why couldn't he just leave me alone?

~ * ~

A cute little black dog greeted me in front of the apartment. I was surprised the other end of his leash was attached to Heather. "Meet JoJo, the most important man in my life."

I'd forgotten she said she had a dog. The object of her affection rewarded my pats and scratches with kisses on my hands and cheek.

"He's adorable. Good boy, JoJo." Heather and the pup restored my good mood.

I was eager to get into my pink bikini and hurried inside to change. When I ran out front to meet her, she tooted the horn and blew my mind. Her ride, a top-down white Mustang convertible, was awesome.

"Wow." I jumped in and ran my fingers across the red leather. "Nice wheels."

"Thanks. I can't help myself. I'm into cool cars."

Today was perfect for a ride in an open convertible. I was glad I'd put my hair in a ponytail. The warm wind in my face blew away all my petty irritations. On the short ride to the beach, I told her about Tom. "What else can I do? I told him we were over the first time he called, and I refused to answer his last one."

"You have to be firm with him. If he calls again, tell him what he's doing is called stalking, and it's against the law. Tell him you'll call the cops if he bothers you again."

"I hate to get him angry. No telling what he'll do. I'm sure he'll get the message if I don't answer him."

"Listen, I work in a law office. Guys like him don't take no for an answer until their butts are in a grinder. Tell him you've talked to a lawyer. That'll shake him."

The day was too nice to waste any more of my breath on Tom, so I ousted him from my mind. While Heather filled me in on the latest neighborhood gossip, she confessed to having pet names for everyone. The redheaded family around the block? The Reds. The little lady next to Mrs. W? Mab, after the Fairy Queen. The paper boy was dubbed Tupper, but I'm not sure why.

Her stories and descriptions had me entertained all the way to Marblehead. When we drove into the parking lot, the tangy smell of the ocean greeted us. I inhaled the heady aroma and thanked my new friend. "This is wonderful. I need a place where no work problems or ex-boyfriends can distract me."

We grabbed our towels and chairs, then headed for the water. I lifted my nose in delight at the distinctive smell of fried clams floating past. Life was good.

From the size of the crowd, I guessed everyone had the same idea. We slogged through the sand. Pieces of it hit my butt as my flip-flops sprayed the crushed stones around. We found a spot near the water where we opened our chairs. Low tide had expanded the beach area. I enjoyed the antics of two young girls as they played around the edges of the surf. They'd run screeching away from the breaking waves then bend over and howl with belly laughs. A couple of other kids boogie-boarded in between the people.

Today was the first time I'd been to the beach this summer. I wanted to dig a hole in the hot sand and stay forever. I leaned back and let the blazing sun beat through the week's aggravations. The cadence of breaking waves, the hissing sound as they dragged across the pebbles, and the contented buzz of conversation put me into a near-coma. I missed most of what Heather said about some good-looking lawyer in her office, Peter something or other.

"Hey, are you asleep?"

"Wha…?"

"I said I might be love. I can't wait for you to meet him at the party."

"Love? Wow. Now I'm dying to meet him."

According to her, Peter was smart, handsome, and had the disposition of a saint. Sounded like love to me. Once she'd filled me in on everything Peter, she gazed around at the busy beachgoers.

I'd begun to drift off again when she poked me. "Look over there."

"Where?" I blinked, hating to disrupt my tranquility.

She pointed toward the water. I held my hand over my eyes to block the sun. A tall, curvy blonde in a tiny black bikini was in a deep discussion with a ripped guy. "Check out who she's teasing…Joe Powers."

"Who?"

"Damn it. I forgot you're new here. The blonde is Trish Gregory, Sam's ex."

That made me sit up. "Sam, the electrician?"

"Yup." She raised her eyebrow. "And that's her best friend's husband."

"Nice," I said. "She must be a real winner. Too bad she's gorgeous."

Heather blew out a noisy breath. "The bitch loves to flaunt her stuff."

The way Trish filled out her scanty bikini, I understood why Sam hadn't been interested in coffee with me. How could I compete if his ex looked like that? The cool dude showing off his dynamite abs was all but drooling over her. "They look pretty chummy."

"Don't they?" Heather said with an 'I've got a secret' smile.

A few minutes later, we trekked to the restaurant she'd suggested. I gave the grilled chicken salad a guilty peek, then ordered a burger and fries.

~ * ~

We hadn't been back home more than ten minutes when I got another call from Heather, who sounded upset. "Put on the news, I'm on my way over."

I left my wet bathing suit in the sink, dragged on shorts and a top, and hurried to the TV to find the news. I lifted my shoulders in confusion. No earth-shattering events.

When she knocked, I yelled, "Come in." I'd left it unlocked for her.

She rushed in. "What have they said?"

"About what?"

"The body."

A minute later, the commentator's words, *Breaking news*, captured our attention.

"Police confirm skeletal remains were uncovered at a construction site near an abandoned house in Salem. Detectives have been on the scene since early this afternoon. We'll break in with updates as we get them."

Heather paced in front of the set as she aired her aggravation. "Salem?" She glared at the TV and yelled, "Where in Salem?" Transferring her agitation to me, she said, "The site could be anywhere. Oh, my God, what if there's a serial killer on the loose?"

I rolled my eyes. Heather spent too much time in front of the TV. "Get over yourself. They found a skeleton. That means it's old. Whatever happened took place a long time ago. We don't need to be concerned now."

Although my voice may have been calm, my insides jangled. Skeletons ranked high in my horror hit parade, right up there with ghosts.

The pacing stopped, but she persisted, spouting out questions. "I wonder who it is. Was it a man or a woman? How do you suppose they died?

Content there was no immediate danger, she centered her interest on the mystery. "Where do you think they found the body?" Her eyes widened. "What if it's the construction site off Derby?"

I suppressed a shiver and shook my head. "I hope not." Even though the crime was old, I wouldn't want the burial site to be anywhere near us.

After another glance at the TV, she said, "They don't have a timeline yet. At least the victim isn't anyone from around here."

"How can you be so sure?

She pursed her lips and gave me an incredulous look. "They'd have been missed. I'll bet the skeleton belongs to a tourist." She worried her bottom lip with her teeth. "I wish I knew who lived in the house at the time the victim was buried."

I had to grin. Listening to her was like tuning in to one of those TV crime shows. I'm sure, with her sense of drama, she pictured us "in the field" àla Rizzoli and Isles.

"You can laugh, but a killer planted the body in our city. You can't dismiss the reality." When I opened my mouth to speak, she stopped me. "Before you say anything, this has to be a murder because someone buried the body to hide their crime."

"Okay, why don't we wait to discuss possibilities until they have more information?"

My refusal to fret irritated her.

"Fine, but we're both single women who live alone. That's who the killers go for."

~ * ~

Saturday morning I poked one eye open, peered at the time, and groaned, but I had to get up. My sister would be here at lunchtime. I ran around the apartment, did the dishes, put away clothes, and dusted. When the place was spotless, I decided to take a walk. If I stayed home, I'd just fidget.

Whenever people talk about Salem, the usual focus was on witches, violence, and the supernatural. Although horror crawled through the city in the late seventeenth century, Salem also had a wonderful maritime history, often forgotten. I read, at one point, Salem was a world-famous seaport in the East Indies trade.

I liked living there. Although Salem was a city, its neighborhoods projected a small-town vibe. Outside my new apartment, I took a moment to appreciate the peaceful atmosphere, until a piercing voice shattered the moment. Heather was right. Mrs. W missed nothing.

I crossed the street, wondering if she ever left her perch. "Good morning, Mrs. Wallace."

"Did you hear about the body?" She quivered with excitement as she expounded on the latest news.

"Happens all the time. Some poor girl gets involved with the wrong man." She shook her head, as if mourning the loss, but the gleam in her eyes belied her words. "It's terrible the way young people today carry on." She pointed at me. "You and Heather better mind your p's and q's. You could be next."

I wanted to inform her nothing would ever happen to us with a nosy old biddy across the street. Instead, I smiled and waved goodbye.

Around the corner on Derby Street, I'd discovered a wonderful coffee shop. The minute I opened the door, the scent of fresh-brewed coffee and baked goods hit me. Saliva filled my mouth. I ordered a latte and a cinnamon bun for later. I had to have a tiny bite now, though, before I put the sweet concoction back in the bag. So good.

I sat down in a comfortable chair to relax. I needed quiet time before my sister arrived. Her unwavering supply of energy was exhausting. Her actions reminded me of a tiny Tasmanian Devil, in constant motion, spinning from one perceived crisis to the next.

After a peaceful interval, I continued my stroll. In one store window, I spotted a sign for a haunted tour of the city. I chuckled. *Imagine people falling for that stuff.*

A couple of hours later, I'd positioned myself on the front stairs to wait for my sister. A pair of skateboarders zipped through traffic, and I shook my head. What kept those long, loose shorts from falling off their skinny butts?

I shifted my concentration to the odd jumble of architecture that lined our street. From my research into Salem neighborhoods, I didn't believe any houses were built later than the early-nineteenth century and a lot of them earlier than that. I'd love to examine time-lapse photography showing the original structures and their changes.

Kirsten's voice startled me. "Hey, I had to park miles away. Who owns all these cars?"

"Hey, yourself, sis. You're late."

"Don't I know it." She tucked my arm into hers and pivoted toward the street. "Which way? I'm starving." No small talk with her.

"Okay. You can check out my new digs when we get back."

The restaurant Heather had suggested gave us a fantastic view of the harbor. The *Friendship* sat docked close by. Enticing smells filled the air. We both ordered the special of fish and chips.

Kirsten sipped her coffee and asked how I liked my new apartment. Then she leaned in and whispered, "What about Tom? Has he tried to contact you again?"

When I told her he'd called me at work, she slapped her hand on the table. "Damn it, Dani." Elbows propped in front of her, she frowned. "You're too nice. Tell him to back off or you'll call the cops. You need to scare him."

"You're probably right. I just don't think he'll listen."

"He will if you're tough enough. Tell him to stay the hell away from you. Never mind that 'please don't call me' stuff. I'll have Rick send him a letter." Since her husband practiced law, she rambled on, emulating an air of authority.

A tinge of anger slipped into my voice as I spoke, "Let's not talk about this right now." I didn't want to ruin our day, so I added, "I'd like to enjoy lunch with my favorite sister."

Her frown slid up at one corner, softening her words. "Your *only* sister."

After lunch, we wandered through stores along the wharf. I mentioned tonight's shopping trip, that Heather was going to help me find a dress. Thrilled I'd found a friend, she wanted the whole story.

After a brief explanation, I said, "You'll love her. She's a trip. Though she tends to be a little dramatic. She almost had a heart attack when they found a body here yesterday."

"I can't believe I forgot about the discovery. What's the latest? My God, they found the remains right near here."

The gravesite was close. Heather and I checked out the place, a mere five-minute drive from our building. Not too far from the condos where my boss lived.

"It's terrible, but not to worry. The crime is almost ancient." My attempt to minimize the news gave my sister the impetus to rehash the dangers of me living alone. When would I learn to think before I spoke?

On our way home, an old storefront with a jumbled-looking window whose sign said, ANTIQUES, sidetracked us. Kirsten was unable to resist anything that predated our parents. I'd always considered these so-called treasures expensive castaways. I never quite understood the attraction, but I followed her across the street.

The inside resembled a church rummage sale rather than a collection of fine old artifacts. From my position by the door, I spied furniture, paintings, old toys, and jewelry in no apparent order.

In a loud whisper, Kirsten said, "I like this place."

I tried not to use the word "junk" in my mind and inspected the "stuff," turning every time she said, "Hey, Dani. How do you like this?" Worried I might get whiplash, I headed to her side of the room.

"Whoops," I said as I tripped over a pot on the floor.

Kirsten lunged and caught me before I did any damage. Her parental glare preceded her censure. "Be careful. You never pay attention to where you're going."

The proprietor, an older woman with jet-black hair—a bad dye job—an ankle-length, flared skirt, and jangling bracelets gave me a nervous stare and moved in closer.

Kirsten pointed to an old desk. "I love this Governor Winthrop. Look at the lines."

An inkwell perched on top looked interesting. Careful where I stepped, I went over, secured my find, and asked the woman who'd been shadowing me since I'd tripped, "How much for this?"

The old writing tool would fit into a 1700s room and might be the beginning of a new appreciation for antiques. I didn't want to start too big.

The price was fair. She said, "I've got an old quill pen around here somewhere I'll throw in." She must have forgiven me for my almost mishap.

"Excellent," I told her.

Kirsten smirked at my attempt to show off my first antique purchase. Not quite ready for the big time.

I wandered off on my own again toward the back of the shop. An assortment of small statues in a shadowy nook caught my attention. In the poor lighting, I leaned closer. When a slight breeze cooled my neck, I swiveled around. No one was near me. Nothing moved.

"Dani, look at what I found."

The eerie atmosphere quashed my interest in the tiny figurines. I was delighted to hear my sister's voice.

"This would be awesome in your bedroom."

Glad to move away from the dark corner, I took care as I navigated the room. "What?"

With a flourish, she raised her arm. Hanging from her fingers was an old metal lantern. One that had seen better days. My face must have shown my displeasure.

In a no-nonsense tone, she said, "It's a housewarming gift."

Pouting like a sulky kid, I said, "What am I supposed to do with a lantern?"

Out of patience, she fell into the familiar role of older sister. Ever since we were kids, we'd disagreed on almost everything.

"I want you to have a special present. This light was made for an old fireplace."

Figures. My description of the bedroom intrigued her. Before I could respond, a voice from behind me said, "That's an interesting piece." The woman I'd dubbed "Gypsy" was speaking to Kirsten. "This came from a house in Salem said to be haunted."

Oh good. Another ghost story. Arms crossed, I glared at my sister, who ignored me and gave the woman her complete attention. "Oh?"

Peering over the glasses on the end of her nose, Gypsy leaned in and lowered her voice. "They say the spirit was a Mooncusser. This is the lantern he used to search through the wreckage spread across the rocks."

My nerve endings zinged. Did the room get darker? I chanced a peek around at all the old stuff in the room and grimaced. Each piece, no doubt, had a ghost associated with it. Although I didn't want to believe in them, the idea of hauntings made me nervous. While I stood there wreathed in discomfort, Kirsten, the intrepid, wanted more.

"What's a Mooncusser?" she said.

Gypsy folded her arms. "A parasite." With a dramatic sigh, she continued, "In the late nineteenth century, there were many shipwrecks along the rocky coasts. A few people made money from salvaging their goods. Mooncussers were different, though. They didn't wait for a tragedy to happen. They used their lanterns on stormy nights to signal a safe haven to ships in trouble, luring hapless vessels onto the rocks, where they pillaged the wrecks." Disgust filled her voice. "They were cold-blooded killers who scoured the awful carnage they created for any items of value."

When the back-room curtain twitched for no apparent reason, I jumped. From beneath the drape, a haughty calico cat glared.

Kirsten's voice dropped to a whisper. "Why did they call them Mooncussers?"

Gypsy pursed her lips. "Moonlight made their gruesome work more dangerous, so they cussed it." Turning to me, she said, "In those days, they used whale oil to light their lanterns. I'd suggest you buy kerosene."

Oh, yeah. That's what I needed. A murderer's lantern.

After the story, Kirsten liked the ugly light even more and bought the thing despite my objections. I decided the lantern would make a great addition to the cellar.

"What if this thing's cursed?" I asked. I didn't believe there was anything wrong with the lantern, but I wanted to emphasize her high-handed treatment of her baby sister.

She poked me. "Don't be silly. It's just an old lantern."

~ * ~

Kirsten approved my apartment and carried on about how great the fireplace was with the addition of her gift. "I told you. This lamp is perfect here."

I hated to admit she was right, but the lantern did fit in. It might have been made for the hearth. I told her so, thanked her, and unwrapped my purchase. "This new inkwell will make a great addition to my office."

I hesitated and gave the loft a wary glance. No smoky blobs. I ran upstairs to place the pen and inkwell on the right-hand corner of the desk, as if I used the quill for writing. I resolved to buy ink and try out my purchases. Now I owned two antiques. For a moment, I gazed at the fireplace, imagining what the hearth must have been in its day with the crackle of the wood and the spray of sparks as a log shifted in the fire.

"Are you going to admire your handiwork all day?" Kirsten said.

I snapped out of my daydream and wondered at the bizarre apparitions my mind conjured, then I regarded the inkwell and pen, crafted so many years ago. After Gypsy's story, I realized the hand that had guided the quill could have been anyone from poet to murderer. I shook off a chill.

"Hey," Kirsten called from the kitchen, "who's the guy in your backyard?"

"What guy?" I ran downstairs to peek out the window. "Oh, that's Jimbo." I recognized his butt. "He's a terrific gardener, and he takes care of Eddie's landscaping."

"What's he doing in your yard?"

"I asked him to put in some flowers. He's okay. Heather vouched for him, and everyone around here likes him."

The ringtone of my phone cut into our conversation. I pressed the button. "Hello?"

"Hi." Heather's voice.

"What great timing. My sister's here. Why don't you pop in for a minute?" To Kirsten I said, "Heather's on her way over here."

A minute or two later, my neighbor arrived a little winded. She must have run over. I'd no sooner introduced her to my sister when she said, "It's a woman."

"Huh?"

Heather and Kirsten swung toward me, my sister with eyebrows raised suggesting she found my friend a bit strange, and Heather, lips pursed, one hand on her hip in her *will you listen* mode.

"The body is a woman."

Kirsten jumped in. "The one they found in Salem?"

Heather spun around to focus on my sister. "Right. The news anchor said the skeleton was a young female, and the police suspected homicide. Like, duh? Why else bury her?"

"Right." Kirsten paused and looked at me. "That means there's a murderer around here."

"That's what I told Dani," Heather said. "If a killer wanted to attack her, she wouldn't even have a dog to bark a warning."

Two annoyed women pivoted toward me.

"Wait a minute," I said. "Don't forget the body has been in the ground forever. The killer is long gone." Heather was on a roll. She flipped her head back and forth between us as she spoke, her ponytail slapping her face with each turn. "There could be any number of reasons why the murderer stopped." She ticked them off on her fingers.

"One, he might be in jail. Two, he might have moved away or died."

I held up my hand to stop her. "Before you go any further, think about what you've said. Those are all valid scenarios, and I'm inclined to agree with number two. The perpetrator, if still alive, has moved on.

She stared at me. "I'm not finished."

She held up three fingers and lowered her voice. "Third, maybe he's still here," she paused and peered at each of us, "but they haven't found his latest victims."

Fingers of ice teased my spine, and I sucked in my breath. That grave was only a short drive from here. I sent up a fervent prayer that Heather was wrong.

Chapter Seven

The shopping trip was a huge success. I bought a cute sundress, beige with big mauve-and-green flowers, and a sweet pair of sandals that looked dynamite on my feet. On the way out of the mall, I snagged a pair of outrageous earrings to complete my ensemble. Bags in hand, Heather and I decided to have dinner at Pickering Wharf.

Our seats had a perfect view of the harbor and the expensive boats docked below us. I was fascinated by the constant parade of people around the area.

After a sip of wine, Heather confided in me she was almost tongue-tied at work around Peter. "Even in a conservative suit, he's sexy and such a nice guy. I can never figure out what to say. At a bar after a few drinks, I have all kinds of courage, but with Peter I'm nervous. The atmosphere there gets on my nerves, too quiet and proper. That's why I'm pinning my hopes on next Friday at the yacht club. I'll be in my element."

After dinner we sauntered along the streets of the wharf, where a cool breeze refreshed us. When we came to a shop that advertised Wiccan jewelry, crystals, and healing stones, Heather insisted we go inside. "I love this place. Awesome stuff, and the prices aren't bad."

She zeroed in on the end of the store, leaving me to poke around on my own. The jewelry was a bit different, silver-shaped moons, wings, and pentagrams, and she was right about the prices. Almost a whole wall held bins of stones in all shapes, sizes, and colors.

In the far corner, I spied a dramatic assortment of colorful velvet capes. Next to the vibrant drapes stood a case filled with books on Wicca. I half expected Harry Potter and his crew to pop into the room. I chuckled. Witchcraft might be a big draw in Salem, but I didn't succumb to the lure of the unknown. To be truthful, seers and fortunetellers made me nervous. I called to Heather to tell her I'd wait for her outside and headed for the door. I almost bumped into the saleswoman behind me. About my mother's age, or a little older, she had hints of gray sprinkled through her long, auburn hair.

When a flyaway strand escaped, she tucked the stray around her ear and smiled. "May I help you?"

I'd been gaping at the beautiful blue and green triangular stone nestled between her breasts. About two inches wide, the striking pendant hung from a fine silver chain. Embarrassed to be gawking, I said, "Sorry to stare, but your necklace is fabulous."

"Thank you. It's my favorite." With a tilt of her head, she said, "I haven't seen you in this store before. You must be new to the area. Did you just move here?"

Ooh, that's weird. I wonder how she guessed I wasn't a tourist. "I did. Last week."

"How nice." She didn't say anything more, just peered at me.

I tugged at my earring, shifted my feet, and glanced around the store.

When she did speak, her voice was more amicable, almost neighborly. "We have quite interesting houses around here, teeming with history. Are you in one of the older homes?"

I had no intention of telling this woman anything. My home address was none of her business. Before I could stop them, though, words tumbled from my traitorous mouth. "I live in the old Gale house."

Her reaction must have been my imagination. Why not? My crazy ideas had been giving me fits since I'd moved here—but I swore her eyes dimmed. She gave a slight nod. "We have a sale on a selection of stones today. I have a wonderful piece you might find appealing."

When I stepped back, ready to leave, she placed a small rough stone in my hand. "The color is perfect for you."

I inspected the piece, a bright emerald shade with different hues of green swirled throughout. "What is this?"

"Malachite. You'll find it's soothing and has protective qualities." She touched her chest. "My necklace has the same stone." Though she held my gaze, her smile didn't reach her dark, almond-shaped eyes. "It never hurts to be safe."

I wanted to tell her she couldn't scare me into buying her merchandise, but she closed my fingers around the gem. "As a welcome to the neighborhood, I'll give you this small piece, and you steer your friends to my store." Her smile faded. "Keep this trinket close."

When Heather asked her a question, she left. The stone I held wasn't polished smooth like the woman's necklace, but I liked my little rock. The ragged green surface sparkled. When it warmed my hand, I transferred the gift to my purse and wondered at the strange incident.

Outside again, Heather opened her bag for me to inhale the sweet scent of the candles she'd purchased. She confessed she used them quite often and recounted the healing properties of each one. In the middle of our aromatic lesson, an insistent tickle on the back of my neck made me swing around.

The woman who'd given me the stone stood at the entrance to her store. I was certain she'd been staring at me. We made brief visual contact, and a tremor of unease disturbed me. I looked away and gave my head a shake. I must have sniffed too many candles. I'd imagined her voice in my mind. *Take care.*

Ridiculous. I gave myself a mental pinch and said to Heather, "She's weird."

"Who?"

"The woman in the store."

Her eyes widened. "She's a witch."

I stopped. "Wait a minute." I gulped as I remembered the words in my head. "A real witch?"

Heather laughed. "Of course. This is Salem."

I couldn't help one more peek behind me. The woman was gone, but try as I might, I couldn't forget her warning.

~ * ~

For whatever reason, I slept well that night and woke refreshed and optimistic. Good thing because the electrician, Sam, would be there at 9:00 AM.

This time I determined to be in better control of my emotions when he arrived. Right. If anything, I was worse. Acutely aware of the muscles beneath his T-shirt as he walked toward the bedroom, I chattered on about the wonderful plug he'd installed and other foolish minutiae. When he turned around with a raised eyebrow and a grin, I stopped talking.

"Any more problems?" he said.

"No concerns other than this room."

He proceeded up the staircase to the loft. I took a minute to enjoy the view. He caught me staring and smirked.

My face grew hot. "Okay, I'll leave you to your work. Yell if you need anything." I spun around and hurried into the kitchen.

A while later, he popped his head into the living room. "I'll be in the cellar under your bedroom. The old fuse box is down there. Be back in a bit."

"In the basement? Where?"

"Come with me, and I'll show you." He led the way. "It's not a very nice place. It's nasty, like a dark root cellar."

We moved past the laundry area to the end of the basement. When he opened a door, the stench of dirt and mold engulfed me, and I backpedaled. I had the strangest urge to break and run.

"Here's the fuse box," he said and directed his flashlight inside the room for me.

I held my breath and leaned in for a peek.

"Uh, thanks for the information. If you need anything, I'll be upstairs." I couldn't get away from the creepy place fast enough. No wonder Eddie hadn't mentioned it on his tour.

Sam spent the next few hours working between the bedroom and the cellar. I ignored the drill's steady buzz and hoped there wouldn't be too much damage to the walls.

When my parents arrived, I gave them a quick tour before we settled in the living room. They liked my new digs and presented me with a great housewarming gift—a certificate to a local home goods store.

In the middle of a conversation on the pros and cons of different kitchen appliances, Sam popped his head in. "I'm on my way to lunch. I'll be back in about an hour."

I hadn't expected the job to be all day. "How much longer will this take?"

"I'm almost done. After I come back, it'll be a couple of more hours. I should be finished before dinner."

My father held out his hand. "Charlie Trent, Dani's father."

"Excuse me," I said. "This is Sam Gregory. Sam, my father and my mother, Meg."

"It's a pleasure to meet you both," he said.

The minute he left, my mother, the matchmaker, appeared. "Oh, I like him. Is he married?"

"Mother! He's here to fix the electricity. I don't pry into people's personal lives." Then I remembered Heather pointing out Trish, the ex of Gregory Electric's owner.

Heat rose to my cheeks, and I looked away. My mother honed in on me like a hungry hawk to a defenseless mouse.

An exaggerated eyebrow waggle and a "You're not fooling me" grin preceded her next words. "Oh. He isn't. Well, I say go for it. Electricians make good money."

Since Sam would be back before long, we opted to order takeout. On this warm, sunny day, my yard looked great, so we ate outside. The daisies and marigolds Jimbo planted added a cheery note to an enjoyable lunch.

Mom was regaling me with stories of their trip to Connecticut when Heather arrived at the back gate. "Hi, everyone. Am I interrupting?"

"No." I waved her over. "Come in and meet my parents."

After the introductions, she revealed a small camera and said, "Want a photo shoot of your first cookout?" She pointed to the food bags and amended it to, "Or eat out."

My mother loved the idea and prodded my father out of his chair. Heather posed us, prompting my mom to ask if she was a professional photographer. "Not yet. I've sold a few photos. I hope to do freelance for a couple of magazines."

Heather ignored my father's grumbling and moved us to different parts of the yard, framing us against the house, forsythia bushes, and the colorful flower beds. She took a few more photos inside. Her businesslike demeanor with much less of her signature chatter surprised me.

She thanked my parents for their cooperation. "I got some pretty good shots. I'll go through them and make copies for you and Dani."

Before she left, though, she mentioned the murder and ruined the mood. My parents exchanged horrified glances.

"Thanks Heather," I said and walked her to the gate to end the subject.

She wasn't finished. She placed her hands on her hips and glared at me. "I wish you'd be more concerned. We have to be vigilant. The killer might be anywhere."

I hoped her words didn't carry. If she was right, the murderer could be someone right in our neighborhood.

I rejoined my parents, told them I trusted the Salem police, and promised to be super careful. Then I unearthed old memories to defuse the situation. I pointed to the forsythia bushes. "Remember when I ran away from home and hid under the one in our back yard? And Mom left a tray with sandwiches and cookies on the table to let me sneak out and eat?"

The story elicited smiles, but Mom wasn't deterred and pulled me aside. "What kind of people live in this neighborhood?"

"It's a great place. There aren't any secrets. Everyone knows each other."

Her lips tightened as worry tinged her eyes. "What's to stop some outsider from wandering in here?"

I chuckled. "If you're worried about strangers, forget it. We have a tenacious watchdog across the street. Mrs. Wallace doesn't miss a trick."

"Make sure you always lock your doors."

"I will, Mom."

When Sam returned from his lunch break, my mother whispered in my ear, "Maybe we should stay until he leaves. This guy is a complete stranger."

I had to assure her of his credentials before she'd go. After prolonged hugs and more admonitions to take care, my parents left.

I put away the lunch leftovers and cleaned the kitchen, hyper-aware of the hottie in the next room. With the kitchen gleaming, I put on a pot of coffee. "Hey, Sam." I poked my nose into the bedroom. "Want a coffee?"

"Thanks. Sounds good. Black is fine."

Yes! A smile strained my cheeks, and I got busy arranging what was left of the cookies from my bake-a-thon the previous night.

I didn't notice him behind me so I jumped when I heard, "How's that coffee coming? Sorry," he said. "I didn't mean to startle you."

His sexy smile brought heat to my face. Dormant romantic urges surfaced. Tom hadn't revved my engine in a long time, and Sam's proximity had my motor purring. *Come on Dani. Get over yourself. He's hot and you're lonesome.*

I put his cup and a plate full of cookies on the table. "All ready. Have a seat."

His reaction delighted me. "I love chocolate chip cookies." He nabbed one, took a big bite and gave a moan of pleasure. "Mmm, good."

The sound went straight to my libido. I took a moment to compose myself and sighed. We may not be relationship-bound, but at least we had something in common.

I gestured toward the bedroom. "What's the verdict?"

He finished the cookie in his mouth before he spoke. "The reason you lost power in there is because it's on a different system." He raised an eyebrow and grinned. "The wiring dates back to Elias."

My mouth dropped open. He chuckled. "An exaggeration. The structure has been here for a couple of centuries."

He filled me in on the house. He discussed the history as if he enjoyed the subject, and I appreciated the way his eyes sparkled when he talked about the man who'd built the room.

"Old Elias began his career as a grunt on someone's fishing boat and later became the owner of a small fleet." He raised an eyebrow, and one side of his mouth quirked up. "They say he made his money when the moon was new."

Confused, I said, "Were there more fish when the moon was new?'

He laughed. "He was a smuggler." When he lowered his voice, he sounded like someone telling a ghost story. "During the new moon, when its face is dark, all kinds of fiends ply their trade. For a smuggler, it's the perfect time to sneak onto the beach to unload illegal cargo."

A cold wave encompassed me, and I rubbed my arms. "The more I hear about him, the less I like him."

Sam winked and tossed back the rest of his coffee. "Elias would have liked you. From all accounts, he was quite the lady's man."

Was that a compliment? I patted my ponytail and prepared to start serious flirting, until he stood up. "I'm moving everything from the fuse box in the cellar to the central breaker panel here in the kitchen. Once that's done, you won't have any more trouble. Oh, by the way, I found evidence of mice in your bedroom closet. You might want to purchase a couple of traps."

"Yuck," I said, almost spitting out my coffee. That wasn't at all amorous.

With a slight twist of his lips, he added, "If you catch any, give me a call and I'll get rid of them for you."

I scrunched up my shoulders and made an icky face, unable to blot out the image of a tiny, gray body squished in a trap.

He grinned at my discomfort. "Thanks for the cookies. They were delicious. Once I finish in the cellar, I'll be done."

Mention of the pit downstairs reminded me of Elias. I bet he stashed his loot in there.

A while later, I sat in the kitchen daydreaming about Sam, who must have a girlfriend, when a voice drifted in from the bedroom. It sounded like my name. Even though daylight splashed through the windows, goosebumps covered my arms.

I edged to the door and listened. It came again, a little muffled, but I recognized it as Sam's voice. "Dani, damn it. Dani, help."

I ran in and swung my head around in an attempt to locate the source. Confused, I shouted, "Where are you?"

His angry retort roared from beneath my feet. "I'm locked in the damn cellar. Come get me."

Oh, boy, I didn't like that musty, dark room. I paused to contemplate the horror of being locked inside, and he bellowed again, "Dani."

I snapped out of my speculation. "Okay. I'm coming."

All the way down the stairs, I reassured myself, *It's only a room.* I hurried to the end of the cellar. Near the door, my footsteps slowed. The air was heavier, like pushing through a wall of syrup. My tattered nerves exaggerated everything. I wrapped my fingers around the door handle then jerked them back. The metal was ice cold. The dank odor beyond the door twisted around me.

"Sam, I'm here," I yelled, as I attacked the cold surface once again, twisting to get it open. The knob wouldn't budge. In my frustration, I tried kicking to no avail. All I did was give myself a sore ankle. "It won't move."

My declaration ignited a stream of swearwords from inside. "I'll try to get help. I'll ask the guy upstairs." There wasn't much else I could do other than call the authorities. "I'll be right back."

I raced up two flights of stairs—exercise I wasn't used to. With the exertion and heightened anxiety, my breathing was ragged when Doug Forman answered my knock. Thank God he recognized me and didn't slam the door in my face.

Doug was weirder, if possible, than his wife. We'd met outside over trash one day. He carried on for five minutes about dogs and raccoons who always managed to get into the barrels and make a mess. His dark-rimmed glasses and messy hair reminded me of a crazed scientist. I didn't mind his tirades so much, but his silent stares made me uncomfortable. A couple of times on my way to work, I'd caught him peering through the shadows. Yuck!

I gasped out what happened to Sam.

Doug frowned. "Okay. Just a minute."

When we reached my *special* cellar, I hollered to Sam to tell him I'd found someone. Doug twisted the knob, yanked on it, and gave the wood a big kick. The door remained closed. He might have hurt himself, but I pretended not to notice. With a savage scowl on his face, he scanned the floor around us.

"Wait a minute." He stormed off to the other end of the room.

Clanks and squeaks echoed as he rummaged around. When he came back, a large metal pipe was slung over his shoulder like a baseball player ready to bat.

He swept his arm around and grinned. "Stand back."

I moved far away in case he lost his grip and let the rod fly toward me. He lifted his arms above his head and slammed his weapon against the door handle again and again. He looked like a madman as he grunted and swung his metal bar.

When the handle flew off, Sam burst from the room like a volcanic eruption. He stood for a minute taking deep breaths then offered his hand to Doug. "Thanks so much. If you ever need any electrical work, I'm your man."

Doug let the pipe clatter to the floor, gave me a sullen frown, and muttered, "No problem."

At a questioning look from Sam, I shrugged. I wondered if Doug and Marie had ever been taught manners.

On the way upstairs, Sam said, "Man, I hate being trapped, and that place is the pits."

Poor guy. I pictured myself stuck in there. No light. No air. Surrounded by dank muck, and closed in with all kinds of crawly, slithery creatures. When I imagined the walls closing in and the ground sucking me under, my stomach threatened to heave. "I couldn't handle being locked in there. I'd go crazy or die."

He twisted his lips in a half smile. "Well, thank God you weren't stuck in there, then. I'd hate it if you died."

Oh, boy, the killer smile again.

He shook his head. "I can't understand how it got stuck. Mind if I take a look at the lock?"

"Be my guest." Now I'd have to call Eddie and tell him something else was broken.

We were in the hall when Heather poked her head out of her kitchen. "What's going on?"

When I told her Sam had been locked in the cellar, her lips pulled together in a grimace. "Oh, wow. That dungeon? I'm glad it's closed off from the main basement. I got a peek in there once when Rose had trouble." She shivered. "That was enough for me." She peered at Sam. "Are you okay?"

He laughed. "Yeah, I'm fine. Other than having to deal with the fact I had to be rescued by a tiny female."

Although I'd never been called tiny, I straightened to my full height. "Be grateful there was a *tiny* female around to save you."

His lips curled in amusement. "Thanks for bringing the muscle." He stopped and examined the floor. "Damn it. I forgot to clean my shoes. The dirt from that stinking place gets everywhere."

Heather promised to sweep up the mess later, then walked us over to my apartment. She and Sam were old acquaintances. They chatted while he gathered his tools.

Before he left, he assured me I'd have no more problems, thanked me again for coming to his rescue, and asked if he might take a couple of cookies with him. I almost tripped over myself hurrying to fill a baggy.

He grinned, touched his fingers to his forehead in his little salute then left.

When the door closed, I tackled Heather on the subject of Sam Gregory.

"Oh, yeah, he'd be perfect for you. He's divorced, and I'm

pretty sure he isn't dating anyone." We both agreed he was a total babe.

"I'd better get back to feed my hungry man. He gets wicked upset if his bow-wow burgers are late." Heather snagged a couple of cookies and gave me a thumbs-up on her way out.

The rest of the evening, I fantasized about Sam. Although I didn't want to jump into a relationship right away, it couldn't hurt to find someone to play with.

Chapter Eight

On my way home from work, I wrangled with the Fischer dilemma. Why was my hateful boss appearing at my complex so often? I decided to contact the other managers to find out if he was bothering them too.

The blue lights of police cruisers in front of my home wiped Fischer from my mind. I zipped into the nearest parking space and joined the crowd gathered around our lawn. "What happened?"

No one had any idea, and their suppositions, including murder, made me sick. I ignored them and sprinted toward my apartment, where a policeman stopped me. "Are you Dani Trent?"

"Yes, what's going on?" Fear made my voice low and breathy.

"There's been a break-in at your neighbor's apartment."

"Oh, my God. Is she okay?"

"Not to worry. She wasn't home when the burglary happened."

Heather's frantic calls for JoJo interrupted us. She spotted me when she came around the corner. "Oh, God. I've been robbed, and JoJo's missing. I can't find him. I've looked all over the apartment." Tears coursed down her cheeks as she peered around. "My poor baby. Where is he?"

"Why don't you take the cellar? I'll do the outside."

"Right." She spun toward the basement entrance.

I ran outside, calling the dog's name. I reached the street and asked, "Has anyone seen a small black dog?"

The sea of headshakes gave me hope he hadn't gotten out there. I tore around the other side of the building and ended in my own yard. I bent over to catch my breath, then called the pup's name. I was rewarded with the sound of pitiful little cries.

"JoJo?" The noise came again from the back. The poor little guy was whimpering underneath the forsythia bush.

I knelt and spoke in a soft whisper. "Hi, JoJo. Easy, baby."

I reached in to let him sniff my hand. After a few seconds, he scootched out on his tummy. Concerned he might be hurt, I took care when I lifted him. I was rewarded with a big lick.

He tucked his head into the crook of my arm, and I rushed to the side door hollering Heather's name. She came bounding from the cellar. "It's okay. He's safe." When I placed him in her arms, her shoulders sagged, and she crooned his name.

Her hands moved over his body as she checked for trauma. Satisfied there were no injuries, she told me what happened. "When I came home, my back door was open and my apartment trashed. What a mess—all my stuff thrown around. Bureau drawers emptied. What would anyone want from me?"

The invasion of her privacy annihilated her self-confidence and kicked a hole in my own courage. I offered her my apartment as a refuge for however long she needed it. "You and JoJo should be comfortable on the sofa bed."

"Thanks, but we'll be okay in my apartment."

Her wan attempt at a smile made me want to put my arm around her and protect her. When Eddie came around the corner, I almost attacked him. He rushed to Heather, concern etched on his face. "Are you all right? The police called."

His abrupt appearance startled JoJo, who bared his teeth and growled. Heather apologized for her dog. "He's traumatized by the invasion. Thank God that monster didn't hurt him. I appreciate your concern. I'm fine, still a little shaken."

Eddie stood there like a prizefighter waiting for the bell. I'd never witnessed his anger. He scowled and rubbed the back of his head. With his dark hair awry, he was kind of cute. I chuckled to myself. Eddie, who prided himself on being professional and tough, would be horrified at the word "cute."

"I'd like to get my hands on the bastard who did this. I can't believe I didn't see him. I was here earlier. I must have missed him." He shoved his glasses to the bridge of his nose and swore. "This is terrible. It makes me furious. Call me if you need any help. I've got new lock sets for your apartment in my truck. I'll install them right away."

After Eddie left, a policeman came to talk to us. "Looks like they figured the place would be empty. Easy enough to jimmy the lock. I'd suggest a deadbolt, ladies. In the meantime, if you see anything suspicious, call us."

Inside my apartment, Heather and JoJo retreated to the living room where JoJo whined, ran to the back door, and scratched.

"He has to go," she said. "Perfect. I've got the makings for burgers. Why don't we cook outside?" I found it easier to breathe there.

JoJo sniffed around the yard, then returned to his mistress who cuddled him in her arms. When she glanced behind me and gasped, I whipped around and followed her stare to the man at the gate. Tall and wiry, the sun glinted off the champagne highlights in his brown hair. He must have had a recent application.

I wanted to run and hide as I screeched his name, "Tom!"

My shout and Heather's gasp made JoJo bark. Tom's smile dimmed. He hated dogs.

He walked in as if he belonged there. "Why were the police here? Are you okay?"

"I'm fine. What are you doing here?"

His gaze strayed to Heather, who'd corralled her snarling dog. "Aren't you going to introduce me to your beautiful friend?"

I ignored the question. "I told you I didn't want to see you again."

"Come on, honey," he said. "This fight has gone on too long. Let's forget the past."

My fingernails cut into my palms as I squeezed my hands. I found it difficult to keep my voice steady when my insides were screaming. "We did *not* have a fight. I left you. There is no more *us*. Now leave or I'll call the police."

His mouth tightened. The light vanished from his eyes. As he advanced toward me, Heather stood up. "Dani asked you to leave." She pointed to the gate. "The exit is that way."

He shot a savage glare in her direction then focused his anger on me. "A housewarming gift." He whipped a package at my head, but I ducked in time. On his way out, he slammed the gate hard enough to break it.

My hands shook as I retrieved Tom's present and threw it in the trash can. I apologized to Heather. "How could I be so naïve? I expected him to confront me at work. In my efforts to keep him from following me home, I never considered the possibility he'd use another car." I frowned. "He's not the man I fell for. In the beginning, he was sweet and engaging, but the charm was bait. Once he hooked me, I lost my independence. He wrapped me in invisible chains that tightened each time I asserted myself." The idea that snake had invaded my perfect nest made me ill. I swallowed angry tears. "I was so sure I'd found a refuge here. I underestimated his determination."

"So that's Tom. I don't like him, and JoJo agrees." He'd calmed down after Tom left and squirmed as she gave him a big hug. When she put him down, he ran to the gate for one last growl. "Maybe he's the one who trashed my apartment," she said with an anxious frown.

"No, that's not his style. Besides, why would he invade your space?"

"I have no idea, but I don't trust him, and I don't believe in coincidences."

~ * ~

After supper, we double-checked the locks on both our apartments. I decided to accompany Heather and JoJo on their walk. Demoralized by the invasion, she didn't want to go out alone. And, after the break-in and the reappearance of Tom, I was a bit needy myself, but JoJo with his little black tail held high emerged unscathed from today's events.

Before we got very far, though, the Cove Street Watcher hailed us. When Heather stopped, I said, "You don't have to speak to her now."

She rolled her eyes. "Best to get it over with."

For once, Mrs. W didn't crave the sensational details. Her concern centered around Heather's safety. "I wanted to apologize. I should have spotted a stranger at your place today. Was there much damage? If there's anything you need, or I can help in any way, just holler."

"Thank you, Mrs. Wallace. They trashed the place pretty good. I'm okay, though." She managed a wan smile. "I appreciate your kind offer."

"Now you girls be extra careful. Make sure to keep your doors locked."

We continued on our journey. I was stunned. "I can't believe what she just said to you. Since when is Mrs. W nice?"

Heather's answer was sincere rather than flippant. "Sure, she's wicked nosy and can be a little grouchy, but she does care about her neighborhood and the people who live here. She's more bark than bite."

When I offered to help her clean her apartment, she put her hands over her face. "Oh, God. I hate to face it. Then she straightened and gave me a wan smile. Thanks. I could use some support."

The place was a mess. Papers and other bits of Heather's possessions covered the floor. Her usually busy desk was bare. He must have swiped his hand across it.

A cry from Heather brought me over to her. "He smashed my camera."

Her face seemed to crumple. I wrapped my arms around her and said, "I'm so sorry."

After a few seconds, she pulled away. "I don't see anything

missing. This Nikon is expensive. Why destroy it rather than take it?"

After we finished straightening up, I repeated my offer for Heather and JoJo to stay in my apartment for the night, but she said she'd be all right. "JoJo will keep watch."

"Okay. I'll see you tomorrow."

I was concerned about her, but there was nothing more I could do.

The evening news provided the identity of the woman's skeleton, and I called Heather right away. "They know who the murder victim is."

"Oh?" The indifferent attitude was so unlike Heather.

"Yeah, her name's Allison Montenegro. She lived in Salem, but she worked for a temp agency in Boston."

"Wait a minute. What's her name?"

Happy to hear a spark of interest, I repeated the woman's identification.

After a moment, Heather sounded almost like herself. "I'm pretty sure that's the chick who skipped out on Eddie, stiffing him for the rent. I remember because he bitched and moaned about it for days." Her excitement dissolved, and her voice became a whisper, "Oh." Then silence.

While I waited for her to continue, small noises around me intensified. As I concentrated on the hollow echo in my ear, the silence around me took on a life of its own.

I imagined eerie whispers in the sighing of the refrigerator. "Heather?"

A tiny voice I'd never have recognized as her, filled the void. "I guess she didn't skip out after all."

~ * ~

Before I settled into bed, I made sure everything was locked. What if a burglar targeted my apartment? Heather's place was less than twenty feet away from mine. The terrible awareness of my vulnerability made it difficult for me to fall asleep. When I did, though, the day's events followed me.

In my dream, sharp cries pulled me from my bed. I crept out to investigate and slid on something. I tried to move, but my bare feet were mired in a sticky goo. Before I looked down, I feared what I'd see. Blood. The floor was filled with the red fluid. I choked back a cry and forced myself to discover the origin. The unfamiliar room confused me. Where was I?

Recognition hit like an explosion. I was looking at Heather's apartment. What a mess. Papers, clothes, even food littered the floor.

Frightened, I called her name. The answer—a sharp bark. I peered through the gloom. JoJo lay on the floor pawing at something. I sucked in my breath. A body? *Oh, no. Please don't let it be my friend.*

I closed my eyes, afraid to find out, but I had to. I edged closer to the bloodied figure. The image changed. Blonde hair receded. The blood disappeared. JoJo remained—chewing on a stick. Oh God. Not a stick, but a bone. And his treat was attached to a skeleton.

Chapter Nine

Clumsy, jumbled thoughts plodded through my head at the unremitting *beep, beep, beep* of the alarm. I shut it off and tried to shake away the remnants of sleep. I dragged my sluggish body to a seated position, then attempted to focus on what to do next—get my coffee or brush my teeth.

I'd best start by getting out of bed. The rain beating against the windows added to my sense of self-pity. I hated to drive in wet weather. Roads flooded. Drivers challenged the water levels and lost, and my travel time to work doubled.

I groped my way to the bathroom. Scenes from my horrible dream replayed in my mind. Damn! Why was I having these nightmares? My sleep-deprived evenings hindered my efficiency at work.

I burned the toast and spilled half my coffee before I pulled myself together. Getting ready for work was a chore. By the time I reached my car, the wind rendered my umbrella useless. My hair hung in soggy clumps. I had to stop and change my route twice because of flooded roads. The delay made me twenty minutes late, duly noted by our resident snitch.

Mary took one peek at me and brought me a towel. Tired and a bit damp, I sat at my computer to work on the end-of-the-month reports when Betty came in. "Hi, Betty. What can I do for you?"

A tiny woman with a sweet disposition, Betty was a model tenant. The top of her head came to my nose; compared to her, I was a giant. Today her usual bright smile was eclipsed by a frown and tear-filled eyes.

Her small hands twisted around each other, and she looked away. "Oh, Dani. I'm awfully sorry."

I was at a loss. What had she done to cause her to apologize? "What's wrong?"

She hung her head and mumbled. "Betty, I can't understand

what you're saying."

In a gush, she blurted out, "I have a little fire in my apartment."

Oh, damn, not today. I called the fire department, then Fischer.

"Did you call the fire department?" he asked.

"Yes. They're on their way."

"I'll be right there."

The situation wasn't bad, more smoke than anything. Betty, in one of her cleaning binges, had switched on the wall oven she used for storage. The firemen placed huge fans around to disperse the smoke and did a final safety check of the apartment.

Fischer's frown and dark snapping eyes made me cringe. He acted as if the fire was my fault. With a disgusted sneer, he scrutinized me, "Whatever is going on in your life, you'd better get it straightened out. This could have been a disaster. You look like you've been on a bender. Pull yourself together. I've got my eye on you."

All I could do was nod. I was a mess today, but the fire wasn't my fault. After he left, I went to the ladies' room and stared at the mirror.

No wonder he'd accused me of boozing. My reflection frightened me. The bright green of my eyes had dulled to a muddy hue, and the skin around them dissolved into deep gray depressions that drooped to my cheekbones. Damp, windblown curls surrounded my head like a crazy clown wig. The face peering back at me resembled a zombie dredged straight from the grave. I needed help.

~ * ~

The storm continued to pound the coast when I left to go home. I drove around the block twice. There wasn't a decent place to park. By the time I reached my door, I was soaked. I left a trail of puddles in the hall and noticed someone had been there before me. Wet spots were visible on the corridor floor. Doug often used the back door.

The inclement weather made the apartment dark. I flipped on the lights, sat at my kitchen table, and leaned my head on my arms, trying to banish Fischer from my mind. A hot bath would wash away the after-effects of his nasty insinuations. I forced my weary body into the bathroom.

The bath salts' tangy fragrance helped relax me. I took my time lowering myself into the hot bubbles. With a moan of gratitude, I submerged my tired bones.

"Ah, perfect." I lay back in the warm, scented water, and my troubles faded away.

I wanted nothing more than to lose myself in the dissolving effervescence. Ten minutes later, the phone's incessant ringing crashed through my peaceful meditation. Damn. I considered ignoring it, but curiosity won out.

I grabbed a towel and stepped out of the tub. I didn't get to the phone in time. The kitchen floor became a tiny river. The phone screen said Possible Spam. I gave myself a mental kick. Why did I have to be so nosy? I'd left the warmth of my soothing bath to answer a call from some stupid telemarketer.

Fatigue threatened to overwhelm me. I dried myself and trudged into the bedroom. My tunnel vision focused on the welcome sight of soft, white pillows.

That was how I missed it. The bulge in the carpet. My toe connected. My body lurched, then a sense of weightlessness enveloped me as I flew through the air. I should never have gotten out of bed today.

My right hand and knee took the brunt of the fall. I suspected I'd broken my toe. Could this day get any worse? I lay there in pain, sprawled on the floor, lamenting my sad state when the phone rang again. I winced in pain as I dragged myself over to check the caller. Kirsten.

At the sound of my sister's voice, I felt better, but she could interpret my tone too well. "Dani, what's wrong?"

I assured her nothing serious had happened and proceeded to outline my day, beginning with the fire and ending with my unfortunate flight across the bedroom. By the time I'd finished my litany of woes, I managed a chuckle. "It's been a hell of a day."

I limped to the bed and assessed my situation. Cuts stung my hand. A lump the size of a walnut protruded from my knee, and my toe throbbed in pain. Not to mention, I was in danger of losing my job, crazy from lack of sleep, and a Nor'easter was beating against my windows. Oh, yes. Let's add the strange events occurring in my apartment.

What else could I do but laugh?

While I'd taken my inventory, Kirsten gave her medical opinion. "Take a couple of aspirin and go to bed."

I hesitated for a second before deciding to tell her about Tom. "So much has been happening, I forgot to tell you. Tom appeared here yesterday."

"Tom!" Her shout almost broke my eardrum. "What did he want? Did he hurt you? Why didn't you call me?" Her questions often came in bunches.

"Calm down. I'm okay. I told him to leave."

"You shouldn't have spoken to him. The time has come for a

restraining order. He's liable to be back."

"I don't think so. I was firm that we are over."

My sister wasn't buying it, and, by that time, neither was I. With her protective instincts peaking, I hated to mention the break-in at Heather's. Kirsten would go ballistic. I spit it out and held my breath.

For a moment she was speechless, but she made a fast recovery. "Oh, my God. You've got to get out of there."

I was almost ready to agree.

Chapter Ten

No matter how weird the apartment situation had become, I wanted to stay. I'd grown addicted to my new digs. I liked being able to walk to the Salem hot spots, but more importantly, I'd found a friend in Heather. Nope. I wouldn't let anyone, or anything, scare me from my home.

After a few minutes, Kirsten abandoned the argument and issued her dire pronouncement. "We'll talk later."

I ended the call, certain she'd be on the hunt for a new apartment for me by the end of the evening.

Before exhaustion took over, I limped across the floor to discover what caused my fall. When I moved the rug, a board stuck up an inch or so from the floor. Mewling in pain, I knelt to peer into the opening. Light winked off a shiny object. Curious, I seized the end of the board and strained to lift it enough to see underneath. It looked like the edge of a book.

After my miserable day, I decided fate rewarded me for my perseverance with a prize. I had to find out what was in there. For a moment, the echo of my mother's voice gave me pause—*Curiosity killed the cat*. Ridiculous. No danger here. Nothing but a book. Paper and ink. However, I did worry a bit about creepy crawlies. I crammed my hand in and yanked the book out.

"Ouch!" Oh, hell, I'd scraped my knuckles.

Sucking on yet another cut, I gazed at my trophy. A small book bound in leather, held together by a brass lock. A sudden awareness dawned while I examined the dusty tome. I'd never noticed a loose floorboard in this room. No matter how crazy my life got, I was sure I would have spotted it.

Why would any sane person hide a book under the floor in the first place? Was it valuable? Maybe that was why it was hidden, and whoever secreted it made the board easier to release. Then, over the years and with all the movers, it loosened more.

An interesting mystery. The old leather appeared to be ancient unless the grungy aspect was the result of its time in a dusty hole.

I tried to maneuver the floorboard back into place but made a mess. I'd have to get a hammer. I swallowed a couple of aspirin, dragged myself onto the bed, and tucked the pillows underneath my back. The book's origins intrigued me. It looked like a journal, old enough to belong to Elias Gale. How exciting. I'd love to read the words of an old smuggler.

All set to dig in, I swore. The book was locked. Damn. I dug through my purse for a paper clip. With the tip of my tongue between my lips, I concentrated on picking the lock. The action seemed easy enough when they did it on TV. I made a complete botch of my attempt.

When I twisted and thrust my substitute lockpick in the small hole, my finger slipped, and I cut myself on the stupid piece of metal. Swear words peppered the air as I brought my finger to my lips. I wasn't quick enough to stop a few drops of blood from staining the sides of the pages. Oh, great. If the book had any value, I'd managed to ruin it.

~ * ~

Wednesday morning a chorus of chirping birds announced the end of the storm and a new day's birth. Under the glare of bright sunlight, my toe glowed a deep reddish purple and hurt like hell.

At work, my pronounced limp elicited sympathy and goodies. One old dear even gave me her mottled, brown cane to use.

I hobbled off to a locksmith at lunchtime. "Hi. I have an old book I'd like unlocked. Can you help me?"

"Sure, we work on all kinds of locks. Let's see what you've got." He opened his toolbox and poked around. He didn't take long.

Once he got the book opened, he scrutinized the lock. "The workmanship is excellent. I'd say this metalwork dates back more than two hundred years. If you want, I can try to make a key to fit it."

"Thanks. I'll get back to you."

When he asked where I'd found the journal, a guilty flush heated my cheeks. The book wasn't mine. I should have given it to Eddie right away, but what harm if I read it first?

I crossed my fingers and gave him my best version of the truth. "Oh, I stumbled on it in my travels." I did fall over a board on a trip to the bedroom.

The man wished me well. I thanked him, paid for the services, and promised to let him know. I wanted to read the book tonight. I didn't need a key. There might even be one under the floorboard.

In the office, I peeked through a few pages. The flowery

penmanship, along with the vocabulary and spellings from two hundred years ago, would make the book difficult to read. I did, however, note the name and date on the first page—Elias Gale, 1695.

That night, when I arrived home, I did a double take at the sight of Heather perched on our front stairs. She wasn't a front-porch kind of chick. That was Mrs. W's style. "Hey, what's up?"

She leaned back and gazed at the sky. "I'm enjoying the awesome sun and soft breeze after the messy rain."

"You sound like your old self."

Her grin was infectious. "I won't let some lousy burglar ruin my life."

I pumped my fist in the air. "Way to go, girl." I turned and tottered toward my door.

"Why are you limping?"

"I tripped over a loose board in my apartment and broke my toe."

"Bummer. You still planning to go to the yacht club Friday?"

"Yeah. No problem. I'm tough."

She pointed to my hand. "What have you got?"

I'd forgotten the journal. "An old diary I found." I opened it and showed her the pages.

"Ugh. How can you read such weird writing?"

"I was hoping a glass of wine would make it easier."

"Right. Good luck with that."

Before I settled in to examine my find, I poured the Chablis and propped my feet on the sofa. Reading the eighteenth-century prose proved challenging. After the first page, the writing deteriorated and became cramped or faded. The inconsistent ink strokes didn't help; I found myself squinting to decipher the words.

The account began with a description of fish. Not surprising since Elias started work on a fishing boat. From a few phrases, I gathered he'd been a proud man. He bragged about his "splendid hand with money."

I skimmed over more information about his excellence and found a transaction to purchase a second boat. From his description, I understood these weren't the large vessels that sailed off to the Grand Banks but smaller craft that worked in and around Salem. I blinked. The crowded writing blurred. I didn't want to read one more account of boats, fish, or finances, and skipped forward a few pages.

Here, the writing became darker and more disjointed as he described the other men who "envee me." He also alluded to a couple of women in the town whose "eyes secretly strayed tord" him. Hmm. This might prove to be interesting.

I was surprised by his derisive attitude toward those he worked with. Although tainted money bought his fleet, he'd begun his career on other men's boats. Yet, in these pages, he scorned hard-working fishermen, as if he'd never had his own hands in a barrel of stinking bait.

After forty minutes of trying to slog through his hieroglyphics, I gave up. I'd have to read it a little at a time or ruin my eyesight. Before I closed the book, it flipped open to another page. This section proved easier to read; he'd taken more care with his penmanship. One name grabbed my attention—Rebecca. My eyes ached from squinting too long, so I bookmarked the page for later and went to bed.

I tossed and turned, until sleep claimed me. I was in a room similar to my bedroom but smaller. As if framed in a movie, a young woman with long, dark hair appeared in colonial garb. Perched on a stool by the fireplace, her body swayed to an internal melody while she mixed ingredients in a large round pot. I recognized the scent of lavender.

For a moment, she stopped and peered at me, then smiled. As her dark gaze found mine, I experienced a deep sense of tranquility. I awoke in the morning eager to face the day.

I drove to work, windows open, singing to the tunes on the radio. I determined to keep a positive attitude despite the recent troubles.

Mary appeared right after I unlocked my office door. "Good morning. You seem better today. How's your foot?"

I ushered her into the office and glanced at my vermillion toe. "I guess it's healing."

We discussed the fire and Fischer's outrageous attitude. Then she took a quick peek around and leaned in to whisper, "I believe he might be spying on you."

"What?"

"He and Mrs. Craigie were huddled together outside the office door. When the building's worst gossip is so pleased with herself, someone—" she pointed to me, "—is in for trouble." Her lips tightened. "I wouldn't be surprised if that man hadn't come out of your office."

Oh great. Fischer snoops around in my things while I'm gone and turns one of my residents into a snitch. Just what I need. Another hostile observer. The woman loved to tattle, and now her radar was focused on me. I spent the day peeking over my shoulder. Mrs. Craigie managed to stroll by the office at least once an hour.

Always nosy, her current actions brought her behavior to ludicrous. The whole idea of Fischer keeping tabs on me made my skin crawl. What about at home? Was he checking on me there too? Why was he doing this?

Before I left my car that night, I scanned the street for any sign of Tom's vehicle and did the same for Fischer's. Oh, this was absurd. I was edging toward paranoia. I'd even contemplated giving Mrs. W a picture of my boss and asking her to be my lookout. She'd love that. Maybe I could pull up a chair with her on the porch and snoop for myself.

I chuckled until I spied Doug slip in the back door. My shoulders quivered, and I hurried inside.

Chapter Eleven

I arrived at work on Friday to a quiet, problem-free workspace. When I called the main office, Fischer's secretary told me he was gone for the day. I grinned and leaned back in my chair. No worries about surprise visits today. I could handle Mrs. Craigie, his white-haired spy.

Later, when she headed out to play bingo, I smiled and waved. They wouldn't be back for a long while. With Mata Hari out of the way, I'd be able to sneak out to get ready for the party. Cocktail hour at the yacht club began at 6:30 PM, and I wanted to fortify myself with liquid courage before Heather introduced me to her bosses at the firm. Since she expected her whole office to attend, I wanted to be prepared.

The escape from work gave me plenty of time. When I knocked on Heather's door at 6:15 PM, she gave me a head-to-toe inspection. "Love the outfit. Totally rad. I'll have to keep you away from Peter."

The myriad hues of amethyst and jade in my dress emphasized the green in my eyes and the dark sheen of hair swirling around my shoulders. Then I limped in.

"Oh, no. Still in pain?"

I gave a short laugh. "It's better. These heels don't help."

She remained undaunted. "If you don't walk much, maybe no one will notice."

"Oh, don't worry. No one will pay any attention to me. You'll take their breath away." My outspoken friend in her bright-red dress, matching shoes, and cascade of blonde hair would have been a standout on Hollywood's red carpet, let alone at a yacht club in Marblehead.

She maneuvered the Mustang through twisty streets to an impressive old building on the waterfront. Inside, the piney scent of polished dark wood combined with the aroma of the sea. People stood around in conversational groups. Wait staff snaked through them to hand out tasty appetizers. The smell of garlic and tomatoes hung in the air.

Heather introduced me to a few of her colleagues, but without much enthusiasm. She scanned the room. "He must be here somewhere." Her radar was set for Peter.

"Come on," she said, "Let's go to the bar outside and get ourselves a drink."

Clomping behind her, I inhaled in surprise when we moved through the door. We'd stepped onto a deck surrounded by water. A moist tang of salt permeated the air. To the left stood a shiny wooden bar with leather-backed stools. Tables and chairs capturing the prime harbor view crowded the rest of the space. Streaks of orange and yellow from the dying sun slashed countless boats as they bobbed in the waves. The scene deserved a drum roll.

Lost in the delicious spectacle, I missed what Heather said. She poked me. "Ow."

"I told you he'd be here."

We approached the bar, and my friend took on the persona of a Southern belle. I half-expected her to whip out a fan and bat her eyes. "Peter. What a surprise. I'm glad you could make it." As if we hadn't been hunting him down.

His hazel eyes widened, and his lips curled in a huge smile at her approach. While his attention focused on Heather, I studied the man who'd stolen her heart. The sunlight behind his slim frame made the bronze in his hair resemble a halo.

"Dani, this is Peter, one of the lawyers in my office."

He rolled his eyes and brushed at a tawny strand of hair. "One of the associates." He shook my hand then refocused his attention on Heather. "What can I get you ladies to drink?"

I opted for wine and promised myself no more than one. My foot gave me enough trouble without adding liquor to the mix.

Drink in hand, I swung around in search of a place to sit and almost spilled my amber liquid on a navy jacket behind me. "Oh, excuse me…"

I halted in midsentence. My gaze traveled from the broad shoulders to the lips forming a half grin. Sam.

"Dani. What a pleasant surprise. I didn't recognize you."

Before I could speak, Heather took over. She introduced Sam to Peter and shot me a wink.

He shook hands with Peter, nodded to Heather, and placed his elbow on the bar, favoring me with a playful grin. "I didn't expect to find you here tonight."

I was so glad I'd bought a new dress. I inclined my head toward Heather. "She suggested I meet new people."

"Smart woman." His voice was soft and intimate as his gaze

traveled over me. This gorgeous man, who regarded me as if I were the special dessert, sent my libido into overdrive.

He ordered another round. With a shock, I realized my glass was empty. I didn't even remember drinking it. Oh, well, one more couldn't hurt. Time flew by, and they announced dinner. We went in together to a table in the dining room.

He noticed I lagged behind. "You're limping. Are you okay?"

"I hurt my toe the other day. I'll be fine. Thanks."

When he placed his hand on my elbow, a line of sparks ignited along my arm. The way he treated me made my heart flutter. Then we were at the table—boy, girl, boy, girl. I became a little giddy; I even giggled.

Oh, no. I'd finished my second glass of wine. The food better arrive soon, or I'd be in big trouble. I caught myself leaning into Sam each time I spoke to him. He didn't seem to mind.

This evening's event was to fund a cure for ALS. I'd glanced at the event flyer and noticed Heather's company under the sponsor lists. I'd missed Gregory Electric on the contributor's page. The more I learned about him, the more I liked him.

When the music began, Sam asked me for a dance. A small hesitation on my part might have been nice, but no, I popped out of my chair. Too late, I remembered my foot.

"Ow," I said as I stumbled. He caught me and held me against his chest. I lost myself in the depth of his aqua eyes. *Oh Lord. I've been staring too long.* I tore my gaze away.

He released me for a minute, then put his arm around my waist and smiled. "I'll support you."

I had no idea if the alcohol or the intensity of those blue eyes were responsible, but the pain in my toe disappeared.

He held me close, his hand on my bare back. The slow, sensual movement of his thumb against my skin drove me crazy. My mind drifted to steamy visions of where else he might choose to stroke, and I missed his next words. All my mind registered was his soft, deep drawl.

I blinked and managed a low, breathy "What?"

Head tilted, his lips stayed apart for a beat. "You look lovely."

My attention stayed focused on his mouth until I noticed we were the last ones on the dance floor, and the music had stopped.

I would have been embarrassed, worried Sam might notice my absorption in him, but thanks to the wine's calming effect, my response was a grin. "Thank you. You do too."

He laughed and tightened his hold on my waist. On the way back to the table, he said, "How do you like living in Salem so far?"

"Oh." I managed a coy smile and peeked at him. "It has its perks."

He gave my waist a squeeze. "Excellent."

He helped me into my seat and excused himself. Heather leaned in to whisper, "You and Sam seem to enjoy each other."

"He's a nice guy."

"You sound surprised."

"I am, a little. I mean he's different tonight. Maybe because there's no business involved."

Her face lit with a knowing smile before she gave her attention to Peter. In fact, they honed in on each other. After a while, he asked if we wanted another drink. I opted for water. Any more liquor and I'd be inviting Sam home. I left to go to the ladies' room, and Heather accompanied me, gushing about her new man.

When we returned to the table, Peter sat by himself. He turned to me. "Where's Sam?"

I shook my head. "No idea."

He scanned the crowd. "Oh! There he is at the bar."

I peered in the direction he pointed. Yup, there he was. Standing at the bar, absorbed in conversation with a supermodel. Her thick, honey-colored hair covered a small portion of her exposed back. The rest of her creamy skin was showcased in a slinky black halter dress. The skimpy attire barely covered her generous assets. She leaned forward and gazed into his face. My scrutiny ended on the hand she held against his chest. Unable to process more without screaming, I whipped my attention back toward our table.

Damn! What a jerk. Playing up to me until he found something he liked more. Too bad. He'd seemed like such a nice guy. The hell with him. I could do better.

Heather shot me a worried look.

"What?" My voice was too loud.

She asked Peter to get her another drink. When he left, she said, "It's late. The party's over. Peter asked me to go for a drink, but he walked here." She shrugged. "I figured he and I could take my car, and Sam would drive you home."

No wonder she was fidgety. The man had other plans. Driving me home wasn't part of them. "Don't worry about me. I don't want to ruin your night with Peter. I'm sure I can get a ride."

She bit her lip and gazed past me in what I recognized as her "I can fix this" mode. "Wait a minute. I'll be right back."

This had turned out to be a great evening. First Sam dumped me and now Heather. I didn't blame her. She was obsessed with Peter, and this was her chance. I'd get an Uber and let them have the rest of the evening to themselves. A voice snapped me out of my contemplation.

"Hey, Dani."

Oh, no, Heather must have badgered him. *I'll kill her.*

Sam dropped into the chair beside me. "I didn't mean to be gone this long. I needed to deal with some unexpected business. I'd be happy to drive you home."

Business, huh? He must have struck out or he planned to meet her later. How embarrassing. "Oh no. You don't have to bother. I'll call a cab."

He leaned toward me, touched my shoulder, and whispered, "No. I *want* to drive you home."

Damn my body. The sound of his voice and his warm touch sent heat pooling to my abdomen.

"Let me get you a drink," he said.

I wanted to tell him no, but he was already headed for the bar. Oh, rats. I didn't need another drink. A few minutes later, he placed a glass of wine in front of me and promised to be right back. Great, now I was alone again, me and my drink. The girl no one wanted.

Most of the tables were deserted. People were either at the bar, dancing, or had already left. One vacant area in the dining room caught my attention. Something about it triggered a sense of déjà vu. In a rush, I remembered. White tablecloths, the sound of water, and the man with the scarred face. A chill rippled through me. I needed to get away from here. My foot ached as I limped out to the deck and sat down.

The moon, like an enormous spotlight, cast a dramatic swath across the water. I listened to the music of the harbor—vessels slapping at their moorings and the jangle of sailboat fittings. Lifting my face to the salty breeze brushing across my cheeks, I inhaled the pungent scent. Every few minutes, a tiny light appeared in the sky; a plane headed along its flight path.

I'd begun to enjoy myself when his voice startled me. "There you are." Sam had arrived a little winded.

"Ooh! Heavy breathing. Is that for me or have you been running?" I asked.

He gave me a sheepish grin. "Although seeing you in the moonlight could induce a bout of breathlessness, I confess I jogged here. I live a few minutes away, and since I'd walked here this evening, I had to run home to get my truck."

"That wasn't necessary. I could have called a cab."

"It's the least I can do for the woman who saved me from a locked tomb."

I leaned back in the seat and smiled. "I would have done it for anyone trapped in that hellish place. Thank you for your effort tonight. Does that make us even?"

He sat on the bench beside me. "You look even more beautiful in the moonlight."

His startling aqua gaze fascinated me. I wanted nothing more than to give in to the enchantment of the moment. I craved his touch and leaned toward him. A flash of gold caught my eye. Sam's supermodel, framed in the dining-room door, glared at us. My hopes evaporated. *The woman must be laughing at the naïve fool who'd fallen for his line.*

I straightened in my seat and pulled myself together. "Are we ready?"

His surprised expression gave me a tiny bit of satisfaction. I'd guess he wasn't used to women saying no. He recovered, though, and held out his arm. "Ready when you are."

Scintillating wouldn't describe the conversation on the way home. The tone ran more to polite. Sam said he'd enjoyed his time with me tonight. I returned the compliment, aware neither of us was sincere. Well, maybe I meant it, but I was certain he didn't.

In front of my apartment, I thanked him and swung around to open my door.

"Wait a minute. Let me help you."

"I'm all set." Before I undid the seat belt, he'd made the trip to my side of the truck.

"Be careful of your toe." His strong hand gripped mine to help me down.

I was embarrassed when he stayed with me on the path to my door like we were on a date. "You don't have to walk me the whole the way. You've done enough."

He ignored me. "Your limp is more prominent now. You shouldn't have worn those shoes."

I bristled. How dare he talk about my shoes. They weren't the problem. Not the whole problem anyway. Although I insisted I was all right on my own, he held on.

"Don't try to be brave. You could hurt yourself."

I hated to seem too needy, but after a couple of steps, I gave in and leaned against him. Might as well enjoy the man while I had him there.

He guided me on the stairs and ushered me into the hallway. When I stopped short, he almost knocked me over. I backed into him in an attempt to get away. Escape wasn't possible. I was stuck.

Leaning against my door as if he belonged there was Tom. The taut lines in his face and his cold glare telegraphed his anger. I prayed he wouldn't make a scene. When thwarted, he became vicious. This evening had all the makings of a never-ending nightmare.

His eyebrow slid up, and there was a nasty tilt to his lips. "Well, well, what do we have here?"

Fixed to the spot, all but paralyzed, pressure in my fingers made me look down. I peeked at my hand crushing Sam's. He squeezed back. His presence, and the fact he continued to hold on, gave me strength to face Tom's hostility.

"I asked you not to come here again."

Anger radiated from his aggressive stance to his narrowed eyes. His scowl moved from Sam to me. I was surprised he kept his cool. "I wanted to find out if you enjoyed the book."

I'd never bothered to open his gift. I'd thrown it away. "Nice. Thank you."

He turned to Sam and put out his hand. "Tom Westin, Dani's boyfriend."

Almost choking on my astonishment, I jumped in to correct him. "*Ex*-boyfriend."

He glared at me, his fake good humor evaporating. Sam ignored Tom's gesture and said, "Sam Gregory."

I took courage from his confidence and prayed my voice wouldn't falter. I stared straight at Tom. "Is there anything else?"

He looked ready to explode. Like a snake, he snapped his hand forward and seized my arm. His tone became sinister as he muttered through tight lips, "We need to talk."

His fingers bit into me. I tugged my arm back and cried out. "Let me go."

Before I finished my plea, Sam grabbed Tom by the throat and slammed him against the wall. "You can walk out of here on your own or leave on a stretcher. Your call."

Tom's eyes bulged in his deep-red face, but he managed to nod. Sam let him go and warned him never to come back.

Tom massaged his neck, flashed me a look of pure menace, and banged the door shut after him.

Sam put his arm around me. "Let's go inside where we can talk."

Once inside, we sat on the sofa. I needed to explain to Sam about my non-relationship with Tom. After I'd finished, I gazed up at him. "I promise you. It's over. I never want to see him again."

Through the whole recitation, I'd quieted my nerves by twisting my fingers together. Sam rescued my restless hands and kissed each one. "I'm so sorry you were treated to such abuse. I should have punched him in the nose."

An image of him championing me brought a smile to my face. I didn't understand, though, why he was still there, why he hadn't run far and fast.

"Thank you," I said.

"You're welcome."

His incredible aqua eyes focused on me. In a tender gesture, he took my face in his hands. His lips touched mine in a sweet kiss, and I stopped breathing.

Though heat raced through my body, my features must have registered bewilderment. He took my hands again. "I enjoyed our night together. I'd like to go out with you again."

"But—"

"I guess you must have been confused this evening."

A huge understatement. I had no idea where I stood tonight. *He likes me. He leaves me for a cutie. Now he kisses me.* My head reeled from the changes.

He took a deep breath and continued, "The woman who corralled me at the bar was my ex-wife." He gave a short laugh. "It must be the night for exes. Anyway, her aim in life is to make me miserable, and tonight was no exception. Trish didn't like me enjoying myself with you and tried to destroy my pleasure."

Now I remembered why she looked so familiar. His ex was the girl with the muscular dude on the beach.

Sam squeezed my hands. "Would you have dinner with me tomorrow night?"

Astonished, I forced the words through my mouth. "I'd love to."

A crooked grin surfaced as he eyed my feet. "We'll find a restaurant where you can wear more comfortable shoes."

He didn't like my sandals? I'd paid almost a week's salary for these puppies. When I frowned, he added, "They're cute shoes, though." Then he became serious. "I'm concerned about Tom. After what he did tonight, I think you might have a big problem with him."

I shook my head. "I don't want anything to do with him. What we had was finished a long time ago."

Sam sighed. "The trouble is, he doesn't believe it. His attitude earlier was proprietary. Tom considers you his girlfriend. He wasn't afraid to claim you. I wouldn't trust him not to come back."

I hoped he was wrong. "I'm sure your actions tonight convinced him."

"I don't like what happened. From his behavior tonight, it's clear he could be dangerous."

Chapter Twelve

Desperate to change the subject, I asked Sam if he'd like a cup of coffee. I limped around the kitchen in my bare feet.

"How did you hurt your toe anyway?"

I put cups on the counter. "I wasn't paying attention. I tripped on a loose floorboard."

"Here?" he asked as he looked around.

"Yup. In the bedroom."

When he headed in there, I tried to stop him. "Where are you going?" My bedroom was a mess.

My foolish question elicited a raised eyebrow. "To examine the floorboard."

With the rug folded away, the uneven piece of wood stood out like a rock in the desert. He zeroed in on the spot and knelt for a better look.

I bit my lip and twirled a piece of hair around my finger. "I was going to buy a hammer to knock it back into place."

When he turned to me, his eyes darkened. "What happened?"

I shrugged. "The movers must have loosened it. It was like that when I came home the other day."

He narrowed his eyes. "This has been pried up."

"That was me, I said as I watched him survey the floor I saw something underneath and tugged at it."

He smirked. "Did you use a crowbar?"

"What?"

He stood up and dusted off his hands. "This wasn't an accident. These boards have been in place for a couple of centuries. It didn't just pop up. Someone helped it."

"But my door was locked. How could anyone get in?" The idea of an intruder in my home, my bedroom, made my stomach sick.

He put his arms around me and softened his tone. "You have to call the police."

"The police?"

"That's what you do when someone breaks into your apartment."

I shivered and looked around in a panic. He held my shoulders and peered into my eyes. "Easy. You're safe now."

I exhaled and leaned into him.

"What was under there?"

I moved to the bedside table to get the book. The nightstand was empty. I checked the floor, under the pillows, and scanned the other surfaces in the room. No book.

This was ridiculous. Elias's journal was somewhere in this apartment. Heat consumed my neck and face. "I put it on this table." I must sound like a fool. An uncomfortable memory flashed through my mind. Rose, concerned about things moving around.

I checked the living room and scouted around with no success. Nothing in the kitchen. Where was it? I stormed at a fast hobble into the bedroom, avoiding Sam and the floorboard. One place left. The loft. It shouldn't be there, though. I'd remember the pain from climbing those stairs, but I was desperate to find my prize. The damn book had to be here somewhere.

I swallowed my aggravation and embarrassment and tottered up to my little-used office. By the time I reached the top of the stairs, my toe throbbed. What light filtered in served to accentuate the deep shadows. I cringed, longing to wobble back down those steps. If Sam hadn't been there, I'd have fled. I forced myself to ignore the dark corners and tugged on the light. I gasped and clung to the rail. The diary was there. Right in the middle of my desk, mocking me.

A second bout of nausea seized me. Someone had moved it.

I grabbed the book and, in my hurry to get away, banged my toe. "Ow! Damn toe."

I grasped the rail, so absorbed in the pain I didn't hear him approach. With gentle hands, Sam helped me down the stairs, sat me on the side of my bed, and held up my foot for inspection. Despite my confusion and apprehension, his warm and tender attention to my foot sent waves of pleasure spiraling through my body.

Pointing to what I held, he said, "The book you found under the floorboard?"

Still breathless from his ministrations, I nodded and handed it to him. "Elias Gale's diary."

His finger slid over the raised writing on the cover. "Is this valuable?"

I shrugged. "I have no idea."

"What about your ex?"

I flinched. "What do you mean?"

"He mentioned a book tonight. Is this what he wanted?"

"No. A few days ago, he discovered where I lived and dropped off a gift. I guess he brought me a book. I'm not sure. I never opened it. Tom's not connected to this. Why would he look for a book under the floorboard? Where would he get that information?"

Sam's voice dropped a decibel as he said, "Who would have that knowledge?"

A terrifying question. I put my head in my hands. "I have no idea." I didn't want to reveal my unease relating to this strange room. I'd sound crazy. In a pleading tone, I said, "I have a headache. If you don't mind, I'd like to take an aspirin and go to bed."

"I'm worried about you being alone here tonight."

"I'll be okay. I'll make sure to lock up after you leave."

"I'm going to do that right now." The smack as he shut each window reverberated in my chest. The heat would be unbearable tonight.

His frown when he came back confused me. "What?"

"You don't lock your windows?"

"In the summer? It'd be sweltering in here."

He peered at me beneath lowered eyebrows. "I can get you a good deal on an air conditioner. Pay me when you can."

Embarrassed, I protested, but he stopped me. "Tomorrow, I'll be back to change the locks and take you to the police station."

"Why?"

The strain in his voice was evident, as he explained once again. "To report the break-in and to find out how to protect yourself from Tom."

I rubbed my bruised arm. "Tom will go crazy if I go to the police.'

As I finished speaking, Sam's face changed. The caring light in his eyes blinked out, and his lips tightened into a scowl. "Sounds like you're not ready to move on from your old boyfriend." With that, he headed toward the door.

"No. You're wrong. I'm dying to be rid of him, but I hate having to involve the police."

He stopped and looked at me. "If you don't do something, he'll continue to terrorize you. A restraining order will either stop him or put him in jail. I'm guessing he's someone who wouldn't like jail." His voice softened. "If you have any problems at all with him, I'll be here. Where's your phone?"

I found my cell and handed it to him. He punched in his digits and gave it back. "I'll pick up the minute you call." He lifted my chin and gave me an exciting kiss. "See you tomorrow morning."

My lips hummed in satisfaction.

I engaged the lock on the front door and frowned. No matter what Sam said, Tom would present a problem. I'd seen his last malevolent glare. Tom, who always got even. Although I was certain the presence of Sam would deter him, I hadn't seen the last of Tom.

At the bedroom door, I froze at the sight of the raised board. Had someone been in my apartment? Oh Lord. Wasn't that what Rose had said?

~ * ~

Last night's goodbye kiss was foremost in my sleep-deprived brain as I turned off the alarm the next morning. Sam would be there in a little over an hour. When I rolled out of bed, pain stabbed through my toe, but, as I walked around, the sharp spasms eased. If I managed to keep from banging my foot into anything, I'd be in good shape.

In the middle of brushing my teeth, I caught the scent of lavender. The fragrance brought back a sleepy, vague memory of the dream woman who'd blessed my sleep a few nights ago. The deepening, sweet fragrance made me lightheaded. My vision blurred.

I dropped the toothbrush and grabbed hold of the sink as the reflection in the mirror wavered. I blinked several times. It didn't help. The image continued to change. My eyes now assumed the color of a cloudy night. My now-black hair swarmed past my shoulders. Unable to move, I gazed in disbelief. My features continued to morph. They settled into the round pale face peering back at me.

Worried I'd contracted some kind of bug, I closed my eyes, hoping I wouldn't faint and hurt myself. I waited a few seconds and then, bit by bit, lifted my eyelids to peek at the mirror.

The face was still there. I recognized her. The woman from my dream. Her dark, almond-shaped gaze held my attention until her lips moved in a gentle whisper. I lowered my head into my hands and prayed, *Please make her go away.*

When I dared another glimpse, she was gone. My face, whiter than usual, stared at me. Then I remembered her words and shivered as waves of ice crashed through my body.

"He wants you."

I gazed into frightened green eyes surrounded by a mop of hideous bed hair, all tufts and flat spots from a restless night. I must be losing it. Why would this woman…Rebecca? Why would she appear to me? I imagined what would happen if I told Heather. "By the way, the woman who stole Elias's heart appeared in my bathroom mirror this morning." Oh, yeah. They'd be carting me away before lunch.

I washed my face with cold water and swung back to the mirror. My still-wild stare greeted me. Was I losing my sanity? Hallucinating? Oh, please no. It must be the strain of Tom's refusal to leave me alone and his aggressive performance last night. My nightmares, awake and asleep, were the result of anxiety and exhaustion. Maybe I should speak to a doctor about the strange smells, though.

I hurried to get dressed before Sam arrived. I'd finished the last of my breakfast when he knocked. I smiled up at his handsome face as he displayed handle sets and deadbolts for the doors.

"Make sure you use both locks." His tone reminded me of my father's parental dictates.

I grinned. At least Sam didn't shake his finger at me, and he looked nothing like my dad. His dark tan set off the turquoise tint of his eyes, and the T-shirt stretched across his muscled chest captivated my mind.

I offered him a cup of coffee, but he was all set.

"I'll get these locks fixed, and then we'll go to the station." It took him no time to remove and replace both locks.

While I pictured those strong hands in a much more pleasurable mode, the reason for the new hardware dimmed my enthusiasm. I had an intruder as well as a stalker.

Chapter Thirteen

Sam insisted I practice engaging the locks before we headed to his truck. I was about to get in when I saw a shadow on the side of my car.

"Wait a minute, Sam. Something's wrong." The problem became obvious as I walked over.

A scratch stretched across both doors. I bent over to see the damage and yelped. A deep gash sliced through the paint. I traced the line with my finger, then swallowed against the lump in my throat. I loved my little Chevy. Minerva was just three years old, and I'd planned on her company for at least a few more. How could someone hurt her like this?

I looked up and down the street. Right. Like the bastard would still be there. I steadied myself, holding on to the side of the car. He didn't have to be standing around. Minerva's attack was vicious. Tom got his revenge after all.

Sam was right. Tom didn't key my car; he gouged it. He'd moved to a different level. The physical disfigurement of my car symbolized what he'd like to do to me. What if his rage didn't end with Minerva? What if this was the beginning of a dangerous siege? I'd have to report him—my safety was at stake.

I leaned into the comfort of Sam's arm.

He caressed my cheek. "Tom must have done this." He took a couple of pictures.

Unable to speak, I just nodded.

"Come on," he said in a gentle tone. "Let's go."

He took me to the police station to report the break-in and the damage to my car. The officer promised to have a detective get back to me on the invasion. When I told him Tom keyed Minerva, the officer raised his hands in a helpless gesture. With no proof, there was nothing he could do. Because he was a friend of Sam's, though, he promised to have a cruiser drive by the house.

Sam shook his hand. "Thanks, Gil."

We headed out when Gil stopped us. "Wait a minute. Did you say Tom Westin?"

"Yeah," Sam said as he turned around.

"Damn, he's the guy we're looking for."

Leaning over the counter, Sam asked, "What do you mean?"

Gil checked the room as if making sure we were alone. "Listen, we haven't released this information yet, but…" He focused on me and lowered his voice. "Did you ever meet Allison Montenegro?"

I blinked. "I'm not sure. The name seems familiar."

"Yeah, it does. It's been all over the news. She's the murder victim we found."

I inhaled in shock and almost choked on my saliva. My coughing fit upset Gil, and he told us he shouldn't say any more.

After he clapped me on the back, Sam said, "You can't stop there. What does she have to do with him?"

Again, Gil peeked around again. "According to the latest report, the woman used to work in Boston for this guy's company." He gestured for them to come closer. "We have it on good authority she dated this Tom Westin before going missing."

This time I didn't choke; I almost passed out. Sam put his arm around me and led me to a chair.

"Stay there for a minute," Gil called over his shoulder. "I'll be right back."

Moments later, a pudgy man with a receding hairline arrived. His suit jacket, slacks, and badge identified him as a detective. Although he was shorter than Sam, his aggressive stance gave him height. "Excuse me, ma'am. I'm Detective Lavoie. Could you please come with me?"

I touched my chest. "Why? What do you want?"

"I'd like to ask you a couple of questions."

I was grateful to Sam when he moved in front of me. "What do you need Dani for?"

"Like I said, I have a couple of questions. Just a few minutes of her time. Who are you?"

"I'm her friend. If you want to talk to her, I'm coming with her."

For the next twenty minutes, Detective Lavoie grilled me on Tom, his actions, and his anger problems.

"He does have control issues," I said. "I was never frightened until the last night in his apartment when he hit me."

As I described his behavior, Sam's lips tightened. I told Lavoie about Tom in my yard and at my apartment and showed him the bruises on my arm where he'd grabbed me last night. Sam jumped in. He spoke in short, angry spurts as he described Tom's actions in my hallway and what he'd done to my car.

Lavoie asked me if anything else had happened. By then, I was upset enough to dump everything. I told him about Heather's break-in and ended my recitation with the dislodged floorboard in the bedroom.

After he checked his notes, he nodded and scratched his chin. "Yeah. I like this Westin guy for the break-ins." He poked his finger at me. "Stay away from him. If comes around again, call me right away."

I had Lavoie's card and the address of the district court to file a harassment petition tucked in my pocket and Sam's arm around my waist as we walked to the truck.

On the ride home, I listened to a controlled rant centered around me being anywhere near Tom. Sam insisted on a thorough inspection of my apartment before he left.

Satisfied the place appeared normal, he took my hands in his and made me promise not to open the door unless I knew who was there. "I've got a job I have to get to right now. I'll be back later to install the air conditioner I have in my truck. Will you be here?"

I opened my mouth to speak, but he stopped me with a kiss, a kiss that silenced me and made me forget I had anything to say. He caressed my cheek and rubbed his thumb across my lips, a gesture so seductive I'd have become his willing slave. From the look on his face, he knew it.

He left with a dimpled grin and his signature two-finger salute. Exciting thoughts of Sam radiated through my insides. His kiss wiped away the day's concerns. A few minutes later, walking by the bedroom, the smoky scent of tobacco jolted me.

My stomach cramped. I'd researched WebMD for diseases whose symptoms included strange odors. Since I didn't use marijuana or heavy narcotics, I couldn't find an answer. My secret fear was a brain tumor. My hope? A musty residue from the old wood or the fireplace stones. Caught between worry and disbelief, the sound of my ringtone distracted me.

Heather asked, "Wasn't that Sam who just left? What's the scoop?"

Her words snapped me back to the police station and Detective Lavoie's chilling revelations. My tongue almost tripped over itself telling her about Tom. When I mentioned he'd dated Alison, she yelped.

"I'm as shocked as you," I said.

"I'm in the middle of fixing lunch. Come over. I'll feed you, and you can tell me the whole story. This conversation needs a face-to-face."

Two minutes later, I sat with JoJo on my lap in Heather's bright orange-and-green kitchen while she chopped salad.

The information I divulged halted her preparation. Her open mouth mirrored the shape of her astonished stare. When I finished, she placed her hand on her chest. "Oh…my…God. I told you he was bad." She pointed at me. "He had a smarmy attitude the minute he arrived in your yard, and then he aimed for your head with that package." She leaned toward me in concern. "What if he comes back? You should stay with your sister for a while."

"My sister." I slapped my head. "I've got to tell her what the detective said."

Heather resumed her lunch prep, while I called Kirsten. I hadn't gotten further than the attack on Minerva when Kirstin broke in. I held the phone away from my ear to protect my hearing. "He's gone too far this time. I'm going to give that no-good creep a piece of my mind."

Her attitude changed, however, when I filled her in on Detective Lavoie's information. When I told her the police wanted him for questioning in regard to Allison's murder, she wasted no time switching to drill-sergeant mode. "Listen to me. Pack what clothes you need and get here right now."

Although I understood her concern, I wanted to stay. When I told her about my new, heavy-duty locks, she didn't care. My sister wanted me back at her house.

"My God, Kir. I'm safe here. The police promised to keep an eye on this place in case he comes back. I'm filing for a restraining order. I'm staying." I made up my mind while we talked. "Besides," I added in a defensive tone, "I have a friend dropping by tonight to install an air conditioner."

"A friend? Who? Where'd you meet him? What's he like?" Her questions teetered between excitement I'd met a guy and worry he might be a serial killer.

After I told her Mom and Dad liked him, she calmed a bit but remained aggrieved I refused to move back with her. At last, she ceded the argument, promising to call me the next day, but my sister never gave up without a fight. I wouldn't be surprised if she dismissed our conversation and showed up at my door.

Heather's eyes sparkled. I recognized her conspiratorial grin. "What?"

She smirked and raised an eyebrow. "Sooooo…Sam's coming by?"

I'd forgotten I hadn't told her. Her worry changed to excited curiosity. The possibility of my murder took second place to romance.

~ * ~

A few hours later, after I returned to my place, I opened every window in my apartment in hopes the breeze would dispel any stale odors, although I no longer smelled tobacco.

When Sam came back, I wanted to ask him if there were any odd smells when he was locked in the black hole of a cellar. The odors in my home might be seeping through the floor from that place. I also needed to tell him about Heather's *special* party a week from Friday.

I half-skipped around the apartment on my good foot. Sam would be there tonight. I caught myself giggling a lot. I took particular care with my outfit and hair. When he knocked on the door at 5:00 PM, I pounced, opening it almost before he finished.

"Hey, Sa…" I swallowed the rest of my greeting and backpedaled in surprise.

The person at my door wasn't Sam. An older guy, who I guessed to be in his forties, with thinning hair and a paunch smiled.

"Hi, Ms. Trent. Bob from Gregory Electric. Sam asked me to give you his apologies and install this air conditioner." He tapped his foot against the machine on the floor.

"Oh, uh. Come in." Disappointment shortened my good manners.

Bob stood in the archway and scrutinized the place. "Nice. I like how you got it decorated. Rose had a bunch of old stuff. Like antiques."

Surprised, I said, "You were here before?"

"Oh, yeah. She had all kinds of trouble with the lights. Sometimes they worked. Other times they didn't." He shook his head. "The old wiring needed to be replaced." He looked around for a minute more, and said, "Where do you want it?"

I pointed to the middle window. "Here behind the sofa."

"Okee dokey. I'll get to it," he said.

While he moved the furniture, I decided to probe for information. "Uh, Bob?"

"Yeah?"

I tried to sound casual. "You met Rose?"

"Oh yeah. We'd have nice talks over tea. She was real lonesome. Liked to have a person to talk to. So, after I'd do my work, we'd chat. A nice old lady."

I chewed my lip and asked, "Were you here when she got a little…crazy?"

"Yeah. I felt bad for her. Should'a figured it was comin' though. She kept tellin' me someone was screwin' with her stuff. Said they were sneakin' in when she was gone." He scratched his head. "But I don't believe she ever went out."

After Bob left, I cursed Sam. At the very least, he should have called me. How hard would it have been to pick up the phone? Oh, damn, what if he'd called when I was in the shower? I dove for the table and snatched my cell. Yes! A message.

"Hi, Dani. It's Sam." Like I wouldn't recognize his voice. "I hate to have to cancel, but I can't make it tonight. Bob will take care of the air conditioner. Give me a call, and we can reschedule."

Reschedule? What was I, one of his jobs?

No way, Sam Gregory. You can damn well call me back. It took all my willpower to keep from punching in his number.

I tossed pillows around on my bed grumbling about men in general, stomped around, and smacked my toe against the bureau. "Ow!"

I bounced on one foot, praying I hadn't reinjured it. First Bob, and now this. My mother always said trouble comes in threes. I hoped not. I couldn't take much more.

Sam and I hadn't even been on a real date, yet. There was no reason to be upset. I consoled myself with a promise to call him tomorrow, then the diary caught my eye. Curiosity trumped pique, and I shuffled to the bed.

When I placed my aching foot on the covers, I sighed in relief. The simple act of opening the book soothed me. Tonight I'd concentrate on Elias.

I began at the bookmarked page. His comments about Rebecca were written in a clear, bold script, much easier to read than the previous cobbled words. His description of the woman bore no resemblance to those of his fellowmen. "Hir feturs aire splended." He described her long, black hair and "tendre" beauty.

Some blood had seeped into the pages, making a few passages difficult to decipher. One bit was more legible. The word, *Blessing*, jumped out at me. After all his vicious ramblings, that threw me. I'd have bet a man like him would have nothing to do with religion. I squinted to read the next bit and was surprised.

He said, "Shees myne." Too bad my blood had smeared the words. This part about Rebecca was the most interesting. To anyone with a heart, the man who'd written those words was obviously in love.

I yawned and glanced at the clock. Almost midnight. I tossed the diary onto the nightstand, where I'd put it before. Had Tom moved it? After what I'd learned, I wouldn't put any nasty action past him. My hand hit my purse and knocked it to the floor. I remembered the pretty green stone was in there. The woman at the store insisted it had protective properties; I wouldn't mind a safeguard for my dreams.

I dug out my sparkly gift and placed it under my pillow. Although I didn't believe all the purported benefits of malachite, I hoped its supposed ability to chase away nighttime demons would work. In the middle of the night, I was jolted from my sleep by a bang.

I held my breath, cowered under the sheet, and listened for more. Nerves on fire, I lay there frozen in place for what seemed like forever. I made a cautious move, and when the apartment remained quiet, I exhaled. What or who had made the noise? It sounded like it came from the next room.

I listened as hard as I could. My heart raged in my chest. I remembered my weapon, the chunky flashlight, and reached down to get it, but no matter how much I strained my ears, there was no other sound. I relaxed. The noise must have come from outside. A car crash, or kids who liked to wake people from their sleep at night.

Logic gave me comfort, and I slid onto my pillow. In the midst of a huge yawn, I choked. Certain I'd smelled tobacco, I sat up and sniffed. Nothing. Was there something wrong with my nose or was it my brain?

~ * ~

In the morning, the source of last night's noise greeted me when I went into the bathroom. My giant, economy-size shampoo lay smashed on the floor. The plastic container had split open and pink goo spread across the tiles. Though I was able to save the little bit of soap lodged in the bottom, I'd need a new bottle, and the clean-up took forever. I couldn't understand how it had fallen. On the bright side, the place smelled like roses and the floor sparkled.

My thoughts turned to the emerging relationship with Sam. Was it too soon? I made myself a cup of coffee as I thought about it. I had to admit I was still a little jealous of his beautiful ex, but I believed him that it was over.

Since I'd decided today would be my lazy day, I still wore my T-shirt and underwear. A puzzling cascade of tiny knocks on my door unnerved me. I held my breath and side-stepped to the door. More knocks, a little louder now. I left the chain on, cracked the door open a bit, and peeked into the hall.

My alarm evaporated at the spark of sunshine standing there. "Let us in, Auntie Dani."

The minute I opened the door, Izzy, the six-year-old light of my life, leaped into my arms. "I miss you, Auntie Dani."

I squeezed her tight and laughed into her yellow curls. "I missed you too."

Arms filled with coffee and a bag of goodies, Kirsten swept by us, deposited her bounty, then faced me. "You didn't ask who was there."

I straightened my shoulders, frowned, and muttered in aggravation, "I kept the chain on."

"Like that would stop a murderer. He'd burst right through that puny piece of metal."

While we squabbled, Izzy ran to the table and opened the bag. "We brought you doughnuts. What kind do you like? I guessed chocolate 'cause it's my favorite." Like a princess bestowing a prize, she awarded me one of the sticky goodies.

"You must be a mind reader because this is my favorite kind too."

Izzy giggled.

Kirsten gave her daughter a fond smile and handed me a cup of coffee. "Izzy's been dying to come here. I hope we haven't interrupted anything." Her gaze lingered on the bedroom.

She was always able to put me on the defensive. "No. Nothing."

Then, she noticed the air conditioner. "Oh, is this the one your *friend* installed for you last night?" Her expression resembled a satisfied cat. "Sooo…tell me about him."

Izzy called from the bedroom. "Mommy, can we get funny stairs like Auntie Dani's?"

I'd forgotten about the spiral staircase.

"No, honey. Those are special. You be careful on them."

"Okay, Mommy."

We took our coffee into the living room. Kirsten pointed to the sofa. "Okay, sit. What's the story with Sam? I already talked to Mom. Is he as gorgeous as she described him?"

I giggled and nodded. I found it impossible to keep anything from Kirsten when she was determined to unearth the story, so I plopped on the sofa, legs underneath me, and grinned. "He is." After a brief description, I said, "He's such a nice guy." I'd already decided to forgive him for his curt message.

She tucked herself on the couch next to me. "Okay, there's got to be more. Give."

I was just describing what a good kisser he was when a scream from the other room spurred us to action. We rushed in to find Izzy's body on the floor at the foot of the stairs. If her arm hadn't been bent at an odd angle, she might have been asleep.

"Izzy!" Kirsten leaned over her. "Oh, my God, she isn't moving. Dani, do something."

My heart slammed in my chest. I dropped to the floor. *Please*

God, let Izzy be okay. I held my breath until I detected movement in her tiny chest.

I wrapped my arm around my sister's shoulder. "It's okay. She's breathing. She must have hit her head. I'll call for an ambulance."

We sat there, next to our sweet baby, and soaked each other with tears. My dislike for this room grew by the minute.

I followed the ambulance in my car. Kirsten called her husband, Rick, who met us at the hospital where Izzy regained consciousness. The diagnosis was a slight concussion and a broken arm. I stayed until the break was set and signed her pretty pink cast. A young man in a white coat with a stethoscope around his neck introduced himself. He asked Izzy if she hurt anywhere else and how she'd fallen.

Shaking her pretty yellow curls, she said, "I didn't fall."

The doctor's focus slid to the adults. "Oh? What happened?"

"He pushed me."

A chorus of "Who?" echoed in the room.

Izzy insisted the "bad man" shoved her off the stairs. Kirsten and I assured the doctor there was no man in the apartment. She was by herself.

When he asked what the bad man looked like, she shook her head. "I didn't see him."

After a few more questions, the doctor smiled and told her not to hit anyone with her cast. While she admired her pink appendage, the doctor reassured us. "Children often experience guilt when they hurt themselves and make up stories of invisible assailants."

When I leaned in to kiss Izzy goodbye, her little lips puckered. "I don't like your house." My skin erupted in goosebumps.

On the way out of the hospital, with Izzy's final words torturing me, Sam called. I let it go to voicemail. After what happened to Izzy, I wasn't ready to handle him and my bruised ego.

Heather must have seen me arrive, because she waited for me in the hall. "What happened to your niece? Such a tiny little thing on that big stretcher."

The memory of Izzy's limp body tortured me. I wiped away tears while I described the accident and Izzy's bravery in the hospital.

"Oh, the poor baby. I'd like to get her a present and sign her cast."

I wanted to buy her a gift, too, but I didn't want to talk about the accident right now. Too much was happening. "Why don't I call you later? We can settle on a time to visit her?"

I entered my home with more than a suspicion all was not well in this apartment. The trouble centered around the bedroom.

When Sam called back, I answered with a neutral, “Hello.”

“Hey, did you get my message?”

“I did.”

“The guy’s an old friend who needed help. Otherwise, I wouldn’t have gone. I’m busy for the next couple of days. I’ve got time later tonight. You want company?”

The after-effects of the adrenaline-fueled trip to the hospital and Izzy’s pronouncement had depleted my energy. I hesitated then said, “Tonight’s not good for me. There was an accident.”

“An accident? Are you okay?”

“Yeah. I…I’m fine. My niece, Izzy, fell on my stairs and broke her arm.”

“Oh, I’m sorry. No wonder you’re upset. I won’t bother you now. I’ll give you a call tomorrow.”

The day’s events crashed in on me. Strain had seeped into my voice. “Okay. That’d be great. Bye.”

I ended the call and flopped down on the sofa. The image of Izzy in a pink cast saying she didn’t like my apartment troubled me. If her accident had been more serious, I’d never be able to live with myself. I was so grateful she was okay.

I got ready for bed, Izzy’s accident preying on my mind. The sight of those metal stairs made me sick. I twisted away then looked back. The rail height did leave room for a child to fall through, but not too much. She should have been able to grab some part of the metal—the handrails, the vertical bars, or the steps themselves. How had a clever little monkey like Izzy fallen?

Chapter Fourteen

My heart did a frantic tap dance as I awoke from another uncomfortable dream. The man tonight was the same distressing person who'd accosted me in my dream about the yacht club. Why did he keep disturbing my sleep? Both his face and voice sent spikes of dread through me. Was the repeat appearance of that frightful character related to my problems with Tom? My nighttime visitor's arrogant demeanor and refusal to leave me alone mirrored my ex's current, abusive behavior.

The unnerving disdain of his laughter followed me out of the dream. I took big gulps of air to quiet my racing pulse and pulled up the sheet. Though the warm night air gave rise to the chirp of crickets outside, a cold wave surrounded me.

Covers tucked under my chin, I flipped my head back and forth, alert for any threat. The nightmare character wasn't real, but it took a few minutes for my heartbeat to slow. So much for the magical properties of the witch's stone.

I forced my hand from under the cover to turn on the light. With the darkness banished, the tightness in my chest lessened. I ignored the "3:05" on the clock and crept into the kitchen for a cup of chamomile to soothe my nerves.

What I found in there made my heart pound all over again. My foot hit a small object that went skidding across the floor. The piece of malachite I'd placed beneath my pillow. I choked. What was it doing there?

When I bent to retrieve the pretty green stone and inhaled an unwelcome smoky scent, I closed my eyes and prayed.

~ * ~

My ordinary office looked good today. The same old gray file cabinets along one wall, my inbox full and waiting for me on my desk, and the lush, green philodendron I'd hung by the window. The everyday stability comforted me.

With an unprofessional groan, I lowered my exhausted body into the familiar depths of the brown leather chair. My butt had almost wiggled into its comfortable spot when Mary appeared holding a cup of tea and a homemade muffin.

I inhaled the warm blueberry scent and heaved a sigh. I loved Mary's goodies, but I'd have to cut down on my breakfast carbs at home. Even with that, I'd need to adopt an exercise routine. "Oh, you're a love. My morning is complete. A sympathetic friend and an injection of sugar."

She placed her offering on my desk before taking a seat. "I hoped something sweet might perk you up. You've looked a little listless. Is everything all right?"

"A new apartment comes with a lot of unexpected worries. My head won't stop whirling." I smirked. "An anxious mind isn't conducive to a restful night's sleep. I'm pretty tired."

"You have to take better care of yourself. Everyone loves you here. We worry about your health."

"Thank you. I'll be fine. Ever since I moved to Salem, I've had one problem after another."

Her sympathy changed to interest. "Did I tell you, dear, I grew up in Salem? Where do you live?"

"It's an apartment on Cove Street, part of an old house."

Her smile faltered a bit as she leaned forward, squinting at me with a troubled stare. In a more brusque voice she said, "What number on Cove Street?"

I paused before digging into my muffin. "Eighteen."

She snapped back in the chair as if she'd been pulled by a string. Her entire face withered, magnifying the wrinkles. In a sharp tone, unlike her, she said, "Is your apartment the original cottage?"

I chewed the delectable muffin and nodded, wondering what had upset Mary.

"When I was a girl, my friends and I used to whisper about your apartment."

Her words rattled me. More information I'd be happy to live without. I tried taking a sip of tea to warm me. The liquid had cooled like my insides. I didn't want to ask about her experience. The answers were bound to be bad, but the question burst from my mouth anyway. "What was wrong with my place?"

In a more normal tone, she said, "Well, dear, don't be alarmed. They're childhood tales of ghosts. A lot of the houses in Salem have them." Her attention focused on my desk as she leaned in to clean up crumbs and throw away my teabag.

"You mean my apartment has one?" My question ended in a little screech.

She patted my knee and pursed her lips. "Perhaps."

"The smuggler? How bad is it?" I'd forgotten where I was. The increasing volume of my voice attracted a couple of residents, but I was too tired to care.

Her lips pursed, and she shook her head. "Oh. Don't mind me. Just a bunch of old rumors."

Fool that I was, I pushed. "Please. What happened there?"

For a moment she hesitated, then closed the office door. "All right, dear. This is the story. The man who owned the original house, Elias Gale, is said to roam the place searching for his long-lost love."

Oh. That didn't sound too bad.

"The poor thing lived in Salem. Her story began a few years after that awful time when they were hanging women as witches. Well, a few neighbors believed she was one and took matters into their own hands. They set fire to her house with her trapped inside. They say her dying screams were pitiful."

No. No. I didn't want to hear this. I wrapped my arms around myself, but Mary was on a roll.

"Salem was a dangerous place for women in those days. Poor Rebecca—that was her name—didn't even have a trial. Her death was disgraceful." She peeked over her shoulder, leaned toward me, and lowered her voice as she said, "After the fire, the revenge was worse."

Oh, hell. How could anything be worse?

Uh-oh, she was patting my knee again. "I'm sorry. You did ask. They say Elias exacted a terrible vengeance on those he held responsible for Rebecca's death." In a dramatic whisper, she said, "They were found with their hearts cut out."

Oh. No. Way. "The guy who lived in my house?"

"Yes, dear. Elias Gale. The townspeople were in a frenzy. They blamed the Devil. One of them suggested Elias as the culprit, and a group marched to his house." She pointed at me. "Your apartment, dear. He was Rebecca's lover, you see. Their relationship made him a natural suspect. It's lucky they didn't burn his house down. Elias was nowhere to be found. He'd vanished. I don't believe he ever surfaced again."

My mouth opened, but no sound emerged. I hadn't expected such a horrid story. Mary sounded like she was reliving her dramatic childhood.

After she left, I spent the rest of the day wondering if our building was haunted.

~ * ~

On my way home, Mary's story monopolized my mind. I was sure nothing like that lived in my space. I intended to talk to someone about it. Not my family. They'd be too worried. I settled on Heather. My friend would give me the low-down. Maybe the resident ghost was an inside joke the tenants shared after the new renter endured a sort of initiation. Mrs. W and Marie had both alluded to something strange, but I was sure those two enjoyed frightening people. I'd ask Heather over for coffee to discuss Mary's revelations.

A quick shower did a lot to restore reason. Captain Elias Gale did not float around my apartment. Heather had lived here for a few years. She'd ease my mind.

A few minutes later, as I tossed salad ingredients, Sam called. The sound of his voice made me smile. "You called at a perfect time."

"Well, ma'am, I aim to please."

I chuckled. I was so glad to have him in my life. He asked about Izzy and how I was doing with it all. "I'm much better, and from what I hear, Izzy is enjoying her celebrity status."

"Glad everyone is okay." He paused for a moment, then said, "I miss you."

His words caused little flutters in my chest. "I miss you too."

"I'm going to be busy most of the week, but I have Friday off. Can I persuade you to go out with me?"

"Hmm," I said through my grin. "Perhaps I could be convinced."

"I'm looking forward to seeing you." His voice softened. "It's been too long."

His sensual tone warmed my soul and other parts of my body. "I agree."

We talked for a few more minutes, and I hated to say goodbye.

After I hung up, I pirouetted around the room. Life was wonderful. I'd forgotten all about Heather. She stopped by after dinner.

We took our coffee into the living room where I recounted Mary's incredible story.

The laughter and skepticism I expected didn't materialize. Instead, she sat there, eyebrows raised, twisting her ponytail around her finger. She shivered. "God, that's news to me. It's horrible." Her gaze darted to the bedroom. "He sounds like a monster."

"What?" I said in a voice way too loud. "Is what she said true?" I leaned in, invading her space. "Do we have a ghost?"

She didn't budge, just stared at her shoes. After an eternity, her gaze met mine. She cleared her throat. "*We* don't have one." The floor seemed to have a special fascination for her tonight as she mumbled, "*You* might."

"*Me*!" I shoved my head forward and dug my fingers into the arms of the chair.

With a furtive glance toward the bedroom, she muttered, "I didn't want to make you nervous because not much has ever happened. The electricity problems, odd noises, and the horrid, creepy cellar. The last tenant, Rose—I told you she was an older woman—kept misplacing stuff and blaming it on some kind of gremlin. I assumed she was losing it, never believed in a ghost, figured the noises were an old house groaning." She paused then gave a slow headshake. "After what you just told me…"

I concentrated. The electricity? Fixed. Noises? The scratches would be the mouse. Whispers might be an old house settling. The basement? That place gave me the chills. It might be haunted and the source of the nasty odors.

"I bet it's the cellar," I said. "Maybe Elias locked Sam in."

She held out her hands palm up. "I guess."

I remembered Doug down there, and the excitement on his face as he swung the metal pipe. "What about the Formans? She questioned me one day in the laundry and made a snarky reference to the bedroom. Do they ever talk about Elias?"

"Oh. I forgot. Doug is a big history buff, works in the antiquity department of a Boston museum. He still carries on about the damage the previous owners caused to the room's historical significance when they removed the second story, and the spiral staircase drives him crazy. I remember him going in there after Rose left, to check the place over. The man is so weird. I'm sure he wishes there was a ghost. He's more into the past than the present."

No wonder he doesn't like me. "Let's have more coffee. I have another concern."

She followed me to the kitchen. I pointed to the floor.

"What?" She leaned in for a closer look. "I don't see anything."

"Last night, after a terrible nightmare, I decided to have a soothing cup of tea." I took a deep breath before I continued. "Remember my malachite, the green stone the witch gave me? I keep it under my pillow, but I found it on the floor out here."

"Oh, my God. Someone snuck into your apartment? Wait—was it the ghost?"

I told her about my dreams—the frightful man and the smoky odor I associated with him. Her gaze traveled around the room as her hands rubbed up and down her arms.

"That's not all," I said. "I researched information on malachite." I swallowed and gave a nervous glance around. "At one time people used the mineral for protection against dark spirits like demons and witches."

Her hand strayed to tug at her ponytail. "Are you serious?"

I nodded. "There's more. The article also said you should keep a piece near your bed to protect against nightmares."

"Are you sure you put it under your pillow?"

I squeezed my arms against me, wishing for a different answer. "Yes."

She snapped her fingers. "I have an idea. A friend of mine has a friend who's a medium. The woman comes into your home to do a reading. She's supposed to be the best. Why don't I call and ask her to do her thing here? She can tell us if the place is haunted. I'll invite a few other people. It'll be fun. I guess she asks for a picture or trinket. Something you associate with the person you want to contact, but you won't need one if there's a spirit here. What do you say?"

Oh brother. I tried not to freak out. I'd always been a baby about anything supernatural. I believe you don't go searching for answers you don't want to find. This ghost business was making me crazier by the minute.

I wished I could afford to move. "No. I don't want to have a psychic in here. It's too creepy."

Heather copped an attitude. Hands on her hips, she pinned me with her stare. "Come on. We'll have fun, and you can find out for sure if Elias is haunting his old home."

I shook my head. "I don't like the sound of it."

Jeez, did I want to poke into the supernatural? Maybe I should leave my problems the way they were. A couple of objects moving around was no big deal. My life wasn't too bad. All I had to do was stay far away from the cellar.

She paced and waved her hands in the air. "Don't you want to be comfortable here? If there's a ghost, she can tell you how to get rid of him."

When I crossed my arms and glared, she caved. "Okay, okay. We'll have the reading at my place, but it won't be the same. Better?"

"Maybe..." I wished the quirky skittering in my gut would go away.

"Good. I'll call my friend tonight."

I walked her to the door, as she discussed a date for the psychic reading, and I wondered how to get out of it.

Chapter Fifteen

Although it took me hours to relax after Heather's ideas about a ghost whisperer, I did fall into a dreamless sleep. The next morning, I decided my pseudo-grandmother had spun me an embellished tale concocted by young girls who thrived on the dramatic. I was sure they'd magnified and embroidered the details.

I'd settled into a good rhythm at work when Fischer launched his latest attack. The phone tirade began right away without him even bothering to say, "Hello."

"Why can't you get your paperwork right?" His current rant referred to the end-of-the-month inventory for the state.

He didn't have to make such a big deal about it. These reports gave everyone trouble, and I hadn't made a mistake in months. "I'll take care of it."

His voice held a nasty sneer. "If you can't do the work, get someone to help you."

I didn't bother to remind him his job was to guide the managers. My anxiety would skyrocket if I was stuck in the same office with him for more than a minute. At the familiar click of his disconnect in my ear, I consoled myself. At least his calls were short.

When Mary and more sugary ambrosia arrived, I grinned. My savior. Between bites of a delicious carrot muffin, I unburdened myself. Fischer headed my list of grievances, and I finished my catalog of troubles with Tom.

She nodded, tut-tutted, and patted my hand. Her maternal concern put me in a better frame of mind. By the end of my pitiful outburst and with the help of Mary's sympathetic attitude, I resumed work in a much better mood.

Around lunchtime, Eddie called. Since he was both my landlord and one of the managers for this company, I wondered which hat he wore today. "Hi. What can I do for you?"

"I'm worried. Why was an ambulance at your apartment this weekend? Are you okay?"

I thanked him for his concern and filled him in on the accident.

Disturbed his stairs had caused her fall, he said, "Text me your sister's address, and I'll send Izzy a get-well present."

"Thanks. I appreciate that."

"Any other problems with the place? How's the electricity?"

"Perfect. Sam did a great job."

"Good. He's a nice guy. Doesn't let his personal problems interfere with his work. It's too bad the way his wife treats him."

I wasn't comfortable discussing Sam and Trish. I tried to keep my mouth shut but failed. "Ex-wife." It killed me to add, "She is gorgeous."

"Yeah, she is. No wonder he keeps going back for more." His words cut through me.

"But their relationship is over."

"It is until she crooks her little finger. You can't blame him, though." He chuckled. "She's quite the woman."

His words were like a roundhouse to my gut. The muffin I'd scarfed earlier threatened to come back up. Eddie must have it wrong. Sam's connection might have been like that before, but he swore he was over Trish.

"Call me if you have any more problems, we'll get them fixed."

"Wait a minute." I remembered Fischer's dictate. "I do need your help."

Surprise lightened his voice. "Sure. What can I do for you?"

"Fischer was kind enough to point out I made a mistake on my end-of-the-month statement. Do you have time to help me with it?"

"No problem. I can come over now or stop by the apartment after work."

"Thanks. I have to get the paperwork at his office. If you want to come by my place, I'll feed you."

"Great. See you around 5:30 PM?"

"Perfect. Thanks a lot."

~ * ~

Eddie arrived with a six-pack tucked under his arm. As we worked on the problem over burgers and beer, I told him about Tom and what I'd learned at the police station. "They said he dated the murdered woman before she went missing."

His mouth opened, then he scrubbed his hand over his face and shook his head. "Poor Allison. What a nice kid. I remember she was seeing some guy in Boston. Pretty weird it turned out to be Tom, huh?"

I agreed. "I just have trouble picturing him as a murderer."

He frowned and sat back in his chair. "You're too naïve. You can't tell what people will do under pressure. Look what the guy did to your car. I've never trusted him."

He was right. Tom had a terrible temper, but killing someone? I hoped not. "Maybe her death was an accident."

His lips pinched together, and he shook his head. "Until this investigation is settled, please be careful."

I promised him I would, then took a breath, mustering my courage, and posed the *big* question. "Hey Eddie?"

"Yeah."

"Have you ever noticed any weird activity in this house, like paranormal?"

For a minute he scowled, then his face cleared into a quizzical stare. "What brought that on?"

How could I explain? I didn't want to go into a detailed account of my experiences. I almost wished I hadn't asked. "A few strange things have happened, and what about the former tenant?" My voice sort of petered off on the last word.

"You've been listening to the local gossip. Okay. Salem is stuck with a bad psychic rep. I can't change that." He chuckled and waved his hand in front of his face. "But, come on! Ghosts don't exist. In this town, they're just a draw for tourists." His smile disappeared, and he sat up. "I can't afford to have my properties associated with hauntings, though. If you're uncomfortable here, I'll be happy to let you out of your lease."

Ooh. I had no idea this would be such a sensitive subject. I glanced around my cheery kitchen. For the most part, I loved the place. I wasn't ready to leave. Was I? Where would I go?

"No. This is a great apartment. I guess I paid too much attention, like you said, to the neighborhood rumor mill."

"Don't worry. It happens." He headed for the refrigerator. "I'm ready for another beer. What about you?"

Glad to be done with the uncomfortable subject, I grinned. "Why not?"

When he came back, he said, "You've been stuck inside too much. You need to get out more. What have you been doing for fun?"

"Fun?"

"Yeah. You know, the stuff that makes you happy? There's been way too much doom and gloom in your life."

I lifted my shoulders. "I've been pretty busy. I did go to a dance at the yacht club in Marblehead last Friday."

"That's a start." He snapped his fingers. "There's a place right down the street here, one of Salem's oldest pubs. Good food. Great music. You should stop in. A fantastic band is scheduled to play there this Thursday. I'm going. Why don't you come? We'll have a great time."

Did he just ask me for a date? No. We'd gone that route one time before I'd met Tom, but we both agreed we're better as friends. "Thursday? Let me think about it. What's the name of this place?"

He laughed. "Mercy Tavern, but it used to be called In a Pig's Eye."

~ * ~

The evening news relayed more information on the murder. I cringed when the announcer said a reliable source revealed the police were questioning "a person of interest." Though he didn't mention any names, I was sure he was talking about Tom. When the phone rang, I expected to hear a news update from Heather.

"Dani, I'm in trouble. I need to talk to you." Tom. He sounded on the verge of tears.

"What?"

His words became a whine. "They believe I killed Allison. They'll put me in jail. You have to talk to them. Tell them I'd never kill anyone. Please."

Oh, Lord. What could I say? I didn't believe he was capable of homicide. Did I? Yeah, I'd seen his anger, but being violent enough to murder? He sounded pathetic. "There's nothing I can do."

"You have to talk to the police. I wouldn't kill anyone. Tell them I never hurt you."

Except for the last night. If I'd stayed, would he have gotten worse? *Damn, he's not going to like what I have to say.*

"I already spoke to the police." I prepared myself for the explosion. "I told them what you did to my car."

"Oh, that," he said in a dismissive tone. "No big deal. I wanted to teach you a lesson. Come on, call them. Tell them I didn't kill Allison."

"I don't have any idea what happened to her. I can't help you." His pleading changed to anger. Tom didn't like the word "no."

Before I hung up, he'd called me some pretty disgusting names, making me wonder if I was wrong about him.

Damn. Why didn't I hang up instead of allowing his abuse? I'd forgotten the man's cunning and his tendency toward violence when he didn't get his way. He blew off the damage to Minerva as nothing, then admitted he hurt her to punish me. Another example of his cruel streak.

I'd experienced his physical abuse. How far would he go? Then the realization hit me like a slap. I glared at my traitorous phone. Tom called me on my cell. He'd found my apartment, and now he had my new, unlisted number. Time to face facts. He was never going to leave me alone. I'd have to take time off to file the restraining order. Since I wasn't about to tell anyone I was going to court, I'd take a sick day.

Sleep eluded me. My mind twisted in eddies. Tom and Elias. Unlike Elias, Tom posed a danger. The pain and anxiety from the last few days circled through my head. I noticed, though, despite the problems, one positive fact emerged. I'd been able to survive some heavy stuff on my own. I was okay.

Three weeks ago, the mere mention of ghosts would have had me hightailing my butt to my sister's. Today I planned to weigh my options until I consulted the psychic at Heather's party. After considering my choices like a sensible grown-up, I slept, but my subconscious clung to the fear.

In the dream I couldn't see anyone, but the tiny hairs on the back of my neck told me someone was there. Like a mouse in a trap, I waited for the cat to pounce. My throat was so dry, I almost choked. The telltale scrape of a shoe told me he was close. My heart pounded in my ears.

I crouched into a protective ball, waiting for the end. The sound of heavy breathing intensified as he closed in, and then a familiar braying laugh. Tom!

~ * ~

For once, I had an easy day at work. No problems I couldn't handle and no Fischer. Even so, I was glad to get home and relax. Soon after I arrived, there was a knock on my door, which was always locked now.

Before I touched the knob, I yelled, "Who's there?"

"Heather."

Since the night at the yacht club, most of her efforts were aimed at her new love interest. When she came in, I expected the low-down on everything Peter.

Instead, she sat at my kitchen table, all bravado gone. She reminded me of a lost waif. "I have to talk to you."

Wondering what new concern derailed my former cheerful, irreverent neighbor, I joined her. "Okay."

After the break-in at her apartment, the announcement that the murder victim was one of Eddie's tenants unnerved her to the point she was ready to find a new place, and she wanted me to join her. She intended to look for apartments for both of us. I had no money for another move, and I'd grown comfortable in our neighborhood, Ms. W included.

When I reminded Heather, she didn't care, so I'd tried reasoning with her. It hadn't worked. She was still ready to move, but at least her attitude had brightened. Now she was in another funk.

She put her head in her hands. "I figured out what he took."

"Who?" My attempts to follow her reasoning almost made me dizzy.

"The bastard who broke into my apartment. Did I tell you he stomped on my camera?"

"Yes. Smashing your property was a rotten thing to do." Her photography equipment meant a lot to her.

She brushed away my words. "I'm insured. That's not what I'm worried about." With an uncomfortable look around, she said, "Let's go outside." Baffled, I followed her into the yard.

She walked to the far end by the bushes. "I didn't want to have this discussion in your apartment."

"Why?"

After a sideways glance at the house, she said, "He might be listening."

When I caught on to her meaning, I said, "Oh, come on. There've been a couple of weird events. It's not like there's a presence in the apartment."

The anxious glance she gave the house made me uncomfortable. She squared her shoulders and took a deep breath. "Remember the other day when I took pictures of you and your parents?"

I nodded.

"And your mother wanted photos from inside your apartment?"

"Sure. She was thrilled."

"Those pictures are missing."

I didn't get it. "Are you certain?"

"I've checked everywhere. They're gone."

"Why would someone want pictures of my apartment?"

Again, silence from my loquacious friend. She ignored my question. Ponytail swinging, she shook her head as if in denial, and sat down. Her lack of chatter spoke volumes. I was worried.

She gave another furtive peek at the house and continued, "I inspected those pictures after I printed them. Two of the photos weren't quite right. They bothered me, but with the break-in and, of course, Peter," her smile made a brief appearance, almost her normal self, "I forgot about it." She lowered her gaze and mumbled, "Why would someone take them unless my hunch was true?"

"What are you talking about?" I hadn't seen her this worried since the burglary.

She ignored my question and continued to talk to herself. "I wish I'd copied them to the computer." I was ready to remind her I was there when she blinked and refocused on me. "I discovered what I believed to be a flaw in the photo of you and your parents outside."

"No problem. As long as our faces are clear."

"It might have been a reflection from the tree, but the closer I peered at the glass, the shadow in the window was more obvious, like a person behind the curtain."

I glanced toward the bedroom. No one had been in there. We'd gone inside a few minutes later and the apartment was empty. Before I uttered a word, she went on.

"Remember how cold it got when I posed you three against the fireplace inside?"

"Yeah, my mother was freezing."

"I noticed an anomaly in that picture."

I waited for her to continue. Her forehead scrunched, exposing a series of wrinkles, and her eyes held uncertainty. "A round orb hovered in front of the fireplace."

"Wha—"

Her hand rose in a *stop* gesture. "I debated with myself about the phenomenon today. At the time, I figured I'd caught the sunlight bouncing off an object. I took other pictures in the room, though, without any flaws. No other shot had the curious glint. A light suspended in the air."

"Oh, come on. Are you telling me I've got glowing balls in my bedroom?"

She bit her lip and pleaded with me. "The sphere was there. Plain as day," she swallowed, "right above your head."

The minute she left I freaked. Should I go to my sister's house for the night? If I believed what Heather said, I'd have to accept the idea my bedroom might be haunted. I'd have liked to see the photos for myself. My friend did have a heavy sense of drama. I didn't blame her, though. She'd been under so much stress since the break-in.

I decided to investigate. I paused in the kitchen, reassured by the sunlight streaming in the window. The daylight bolstered my determination. What had my life come to, that I balked at entering my own bedroom? I shook off the tension and marched in. With my nose in the air, I sniffed. No smoke. I was ready to bolt if necessary.

The cool air no longer bothered me. I listened for foreign noises. Silence. No threat. I edged closer to the fireplace. Did the temperature drop? I swung toward the window where Heather had spotted the silhouette, and the room dissolved into darkness. *Oh, God, he's here.*

Terror held me in place. My heart drummed in my ears. I closed my eyes, unable to face him. When nothing happened, I chanced a quick peek, ready to flee. The descent into darkness wasn't caused by an evil spirit. A big, black cloud had covered the sun. With the shock of returning light, I blinked and blinked to readjust to the brightness. No villains in my face. Except for my shaking carcass, the room was empty. I slumped in on myself and sat on the bed. This was ridiculous. If I kept this up, I'd give myself a heart attack.

I worked up a surge of courage, swallowed my anxiety, and headed for the loft. Even during the day, the place made me uncomfortable. I tended toward claustrophobic, so I hunched my shoulders against the dark rafters and forced myself to breathe. I peeked at the desktop. Nothing unusual there.

I looked out over the room and released my breath. No wraiths at the window or any other psychic problems. I sniffed. No acrid smell. A ghost-free area. Now I doubted my own senses. I'd do one more inspection from the outside. A shadow or trick of light might have resembled a person to Heather.

I moved about the yard, checking the window from different angles, looking like a fool. No matter where I stood, the windowpane remained clear. The whole "person-in-the-window" thing was her imagination. Relieved, I headed back inside. A loud voice stopped me. I let out a little screech and spun around. Jimbo. I patted my chest to ease my racing heart.

Took me a second to find my voice. "Hi, Jimbo."

"I…I didn't mean to scare you." He spoke to me from the gate.

As I walked over, the nervous glances he threw toward the house prompted me to ask, "Are you okay?"

He studied his hands, clasped them together, and took short, heavy breaths. "I can't work for you anymore."

"I don't understand. You don't enjoy working here?" Before I could ask for an explanation, he opened the gate to leave. "Wait a minute. Why?"

He gave a quick peek at the house, then shook his head. "It's not good here." Then he hurried away.

The break-in must have upset him. Although I hated to see him frightened, I didn't have the means to reassure him. The place made me nervous too.

Another uncomfortable situation out of my control. How did my life get so out-of-kilter? Although I believed Tom was behind most of my problems, Heather's crazy photos and Jimbo quitting weren't his fault.

I'd just have to add today's revelations to the crap pile I'd collected—Tom, Fischer, Izzy's accident, and Mary's tale of horror. No wonder my dreams were such a mess. I found it astounding I was still sane, but I refused to buckle under because of ghost stories. I'd wait to see what the medium had to say.

Instead of running, I settled on a compromise. I'd spend the night in the living room on my brand-new sofa bed.

Chapter Sixteen

An escalating dispute at work over parking spaces ate up most of my morning. I appeased both parties and got back to my office before Mrs. Craigie found out and tattled to Mein Fuhrer.

I checked my calendar to make sure everything was done when I remembered Eddie's invitation. I'd forgotten to mention it to Heather. After a day filled with spiteful sniping, I deserved an evening of fun.

I phoned her at work. "Are you busy?"

"I've got a few minutes. Why?"

"Eddie mentioned a pub called Mercy Tavern," I said.

"Oh yeah. That place is a lot of fun."

"Good. Do you want to go there tonight, listen to the band, and have dinner?"

"Outstanding suggestion. What time?"

"Six PM?"

"You got it, girl. I'll be ready."

The promise of music and drinks with friends brightened my spirits. A popular neighborhood pub was another benefit of living here. I checked it off in the air with my finger and mentally added a few more—walking distance to Pickering Wharf, a private yard, and a friend across the hall.

My choice of clothes reflected my mood. I'd chosen a bright striped blouse, white fitted jeans, and gold hoops for my ears. I was ready to enjoy myself. When I popped over to Heather's, her outfit proclaimed she had the same idea—tight red jeans, a black clingy top, and large red feather earrings.

Heather waved me into the kitchen. "Come in for a minute and sit down. I've got something to tell you."

JoJo came over to welcome me, and I picked him to cuddle him. "I've been dying to tell you the good news." Words spilled out of her mouth in an excited rush. "I've been with Peter three times since the dance, and he invited me to his cottage on Cape Cod for the weekend. It's right on the beach. Just a sec." She shoved her chair back and jumped up, startling JoJo into a series of barks. On her way to the bedroom, she threw words over her shoulder. "I made an emergency trip to the mall. Thank God for Victoria's Secret."

With a look of triumph on her face, she exhibited her prize, a black gossamer triangle and a tiny stringy thing. My mouth fell open. I blinked to wipe away the image her lingerie conveyed. "Oh my God!"

"I intend to knock his socks off."

I covered my mouth and giggled. "It'll knock more than his socks off."

She grinned and raised an eyebrow. "That's the idea." She sat down, elbow on the table and chin in her hand. "So, how was your week?"

I frowned. "To begin with, I've seen too much of Fischer. He appears at the complex at weird times for no reason. The other day I spotted his car in the lot, but no sign of him. He has me second-guessing every move I make. It's like he declared open season on my life. Then there's Tom."

When I told her about the phone call on my unlisted number, she drummed her fingernail against the wooden surface as she gave me her opinion of Tom and my willingness to talk to him.

"He won't be a problem much longer," I said in a rush. Nervous flutters teased my stomach at the huge step I was about to take, but it was necessary. "I filled out the paperwork to stop the harassment, and I'm taking a sick day tomorrow to get the restraining order." I let out a huge breath as I finished my pronouncement.

"Atta girl! You take care of Tom, and I'll help you get rid of Elias."

"Right. How are you going to do that?"

"I got in touch with a medium and scheduled a reading for a week from Friday at 7:00 PM. I have some friends who are interested. How about you? Got any people to invite? Maybe from work? Hey, why don't you ask Kirsten?"

Oh, yuck. "Let me get back to you."

Sheesh, I didn't want to meet someone who talked to ghosts, let alone a bunch of believers.

She reached for her purse and said, "Seriously, though, I'm here for you. I'll be on the lookout for Tom. If he killed Allison, he won't respect a piece of paper."

Her words rattled my nerves. "The police would arrest him if he ignored the order. Right?"

"I'm just saying you still have to be careful."

I followed Heather to the door but stopped. "Wait a minute. What if he's out there now?"

"Whoa," she said. "Stay put while I check."

She came back smiling. "No problem. It's safe."

~ * ~

I took a deep breath and ignored a flash of anger. I would not let that bastard bother me. After I went before the judge tomorrow, my problems with Tom would be over. A nip in the air boosted my energy. This evening promised to be fun.

As we walked along Derby Street, I had the urge to skip across the sidewalk. With the shadow of Tom gone, and the medium helping me evict the poltergeist or whatever lived in my bedroom, my life could return to normal. In the meantime, I'd concentrate on enjoying what I had. Tonight, music and friends would erase those two terrorists from my mind.

Noise surrounded us the second we entered the pub. The buzz of eager conversation and laughter from the good-sized crowd created a comfortable atmosphere. The excitement was contagious. Tantalizing odors of grilled burgers and deep-fried food swirled through the air as we looked for a seat. Hunger growled through my stomach. I had to resist the urge to steal a French fry from a nearby plate.

Heather leaned in and yelled in my ear, "There's Eddie waving us over."

What should have been a short journey to our friend, only a few tables away, took forever, because Heather stopped to introduce me to all her pals. Unfamiliar names spiraled around in my brain, and my belly grumbled in revolt as I squeezed myself into a chair next to Eddie.

"There you are," he said. "How come you brought Heather?"

"She loves this place, and I'm amazed at how many friends she has. I'll never remember all of them."

He shrugged and began talking about the different bands that played here. "You'll have to come more often."

Heather slung herself into her seat. "This is great. What a good idea, Eddie." We ordered drinks and food. A short while later, while the band was tuning up, she peered into the crowd and said, "Isn't that Sam?"

"Where?" I looked in the direction she pointed. "It is. What's he doing here?"

She raised her hand to wave, but the ex claimed his attention. Trish touched his arm, and he turned toward her. My food stuck in my throat. He'd said he was working all week, but there he was meeting *her*!

I had enough. I pushed my plate away and grabbed my purse. I should have listened to Eddie. The bitch wins.

Heather poked me. "What are you doing? He's coming over."

"What?"

"Sam. He's seen us."

I glanced up to find the handsome man next to me. "Hi. Do you mind if I join you?"

Eddie grunted, and Heather moved over so Sam could sit beside me.

I was confused. "I thought you had to work."

"I did, but I finished early."

"What are you doing here?" Heather asked.

"Looking for Dani."

Me? "How did you know where to find me?"

He grinned. "Mrs. W."

I was astounded. "Who told her?" I looked at Heather. "You?" She shook her head.

Sam still had a delighted grin. "When I showed up at your place, she called me over. She's something else." He chuckled. "She said she figured you were here, because it was a favorite of Heather's, and your clothes suggested a pub kind of night."

Heather shook her head, and I laughed. "I'll have to thank her."

Sam stole a couple of fries from my plate and ordered a sandwich. He smacked his lips. "They have good food here."

"Weren't you with Trish earlier?" Eddie said as he sipped his drink. "She looks good tonight."

Sam raised an eyebrow and pursed his lips. "I don't think she's with anyone, if you're interested."

At the detached tone of his answer, I smiled and stopped worrying about his ex. I wanted to hug myself. Eddie was wrong.

By the time Sam's food arrived, Heather had deserted us for some of her friends, and Eddie checked his cell and grumbled something about business before he shoved his chair back. "See ya."

Sam draped his arm around my shoulders. "This turned out to be a great night. Good food, a jazz band, and a beautiful woman."

I offered him the rest of my fries and leaned into his shoulder while we listened to the music. During the musicians' break, when we could hear each other, Sam surprised me with a tidbit from the pub's past. "In the early eighteen hundreds, when Salem was a thriving seaport, Derby Street businesses catered to sailors who'd been away for months. This district was famous for drinking, gambling, and prostitution."

I smirked. "How nice."

He grinned and squeezed my shoulder. "There's more."

"I can't wait."

"Smugglers built secret tunnels to the wharves to transfer illegal goods from the ships."

A scary idea popped into my mind. "Maybe Elias built one underneath our place? You said he was a smuggler."

"No. Don't worry. The city mapped the underground routes. They don't go near your building, but I understand those byways served *another* purpose."

From the mischievous look on his face, he was about to tell me something I wouldn't like. "Isn't it time for the band to play again?" I said as I looked around.

"We have plenty of time." He carried on with his history lesson despite my concern. "In those days, a lot of men either died on board or deserted their ships. Captains, desperate for a crew, would hire men to shanghai drunken sailors." He leaned in close. "This building was a popular tavern." He wiggled his eyebrows in a suggestive gesture. Warmth crept up my neck as he continued, "It's tunnel still exists. Some of the drugged sailors died during their abduction, and for years, people have claimed to hear the cries of their souls." He pointed to the floor with a flourish. "Right beneath our feet."

I peeked down and rubbed my arms. "This city has too many ghost stories." Now might be a good time to talk about my resident phantom, though. "I'll bet a lot of them are true."

He laughed. "Don't be ridiculous. There's no such thing as ghosts."

His answer made me furious. I knew spirits were real. I had one.

What was the matter with him, anyway? Just because he'd never experienced an ethereal being, didn't give him the right to deny their existence. What would he say if I told him about Elias? Would he call me crazy and distance himself from me?

While I tried to come up with some way to convince him there might be genuine hauntings, the band started up again. I checked my cell. 11:00 PM.

I'd have to wait for that discussion. "Time for me to leave." On the way out the door, I caught a glimpse of Trish cuddled up to a guy by the bar and smiled. Sam was leaving with me.

Out on the street, intermittent illumination cut into the black night. The temperature had cooled, and I was glad for his arm warming my shoulders.

"Hey." A shout from behind.

Heather came jogging up to us. "Can I butt in for the walk home? There's still a killer on the loose, you know."

I shuddered and peered at the myriad places of concealment made invisible by the dark. This was not a safe area to travel at night. I leaned into Sam, glad Heather and I weren't walking back alone. She chattered on to him about acquaintances they shared. By the time we arrived at our building, I'd learned the dating history of at least six people. Heather wished us goodnight, and Sam walked me to my apartment.

I turned, expecting a kiss, but he said, "I'm coming in to make sure it's safe."

Pleasure rippled through me as I opened the door. I considered shanghaiing him, but I had to get up early.

"Have you had any more problems?" he asked.

Mary's revelation and Heather's photos came to mind, but I didn't dare tell him. He wouldn't believe me. I hated to lie. "Nothing."

As he inspected the rooms, closets, and locks, I had an inspiration. If I moved away, I'd never have to divulge my ghostly secret at all. Satisfied the apartment was all buttoned up, and no intruders lurked in the shadows, he stood in front of me, gazing down. I hoped my body's instant reaction didn't show in my face.

His breathing deepened. "It's late and we both have to work in the morning, so I'll say goodnight."

He gathered me in his arms for a heart-pounding kiss that left my body crying for more, but Sam was right. Although I wasn't going to the office tomorrow, I wanted to get to the courthouse early. I had no idea how long it would take to see a judge.

As we stood there, he brushed his hand across my cheek and said, "Do you like Chinese food?"

"Huh?" I stirred in his arms. He smiled. "Do you?"

"I-Yes. I love it."

"Good. Since we ate out tonight, I figured it would be nice if I brought dinner to you tomorrow night."

"That sounds wonderful."

He captured my lips for one more killer kiss, then added in a deep, husky voice, "Sleep tight."

Chapter Seventeen

After hours at the courthouse with my nerves on fire, I drove to my sister's to show her the restraining order. She gave me a big hug, and Izzy insisted I examine all the artwork and good wishes on her cast.

"This calls for a celebration," Kirsten said "What do you think, Izzy? Should we take Auntie Dani out for a treat?"

My niece jumped up and down and clapped her hands. "Yes. Yes."

We went to Izzy's favorite ice cream parlor. My mouth watered for a hot fudge sundae, but, an image of my tight jeans popped into my head, and I settled for a single scoop of frozen yogurt. On the way home, memories of Sam monopolized my thoughts, how his sensuous gaze traveled over my body and what his kisses did to me. Lost in erotic daydreams, I almost forgot to stop at the packy for beer.

Six-pack in hand, I hurried into my apartment and stowed the cold bottles in the fridge. Cleaning came next. I rushed to finish, caught my breath, and looked around in approval. Now, what to wear? I agonized over choices, dragging out half my closet. The night was cool, so I settled for a forest green sweater and jeans. I confirmed the time, fifteen more minutes, checked the beer in the fridge again, and sat on the sofa bouncing my leg.

At 6:01 PM, a knock brought me to my feet. I was at the door in seconds. "Who is it?"

"The man of your dreams."

I flung open the door. He looked more delicious than the promised feast. Tight slacks and an open-necked white shirt emphasized his lean, muscular body. I stood there ogling him, and his dimple appeared.

He held out two large shopping bags. "We should eat this while it's hot."

"Mmm, smells wonderful."

He gave me a quick kiss on my lips and plunked his bounty on the counter.

"Oh, no. Not there. We're dining outside. I've got everything set up."

"Lead the way," he said, with a sweep of his arm.

The table was ready. He secured the tongs and insisted on serving. I sat back and let him. There was way too much food, and I smiled. My fridge would be filled with yummy leftovers.

After I ate my way through sweet and sour chicken, spareribs, fried rice, and lo mein, I grinned and patted my full stomach. "Thank you. A perfect meal. Delicious food, no cooking, and no dishes."

He raised his beer in a salute. "I'm happy to do it. Being with you is a trip. I can never tell what to expect—locked in a cellar, a dance under the moonlight, or a morning at the police station."

I chuckled when he lifted my hand to his lips for a small kiss.

We talked for a bit about favorite pastimes. Music. He was country; I was rock. Movies. I'm into romcoms, and Sam prefers action films. Sports. Football was good. We both love the New England Patriots, but we agreed to disagree on baseball. I'm fanatic about the Boston Red Sox, and Sam is a diehard New York Yankees fan.

In the intimate shadow of twilight, each new revelation brought us closer, but with the descent of darkness, our flirtatious discoveries were frustrated by a swarm of hungry mosquitos. We grabbed the food and hurried inside.

Sam placed the boxes in the fridge and said, "How's the A/C?"

"Works like a charm."

A moment later, in the living room, a frown marred his handsome face. "Don't you want the air in your bedroom?"

I shook my head. "No. It's always cool in there."

Before I could stop him, he'd walked in there like he didn't believe me. Men!

"Hey, you're right. Weird how it's cooler in here."

I shook my head. *Next time take my word for it, dude.*

On the way back through the kitchen, I grabbed a couple more beers. We settled in on the sofa. For a minute, Sam sprawled next to me in a lord-of-the-manor pose. Then his air of contentment changed. He sat up, took a deep pull on his beer, and cleared his throat. "Have you had any more trouble with Tom?"

"I don't have to worry about him anymore." I leaned forward and grinned. "I got a restraining order this morning."

Worried wrinkles dissolved, and his dimple reemerged. In a tender gesture, he caressed my face. I closed my eyes to savor his touch and breathe in his scent. A heartbeat later, when I opened them, his warm smile became a tentative kiss, then a sensual embrace. The slow, deliberate movement of his lips ignited a long-dormant hunger. He deepened the kiss, and I leaned in, wanting more. Heat radiated through my body. I melted against his chest. His hands moved across my back and slid under my sweater.

At his touch, an aching heat pooled in my abdomen. I rubbed my fingers along his neck and through his hair. When he leaned me back on the cushions, a deep, pulsing need overwhelmed me. I moaned his name. The beep of a phone intruded. I chased the sound from my mind. All I wanted right now was Sam. I told him to ignore it, but he groaned and sat up.

He glanced at the screen, then back at me, apology filling his face. In a low, husky growl, he said, "I'll shut it off. Wait a minute."

I wanted to cry, "No!"

"Bob would never call unless he had something important to tell me." He answered with a resigned, "Yeah, Bob. What's up?" and ended with a yell. "*What*?"

He disentangled himself from my arms, his body rigid, his tone tense. "Okay. Right. Okay. I'll be right there." Disbelief and fear played across his face. His voice held a small tremor. "I have to go. My building is on fire."

"Your apartment?"

"My business." He looked ill. He wrapped me in his arms and gave me a satisfying kiss. "We'll continue this later. I'll call you."

He was halfway to the door before I processed what had happened. "I'm so sorry. What can I do? I'll come with you."

"No. I have no idea what I'm walking into or where I'm going to be. I'll call you later."

"But..." The click of the closing door finished my sentence.

I prayed the fire wouldn't do serious damage. His face had held a terrible insecurity. The urge to hold him, to comfort him, hit me hard. In a short time, he'd become very important to me. I paused to assess where our relationship was headed. It happened so fast. We'd known each other for less than a month. I came to the sensible conclusion we should take things slower, but my body rebelled. The hell with reason. Three weeks, three days—it didn't matter. I wanted Sam.

Worry propelled me through my apartment, back and forth from the living room to the bedroom. On my third trip, the room started to spin. I lurched toward the sofa, sat down, and waited for my mind to stop whirling. I leaned forward and cradled my head. I needed to come up with a plan. What could I do? Heather! She'd help. I dialed her number.

"Dani, what's wrong?"

"Sam's business is on fire."

"What?"

"Bob called, and he ran out of here. I have no idea where his business is located."

"Oh, how awful." She told me his place was on North Street but cautioned me not to leave the house alone in case Tom was around.

"I don't know what to do. Sam's in trouble."

Her voice became a harsh whisper. "Damn it. What do you want me to do? I'm on the Cape with Peter. We're in the bedroom. Get a grip. Sam will call you. Until then, let it go."

She hung up. No wonder she was upset. I'd forgotten she was with Peter this weekend. What a terrible time for me to call. Heather was a good friend. I had to stop looking to others to solve my problems. With the information she'd given me, it shouldn't be difficult to locate the fire. I'd go and offer my support. I didn't want Sam to bear this calamity alone.

I checked the clock. After 9:00 PM. Not a good time for me to go outside alone. If I stayed here, I'd go crazy with worry. I needed to find out how bad the fire was, and I wanted to be there for Sam. Besides, Tom would have no idea I'd leave my apartment tonight. I found my purse, which was never in the same place I left it and headed for the car. When I reached the sidewalk, Mrs. W's voice stopped me.

Tucked on her porch in the dark, she was almost invisible. Did she spend her whole life there? What did she want now?

I marched across the street, my mother's words prominent in my mind—"Always respect your elders." I refused to give her any information. My life was none of her business.

Her first words surprised me. "Sam Gregory's business is on fire. It doesn't look good. They've called in engines from surrounding communities."

"Where did you hear this?" The woman was such a gossip; I hoped she was wrong.

"The call came over my scanner."

I gave myself a mental head slap. Of course she'd have a scanner. Wasn't it one of the busybody prerequisites?

"It's too bad. He's a hardworking boy." Surprised to hear her utter another caring remark, I wondered if I'd misjudged my neighbor. I nodded in agreement, then caught the change in her manner. An inquisitive gleam shone in her eyes. "Didn't I notice his truck in front of your place?"

Ah ha! There's the real Mrs. W, itching for more gossip. I wasn't falling for it. "Thanks for the news, Mrs. Wallace. I've got to go."

From habit, I scanned the empty street before crossing. Halfway to the curb, I paused, then broke into a run. I recognized a familiar Buick and Tom's tall figure heading my way. I sped up.

At the apartment door, my hands shook so much I dropped my keys. Bending to retrieve them, I let out a yip of terror at the sound of his feet on the stairs. Oh, God! My heart pounded as I snatched up the keys, found the right one, and fumbled with the lock. "Hurry. Hurry," I whispered. The hall door opened. He lunged toward me. The key turned.

"Dani, wait. I want to talk to you."

I burst into my apartment and slammed the door behind me. I flicked the lock seconds before the doorknob twisted. My fingers shook as I engaged the deadbolt. He banged on the door. I bent over. My breathing was ragged, and my heart galloped in my chest. All the while he pounded on the door, yelling at me.

Tom's actions tonight chased away any ideas I'd nurtured about my ability to take care of myself. What was he doing here anyway? What about the court order? I backed away from the door, afraid to get too close. I had to try twice before I managed to scream above the noise, "Leave me alone. I'm calling the police."

He tried once more to talk himself into the apartment, but left when I said, "That's it. I'm dialing."

The officer listened to my story and asked if Tom had gone. "I'm not sure. The outside door banged, but I didn't look."

"Stay inside. I'll send someone over."

I sat down to decompress, but after a few minutes of quiet, I disengaged the lock and took a quick peek. A noise from the other direction made me turn. Doug's face squinted at me from the end of the hall.

I ducked back into my apartment. Despite shaky fingers, I managed to call the one person I trusted: my sister.

"Dani? What's wrong?"

"Sam's business is burning, and Tom tried to get me." I explained what happened and how Tom had battered my door.

"Is he gone?"

"I'm not sure. He slammed out of the house, but he may not have left the area."

"Can you have Heather drive you here?"

I explained my friend was on a weekend date and sulked while Kirsten took the time to applaud her new pal's relationship. Her next words shouldn't have been a surprise. "Did you call the police?"

"I did. They're on their way." I finished on a sigh. The

adrenaline high had dissipated. I was tired, and my head ached.

"Okay. I'll give Rick the details and come by to get you. You can't stay there alone tonight. No arguments."

I hated to put someone in jail, but Tom was out of control. Maybe that's what happened with Allison. I flashed back to the overgrown yard a few minutes down the road and the dark, anonymous hole that was the final resting place of a young woman whose last boyfriend was the man who now stalked me. I'd made the right move.

By the time Kirsten arrived, Detective Lavoie and another officer were in my kitchen taking notes. They'd already scoured the neighborhood for Tom who'd vanished. Lavoie questioned Mrs. W, who acknowledged she'd seen me bolt and Tom run after me. Her impression was that she'd witnessed a lovers' spat, since I'd been with another man earlier. She'd had no problem telling Lavoie Sam was at my apartment for most of the evening until he hurried away because his business was on fire.

Lavoie wanted to check the facts. Although there was no reason to be embarrassed, my face burned. "Yes, I guess she's right, Detective, except I broke up with Tom over a month ago."

He consulted his notebook. "Wasn't Mr. Gregory at your apartment the night your car was scratched?"

What was he insinuating? I bristled as if I'd been accused of indecent behavior. "Yes."

"Easy, Miss Trent. I'm not interested in your dating habits. What I find fascinating is your car was damaged the night you were with Mr. Gregory. Now he spends the evening here and his business goes up in flames."

My sister jumped in with the same idea exploding in my head. "I bet Tom set fire to Sam's place."

"Ms. Morrison, is it?" Kirsten gave a quick nod. "We have no reason, at this point, to consider the fire at Mr. Gregory's business suspicious. I'm expressing my distaste for coincidences. If Mr. Gregory's fire should prove to be arson, we will question Mr. Westin." With a synthetic smile, Lavoie closed his notebook. To me, he said, "I'd appreciate it if you'd stay inside until we can pick him up."

"What happens then?" I asked.

"We'll keep him in custody until his arraignment Monday morning. It'll be up to the judge what to do with him."

"Don't worry about Dani, Detective." Kirsten said. "She'll be spending the night at my place."

Lavoie copied my sister's phone number and address before leaving.

Her eyes glittered with an emotion akin to excitement. "My God. You were living with a monster."

I hustled to get what I'd need for the night. Kirsten's words echoed in my ears. "I know," I murmured. "I know. I know."

Chapter Eighteen

That night Kirsten showed me listings for a couple of apartments that might work for me. One was in Beverly, only a few minutes from my job at Beach Street.

"You could probably walk to work," she said.

Each night I'd checked the *Salem News* to see what was available. So far, nothing jumped out at me. Either too expensive or in an iffy neighborhood. I thanked her and said I'd keep looking.

The next morning found me stuck in the Molasses Swamp. A crowing Izzy moved her gingerbread man closer to the Candy Castle when my cellphone rang. Sam's worried voice greeted me. I told Izzy we'd finish the game later, then hurried into the guest bedroom to listen to his agitated questions.

"What happened? Mrs. Wallace told me Tom chased you into your apartment and the police arrived. Did he hurt you?"

The concern in Sam's voice made me almost forget the terror of the moment. I assured him I was fine. "I made it inside before he got there. Kirsten picked me up, and I spent the night at her house."

Then I became the inquisitor. "What about you? How are you doing? How bad was the fire?"

"Couldn't have been worse. I lost everything."

"Oh no. What will you do?"

"Can I come to your place? I'm hungry. Do you have any leftovers from last night? I'll supply dessert."

"Sure. I've got plenty." Whew! I was glad I hadn't been home yet to raid the refrigerator. "I'll meet you at my apartment around noon."

Yikes! I had just over an hour to throw on my clothes from last night, get home, and make myself beautiful. I'd have to hustle.

Kirsten said she'd drive me. Izzy, who hated to see me leave, gave me a hearty one-armed hug.

"It's okay, honey. I'm not far away. You've been to my

apartment." The minute the words were out, I winced. My gaze slid to her pink cast.

"Is the bad man still there?" Her little face puckered.

She'd listened to her mom's and my conversation regarding Tom. "No, sweetie. Don't worry. The bad man isn't there."

I thanked Kirsten, kissed Izzy, and surveyed the area for any signs of Tom as we left. Lavoie said they had him in custody. I didn't dare trust he'd stay there.

By the time Sam arrived, I'd cleaned the apartment and transformed myself from Saturday morning lay-about to what I hoped was a cute chick.

He hadn't done the same. Although he'd changed his clothes, he bore little resemblance to the man who'd left me last night. Every few minutes he'd run his hand through his tousled hair. His restlessness, the smudges under his tired eyes, and hollow stare, told the story.

He rubbed his hand across his face. "Sure, I've got insurance." He gave a harsh laugh. "It won't take care of my customers right now. The rest of my inventory is gone, although I do have a few tools and some stock in the van. Thank God some equipment was saved from the fire. My accountant has all my records on her computer. It's not much, but I'm grateful. The problem is I won't be able to get back to work for weeks." With a deep sigh, he continued, "Then, there's the cause of the fire."

Oh, no. Please don't let it be arson.

"The fire chief believes it was deliberate."

The words slammed into me. I wanted to curl up like one of those little pill bugs to hide myself from everyone, but he deserved the truth. His business was gone because of me. If he hadn't met me, his business would be whole and thriving.

"Sam, I…I can guess who torched your business." He stared at me, his jaw tense. "It might have been Tom."

"Tom!" The word exploded from his mouth.

"The police agree. They believe he's been surveilling me, and your presence at my apartment was the last straw, so he decided to get back at you."

"Shit, he must be crazy. He'd burn my business because I'm dating you? I don't get it. Did he confess?"

"No, he swore he didn't do it. The police haven't found any evidence to connect him to it yet. No one believes him."

He studied his shoes for a few seconds, then gave me a quick glance. He couldn't hold my gaze. "I'm all confused right now. Listen, I don't have the time to eat. I've got a lot of calls to make. I'm supposed to meet this insurance guy…"

"Oh, Sam, please stay. You have to eat, and there's all this food." I gestured to indicate the white boxes lined up on the counter.

He made a point of checking the clock and shook his head. "I can't. I have to go. I'll talk to you later. Oh, here." He handed me a bakery box, gave me a perfunctory kiss, then left.

I stared at the door and cursed Tom. He'd struck out at the man I cared for, and now Sam was afraid to be with me. I couldn't blame him. No one wanted a crazy person after them, but dammit, I wasn't the enemy, and I ached to put my arms around those broad shoulders to comfort him and help make his pain go away.

After a few minutes, anger took over. It wasn't my fault Tom was crazy. Besides, if he torched Sam's place, the police would find out. He wasn't clever enough to fool them. They'd throw him in jail for a long time. End of story.

As I continued to obsess over the jerk I'd spent half a year with, I hit the kitchen and surrounded myself with takeout boxes. I bit into a cold sparerib. Men weren't worth the pain they caused. After I'd stuffed the last bit of food into my mouth, guilt seized me. No way could I afford those calories. I noticed the strained zipper on my pants. I needed exercise. A good walk would help work off those unwanted calories and clear my overwrought brain.

The street held no men, crazy or otherwise. I countered the yoo-hoo from across the street with a wave of my hand. I wasn't in the mood for Mrs. W's questions.

Earlier, on this cool September day, I'd decided to wear jeans. Now, in the full afternoon sun, I wished I'd worn shorts. I drifted toward one of my favorite spots, the Salem Commons. The purposeful exercisers, casual strollers, and boisterous children surrounding me gave me a sense of comfort, like I was part of something special. My mind strayed to the crisscrossed walkways and resplendent trees. I wondered, not for the first time, who planned this popular maze.

I circled the Commons twice before I crashed onto a bench. My rubbery legs reminded me exercise wasn't my forte. When my chest stopped heaving, I ambled to the waterfront to people-watch along the busy harbor. In some northern cities, September signals the end of tourist season. Not in Salem. Here, fall festivities take over. Traditional harvest festivals, corn mazes, and haunted houses dot the area, culminating in the arrival of ghosts, goblins, and everything scary on Halloween. Pickering Wharf hummed with pre-autumn activity.

I sat on a bench by the water with a yummy cup of chocolate ice cream, destroying the positive effects of my brisk walk. The activity on the crowded pier captured my interest. I'd almost forgotten my troubles when I caught sight of the witch's shop. The dessert's creamy comfort dissolved. I tossed the cup into a trash bin and fought a rush of nerves. Time to leave.

The woman struck me as odd, and a bit too curious, but she had given me the piece of malachite that helped me get some rest, and Heather swore the proprietor was a good witch. There was no reason for me to be nervous. I shook off my childish angst and changed direction. I'd just peek in her store. I might buy another colorful gem. In the back of my mind, though, I was hoping she might have information about the spirit world to help me.

The moment I stepped inside, her gaze found me. She projected no welcome in her dark eyes. This was a mistake. I'd decided to leave when an attack of vertigo hit. I hung onto the door to stay upright.

"I'm glad you decided to visit again." The saleswoman or *witch* stood there. How did she get there so fast? "You look a bit unsteady. Would you like to sit for a minute?"

"N-no. I'm fine." As I said it, my head cleared. No more dizziness. Very strange. I let go of the door. "I wanted to stop in and poke around."

Her expression held nothing but acceptance and comfort. I must have been mistaken earlier. "I'm finishing with a customer. I'll be right back."

I found myself drawn to the bins of stones. The variety, textures, and colors intrigued me. I chose one and then another of the small beauties and stroked their surfaces. Engrossed in the unusual assortment, I didn't hear the woman approach, but her lavender scent alerted me.

"Has the malachite helped you?"

The stone slid from my fingers. A picture of green skidding across the kitchen floor spun through my mind. I'd put it away in the nightstand drawer, hoping it would stay there.

Before I said anything she held up her hand. "Don't worry. I have a better alternative. Follow me."

We moved to the jewelry counter, where she reached beneath the display cabinet, then laid a dark blue velvety box on the glass. With great care, she extracted a delicate necklace. Though the woman's voice held a soft lilt, an air of concern surrounded her. "This is a rare piece. Made by the Navajos, it intermingles turquoise to guard against negative magic and coral to protect against demons."

I might have gasped because she smiled and touched my shoulder. "Turquoise is also used for love spells."

My immediate concern about demons dissolved as ideas about

enchantment and Sam took over. Her voice broke into my musings. "Coral is said to produce courage, wisdom, and peaceful dreams. This special work of art is beautiful and practical." She held it up.

An almost-transparent silver strand held a medium-size pendant composed of one blue and one white stone cocooned in a silver web. I ran my fingers over the surface of each stone, one smooth, the other rough. Impressed with the artisan's skill, I lifted it onto my palm and smiled. The pendant warmed my hand, and a spurt of hope bloomed. I closed my fingers around its warmth, and my anxiety lessened.

"Good. I suspected you were the right person for this. The pendant will help deflect any harmful intentions sent your way."

I sensed the magical piece was a part of me. I rubbed the stones once more and secured the beautiful pendant around my neck. The stones nestled against me and radiated heat deep into my chest.

On my way home, I opened the blue container to read the list of properties for turquoise and coral. I grinned. It did say love spells. I should try one on Sam. I wondered if the library had any books on how to practice magic.

~ * ~

After my long walk, I popped my ear buds in and sat down to relax. So much had happened in such a short time—Tom and the restraining order, the fire, and Sam. Anger, worry, and a sense of loss warred within me. In the meantime, I swiveled my shoulders and sang to Tayler Swift's "Shake it Off." A knock on the door interrupted my therapy session.

I removed the buds and hollered, "Who is it?"

"Eddie."

What was he doing here at this time? I unlocked the door. "Hey. Come on in. What's up?"

Instead of his usual grin, he scowled at me. Oh, Lord. Another irritated man.

Towering above me, he planted his feet apart and spoke through tightened lips. "What did I tell you about ghost stories?"

"What are you talking about?"

"What did you say to Jimbo?"

"Nothing. I was disappointed when he came to me and quit."

"What reason did he give?"

Eddie's annoyance surprised me. "He told me the place was bad. I assumed he was talking about the break-in."

"You didn't mention a spirit or entity in the building?"

"Of course not. I'd never do that after you asked me not to. Maybe he got it from Mrs. W."

His body relaxed, and the side of his mouth quirked in a grin. “Oh. That old biddy. She’s full of it. Nobody pays attention to her dramatics.” He scrubbed his hand through his hair. “I’m sorry. When Jimbo said he was quitting, I assumed you must have blabbed that ghost nonsense and scared him.” He ran his hand around his neck. “He does a great job at my properties. I hate to lose him. I’m always worried about unsavory rumors regarding my buildings. Please forgive me.”

“No problem. I understand your concern.”

I offered him a cup of coffee, but he said he didn’t have time, then apologized once more before he left. I sagged back in my chair, happy to have relieved Eddie’s concerns. One less man to worry about.

Later, when the prospect of another Saturday night all by myself depressed me, I remembered my necklace. I’d decided to always wear the beautiful piece of jewelry. When I wrapped my fingers around the pendent, I found my tension relieved. I willed myself to be more positive. Somehow it worked. I stopped obsessing over all my aggravations and popped into the kitchen for a cup of tea.

At the cabinet, I paused. The hell with tea. A glass of wine sounded much better. Tomorrow was Sunday. I could sleep late. Jug of vino in hand, I was ready to face more of Elias’s story. It had been a while since I’d read it. Intrigued about his relationship with Rebecca, I flicked on the living room light, set my wineglass on the coffee table, and went for the book.

My imagination came out to play when I moved into the dark bedroom. Whispers filled my ears. I tested the air for unwelcome smells. As I searched for the origin of the murmurs, movement to my right made me freeze. Eyes closed, I prepared for a spectral attack. I was relieved when a cool breeze played across my face and revealed the origin of the spooky motion. Curtains billowing into the room. The whispers? The silky material rubbing together.

I shook off the fright and hit the light switch. In the bright glow, an empty room mocked me. Not a ghoul in sight, and since I didn’t want any other unwelcome visitors, I closed and locked the window.

Tension mounted again as I contemplated circling up to the loft for the diary. At each turn, I peered around the room. After I seized the journal, in my hurry to get away from there before darkness closed in, I tripped and almost fell. When I clutched the rail, Izzy’s face swam in front of me. I remembered the way her tiny body lay crumpled at the bottom of the stairs.

The pain of her accident returned and, with it, guilt. “Poor little Izzy.”

No sooner had I spoken those words, than my remorse twisted

into a gloating sense of dominance and triumph. What…? I slumped to the stair. I shook my head to scour those despicable emotions from my mind.

When I closed my eyes to inhale a more positive aura, the bitter scent of smoke drifted around me. I choked and held my breath. Was Izzy's fall deliberate? No. That was ridiculous. I didn't want to believe in a malevolent presence. I couldn't imagine a spirit having the strength for a physical attack on someone. My sweet Izzy was small, though. She weighed next to nothing.

Had some nasty phantom tried to hurt her? A surge of anger rippled through me. I stood on the step, book in one hand, the other waving in the air and yelled at whatever haunted this room. "You son of a bitch. You'd better not have pushed Izzy. Who the hell do you think you are?"

My lips hadn't closed on the last word when a rush of cold air surrounded my neck. I opened my mouth to scream, then remembered the necklace. I held tight to the pendant and prayed. Warmth seeped through my fingers. The cold on my throat shifted, becoming a cool caress along my cheek. Then it faded. The temperature shifted back to normal. The bitter stink of his pipe dwindled, and the name "Rebecca" filled my head.

Adrenaline kicked in. I clattered down the stairs, making an expeditious, if undignified, retreat to the living room. That did it. When Heather came home from the Cape, I'd join her in the search for a new apartment. No way would I live with a dangerous ghost.

Afraid my limbs might vibrate off my body, I took a huge gulp of wine and blew air through my nose. I needed to eliminate the memory of his wretched stench. After a moment and a cautious sniff, I detected no more evidence of his nasty presence. As I caressed my enchanted pendant, I sent a silent prayer of thanks to my real-life guardian angel, the woman who called herself a witch.

Chapter Nineteen

Between trembling hands and having to check behind me every few minutes for a smoky assassin, it took me forever to make up the sofa bed. I took another long sip of wine, then settled in to discover more about the bastard who infested my bedroom.

The relaxing effect of the alcohol and my sense of safety in the living room worked to soothe my jangled nerves. I reflected on my supernatural experiences in the apartment. I'd never sensed him anywhere other than the bedroom. There and the horrible pit in the cellar must be his primary haunts. Ha! There's a word I'd never again use casually.

After a fervent prayer I'd found a haven, I propped a pillow behind my head, flipped open the diary, and searched for any entries mentioning Rebecca. I didn't have far to look. The woman had captivated Elias. Her name appeared in page after page. In one spot, he described her "modish" attire and "jonty" manner of walking. On another page he mentioned her "carefree" laugh. Later he wrote "the mesmerizing touch of her eyes, dark as nite."

I cringed when he fantasized about having his hands on her "genrus bosum." The further I read, the more interested I became. I decided she must have been at least ten years his junior, maybe in her twenties. The year this was written, 1698, Elias would have been thirty-seven. After I'd found the diary, I called the Salem Historical Society and asked for information on Elias. They got back to me with his date of birth—1661.

He first noticed Rebecca when she came to Salem Town for supplies. Later he discovered she was a recent widow who lived alone in Salem Village.

I scanned my memory of Salem history. From what I recalled, most of Salem Village had been the area now named Danvers. The descriptions in the diary of Salem Town fit present-day Salem. When he rhapsodized about Rebecca, his descriptions and emotions read like any normal man falling in love. Whenever he cited other residents, though, there was a drastic change in the tenor of his words. He despised anyone in power and referred to the rest of the town's inhabitants as "fools."

But Rebecca fascinated him. One look, and he became determined to have her. "She will be mine," he wrote.

I didn't understand his certainty. There was nothing I'd read to suggest he had any interaction with her. In one sentence he referred to the young men near the dock who flirted with her. "Let the popycoks strut. By one week next, she will desire only me."

Perhaps he believed his money would win her over or he might have been quite handsome. There was no way to verify my assumptions, but what else could it be? His own pen revealed he wasn't the most personable man.

He continued to extol Rebecca's virtues in between his day-to-day diatribes about "deevius" business associates, whom he called "sly felloes." When the lines of text became blurry, I rubbed my eyes and put the book aside. I'd continue later.

I lay back on my pillow, the pendant warm against my chest. No way would I take my necklace off in this apartment. My eyelids closed, and my breathing slowed. Visions of Elias and Rebecca followed me into sleep.

I was lost in a dream, but it wasn't my dream. Someone else was in my head.

My feet teeter on uneven cobblestones, so different from the dirt roads of my home. I put my handkerchief to my nose to keep out the dust stirred up by horses and carriages, but I find the busy streets exciting. The back of my neck tingles as I walk by the good folk of Salem Town. Censure radiates from the women for the new widow, but the men's gazes speak with lust. I don't care. I have money and property now, and I intend to enjoy the attention of virile young men.

Oh, look, Will Bartlett can scarce keep an eye on his task. He almost walked into a cart. I try to squelch an impertinent smile, but I am certain everyone can see the merriment in my eyes. I stare at his strong arms and muscular back. Hmmm? We might do well together.

Ho! There be the high and mighty Captain Gale puffing on his pipe. There are whispers. His black eyes follow. Oh no. Not this time. I have no need for a master near twice my years. I prefer a malleable young pup to warm my bed.

Then everything in the dream changed.

Nighttime with a full moon. A man clothed in a dark robe

intoning unintelligible words. When he tossed something into the fire, the bright flash illuminated a dwelling in the background and the scar on his face.

Tendrils of smoke, like fingers reaching into the night, hovered for a moment above the flames and then drifted toward the house.

A short time later, the woman I'd seen earlier appeared, the white of her nightgown a beacon in the shadows. With a broad smile on her face, she walked into the waiting man's arms.

Her soft whisper carried through the air. "I heard your call, Elias."

"Yes, my Rebecca," he said, triumph in his voice. "Now you're mine."

~ * ~

After a comfortable night's sleep, I congratulated myself on an excellent solution to my latest predicament. I'd discovered an Elias-free zone. Until I found another place to live, I'd use the pull-out sofa to sleep and spend as little time as possible in the bedroom.

Memories of Rebecca from last night's dream resurfaced while I folded the sofa bed. A cold sense of dread seeped through me. Elias had performed some kind of magic on Rebecca. Then common sense prevailed. What I'd witnessed had been a dream, a fantasy drawn from the ghostly activities in my apartment and the words in Elias's diary.

I had to force myself to move. With my hand wrapped around my necklace, I took a deep breath, and braved the bedroom. Senses alert, I grabbed my clothes and rescued my green stone from the nightstand drawer. My poor nose was sore from sniffing the air. Although my safeguards proved unnecessary, I wasn't fooled. The hairs on the back of my neck told me he was there. After breakfast, I drove to Gloucester to visit my family.

Kirsten wasted no time in regaling my parents with the details of the police report. "Thank God they arrested that maniac. Dani might have been his next victim."

In an effort to introduce a dose of sanity, I said, "We can't brand him a murderer. Jeez, he dated Allison before she disappeared. It doesn't mean he killed her."

My sister was on a roll. "Oh, come on. He must have done it. What about the way he's stalking you? You're lucky he didn't catch you last night."

"The police haven't found any evidence…"

"Danielle!" The steel in my mother's voice silenced everyone. "I don't care what anyone believes. Your safety outweighs any possibility of innocence on Tom's part. Assume he's dangerous and proceed from there."

I closed my mouth, chastened. Mom was right. To defend someone who might want to kill me was foolhardy. She went on to insist I stay with them until I found a new apartment. Kirsten chimed in, seconding my mother's decision.

For a minute, the offer of my old bedroom sounded like a good idea. I'd have no problem with Tom or Elias there, but I hated to run away. My pride and the desperate hope Sam would come back reinforced my decision. "My apartment is safe," I said.

My declaration was made more positive by my hope for Sam's return and a blind faith in Heather's medium. Although, I did falter a bit on the last word as I caressed my neck at the memory of yesterday's cold menace.

I left my parents later than I'd expected and worried that I wouldn't be able to see Tom or his car at night. When I reached home, the light was almost gone. Damn! I hadn't been afraid of the dark since I was a kid.

Now I darted from the car to my apartment, unable to relax until I put the key in my lock. The minute I opened the door, a different kind of alarm choked me. A blast of cold air that would put the frozen tundra to shame greeted me. I'd shut the air conditioner off before I left. No matter how much I pretended, the icy chill was confirmation. The comforting light spreading across the kitchen couldn't hide the source of the cold. Frigid air poured from the black rectangle defining the entrance to the bedroom. Without hesitation, I slammed the door shut and moved far away. I found some warmth at the end of the living room and rubbed my arms.

I gave serious consideration to driving back to Gloucester and admitting defeat, but I'd be damned if I'd let some stupid ghost chase me off my turf. Okay, he'd run me out of the bedroom, but that was it. Unless the medium failed to help me eliminate Elias, this was my home, and I would stay.

I picked up my phone to call Heather, who must be back by now. I paused as a flash of guilt for interrupting her weekend nagged at me. No sense to bother her now. What could she do? I snatched the blanket from the back of the sofa, wrapped it around me, and turned on the television. Since my favorite shows weren't on until later, I surfed channels.

A picture of Allison's grave flashed by, and I flipped back to that station. "The police are still seeking any help with this heinous crime." A photo showed a beautiful young woman with long chestnut hair laughing into the camera. "If you have any information pertaining to Allison Montenegro, please contact the Salem police."

When the announcer rehashed the case, I moved on, in no mood to listen to a discussion of murder. On the National Geographic channel, a gentle deer-like creature leaned down to drink from the lake. A sudden strike by an alligator/crocodile—I can never tell the difference—felled the defenseless animal. Before I changed the channel, the brutal killing was imprinted on my brain.

Screw television—I'd read instead. I selected a light romance from the bookcase next to the TV then braved the cold kitchen for a hot cup of cocoa. Heat to counter the cold and chocolate to make me happy.

When I sat down again, I noticed the diary. Rats, I'd have to give it to Eddie pretty soon. If I wanted to finish the story, I'd better hurry up. The romance novel stayed on the table. A slight tremor rippled through me when I touched diary. Was I delusional? Could the man speaking to me through a two-hundred-year-old diary be a pipe-smoking spook haunting my bedroom? And if it were true, why? What did a dead smuggler want from me?

I hoped the diary might give me answers. Tucking the blanket around my shoulders, I took a sip of hot chocolate and dipped into the words of my eighteenth-century roommate.

Before I continued, I wanted to reread Elias's beautiful tribute to Rebecca. Would a soul, longing for his lost love, be so nasty? Any brokenhearted ghosts I'd ever heard about, floated around in the moonlight, moaned, and looked sad. What I'd read about Elias suggested a mean-spirited snake of a man who wouldn't pine if his life depended on it. After the incident with the malachite and Izzy, I wasn't fooled. Elias was no misty lovelorn specter. I wish he'd leave me alone.

A few pages later, I discovered a strange entry. "My bisness with the full moon is done. She'll welcum me now."

Oh, God. That was my dream.

A loud bang startled me. I dropped the diary and grasped my chest. What happened? Where did the noise come from? My attention snapped to the back door. I stood up, ready to run, but the outside held its own threats. With my heart drumming in my ears, I crept toward the kitchen, keeping my options for the back door open. Wait a minute. I needed to protect myself.

I scanned the room for a weapon. The loud thudding in my chest threatened to hide the sounds of danger. I wrapped my hand around a pretty, aqua glass ball on the bookcase. Heavy and easy to maneuver. I was ready for battle.

An icy pall hung over the kitchen. When I sidled in, my foot slipped. There was water everywhere. What was going on? I spied a flash of red. My beautiful teapot sat in the midst of the puddle, water leaking from the huge dent in its side.

Anger bubbled up. I wanted to scream out at the damned entity who was plaguing me until I remembered what happened the last time I threatened him. I kept my mouth shut. I got a mop, cleaned the floor, and tossed my injured pot into the trash.

As I finished up, I managed a relieved snort. At least it hadn't been a murderer. My nerves eased until I noticed the bedroom door I'd slammed shut an hour ago was wide open.

I ran back to the living room, clutched the pendant, and prayed. I glanced at the clock. Almost 11:00 PM. Too late to go anywhere tonight; besides, my purse with the car keys was in the kitchen. No way would I go there again. I ignored the nasty, wood-burning stench, opened the sofa in my substitute bedroom, and prayed for a restful oblivion.

~ * ~

If anyone had seen me the next day as I got ready for work, they'd have worried for my sanity. Between running around the bedroom trying to select an outfit and twisting my head back and forth on high alert for my invisible roommate, I looked like a paranoid clothes burglar. By the time I left the apartment, I was winded and a little dizzy.

Two determined faces greeted me at my office. "Good morning, ladies. What can I do for you?"

Clara, the tall, angular one, tilted her head and softened her voice. "It's Mary."

I clutched my chest. "What's happened to Mary?"

"Calm down. She's fine." This from Anya, the plump sprite next to Clara.

Clara stepped in front of her, the corner of her mouth scrunched up in annoyance. "She fell on Saturday." She raised her hand to forestall any reply from me. "Don't worry. Nothing broke. The doctor wants her to stay in rehab for a few days to make sure she's okay and to adjust her medication."

Mary, my friend and cohort in the war against Fischer. The woman whose delicious baked goods helped me through the tough times at work. She'd been my rock in the face of crazy boyfriends and complaining tenants.

My chest tightened with worry. "Where is she?"

"Doane House."

Not the best nursing home in the area, but it had a good reputation, and one of the nurses there was a friend. I'd ask her to look in on Mary.

In a tiny voice, Anya, who managed to peek around Clara, said, "I spoke to her. She's doing great."

I thanked them and started my day. Part of a manager's job was to keep tabs on the residents, which also meant a visit to hospitals or rehab centers when one of them was ill. At 3:00 PM, I closed the office and alerted Fischer's secretary. On my way to Doane House, I stopped to buy scented hand cream and two magazines.

Mary's greeting was predictable. "Oh, dear, you shouldn't have come. I'm fine."

I suppressed a relieved chuckle. She looked wonderful, not a hair out of place or a flaw in her makeup. If not for the pink satin bed jacket, she could be waiting for a date.

"What happened to you?" I asked.

"Oh, just a foolish accident. I climbed up on the chair to clean the window and slipped. I caught hold of the counter, and it saved me. I told the doctor I was fine," her face pinched up as if she smelled something bad, and she waved her hand around, "but he insisted on sending me to this place."

I stifled a smile. "It's nice here."

Her lips thinned in response. In the middle of thanking me for my gifts, she stopped in mid-sentence. "I almost forgot. You'll never guess who's here." I must have looked concerned because she said, "Oh, no dear. None of our residents. A woman who used to live in your apartment."

"Rose?"

"The very person." She lowered her voice and leaned toward me. "I planned to have a chat with her to get details of your unwanted visitor, but," she raised her eyebrows, "she might be more forthcoming if you asked."

Before I left, she made me promise to repeat everything Rose said. As I moved along the hall, I wrinkled my nose, saddened at the unpleasant odors of an institution that catered to the aged and infirm. At least Mary would be able to leave in a few days.

I checked the room numbers, while I worried about how to broach the subject of Elias with Rose. Should I be direct and ask, or should I play dumb and wait for her to mention the trouble at the apartment? Oh, rats. There was her room. I still hadn't decided. I peeked around the corner of the door.

A tiny lady dressed in slacks and a sweater sat in a wooden chair with bright cushions, shaking her finger at the TV. Gray streaks peppered the white hair she wore parted in the middle, fashioned into a bun, and sharp angles defined a face with few wrinkles.

I took a tentative step into the room. The woman hollered at the *Jeopardy* contestant in the voice of a frustrated teacher—"What is the UN?"

I cleared my throat. Her face scrunched in disgust. "Can you believe they can't identify the UN? We're fostering a generation of dimwits."

What could I say? She might be right.

"You're not a nurse," she said. "Do you have the wrong room?"

"Are you Rose?"

"I am, young lady. How can I help you?"

"Uh…I was here to visit a friend who mentioned your name." She tilted her head as if to say, "And?"

I confessed in a rush. "I live in your old apartment on Cove Street."

"Oh. I see." Rose sat back and lifted her shoulders. "You'll have questions. Have a seat." She reached for the remote, clicked off the TV and peered at me. "You've seen him, haven't you?"

I dropped to the chair. "Yes."

"Well, girl, if you tell anyone, they'll say you're batty. I don't talk about it nowadays. I don't need any more medication." She heaved a sigh. "But there was something there."

Hearing her was like touching a live wire. Her words reinforced everything I'd experienced. I wasn't hallucinating or losing my mind. An entity did haunt my apartment. She told me about the strange, inexplicable noises from the bedroom.

"Was it the ghost?" I asked.

"I'm not sure what I saw. Twice a foggy mass floated across the room. Not for long, mind you, but I didn't imagine it. Both times a pungent smell buggered my nose. I'm a sensible woman. I decided someone had been smoking in my apartment and the old peepers misinterpreted the haze. I made the mistake of telling my niece someone had snuck into the place. Before I could say, 'I might have been mistaken,' she'd parked me in here."

"Did it get cold in there?"

"Oh, my, yes. I kept piling on sweaters." She winked. "Old ladies do tend to get cold once in a while."

I noticed the heavy sweater around her shoulders and gave her a quick smile. "Did it escalate?"

"How much worse could it get?"

Oh, Rose, if you only knew.

Chapter Twenty

On the way home in the middle of traffic, I recalled Rose's words— *"Leave that place and find a nice man to marry."* I'd found one. Sam. Acting like a high-school teenager, I tried his name on for size. When I said it out loud, "Dani Gregory," the result was perfect. My temporary euphoria soon faded, though. He'd given up on me.

I rounded the corner onto Cove Street and spotted Heather talking to Mrs. W. The old gossip must be regaling my friend with stories of Tom on Saturday night. I assumed she was embellishing the details, but I couldn't blame her. Since I'd moved in a few weeks ago, the police had been there twice, and Sam's business was destroyed. Enough excitement to keep Mrs. W in morality tales for the rest of her life. I pitied the next young women who moved to this street.

With all that happened in the past few days, I marveled today was only Monday. I discovered my apartment was back to its normal temperature. No strange smells, no broken appliances, and no obvious occult activity. Thankful for the respite, I changed clothes. Trash pick-up was tomorrow. I wanted to get my stuff to the sidewalk before dark.

First, though, while the place remained quiet, I dashed into the bedroom to gather an outfit for the next day. The idea to collect clothes I needed for work from Elias's lair in daylight hours was working.

Headed out the door with my rubbish, the sound of voices from around the corner of the hall stopped me. I recognized Marie's shrill tone. "I'm telling you the noise was terrible. Loud banging and yelling. Then the police! They came to *our* apartment to question us. They were all over the building, searching for her crazy boyfriend.

There's been nothing but trouble since she moved in. Look what happened to you."

Heather's familiar voice answered, "You can't blame my break-in on Dani."

"What about the ruckus on Saturday night with the police and everything? Her fault. If she didn't live here, it wouldn't have happened."

"Come on, Marie. Can she help it if some crazy guy is stalking her? She wants to get away from him."

"Yeah, well…what about Sam Gregory? I'm telling you, she's bad news."

While Marie continued her rant, an itchy sensation on the back of my neck made me swing around. Doug hovered behind me. I jumped as his freakish stare bore into me. He grinned at my reaction, and in a soft sing-song voice said, "Eavesdroppers never hear good of themselves."

His mouth and nose were pinched in, as if he smelled a foul odor. He made me uncomfortable, always looming where he was least expected. Now he'd caught me listening to Heather and Marie's conversation and alerted them to my presence. Marie rounded the corner first and put her hand on one large hip.

"Well, well, nosy parker, did you hear enough?" With a dramatic swish, she grabbed her husband's arm and marched toward the stairs to their apartment.

My face burned in shame. I apologized to Heather. "When Marie said my name, curiosity trumped polite behavior. I didn't even hear Doug behind me."

"Oh, he can be sneaky. You've got to be careful of him." Pointing to the bag in my hand, she said, "Hold it right there. I'll get mine. We'll go together."

I was happy to see her and grateful she'd taken my side with Marie.

As we walked outside, I questioned her about her weekend.

Satisfaction glowed on her face. "Peter was wonderful. He treated me like a queen, and he's such a good lover."

I held my hands in the shape of a cross. "Too much information."

She laughed. "I'm falling for him." She hugged herself. "He's sooo awesome."

My normally shrewd friend acted like a lovesick teen.

"I'm happy for you. About time a handsome cutie snagged you."

"Your turn. What's new in your boyfriend department? How's Sam? Got him in the sack yet?"

Oh, hell. A couple of tears snuck out. "It's over."

"What? No way."

"Yeah. It's true."

Before I launched into the whole sad tale, the man, himself, appeared through the twilight. “Hey, why the serious frown?” he said. Surprise kept me quiet until I noticed Heather’s stance. She was ready to do battle. I put my hand on her arm before I answered him. “I didn’t expect you back again.”

He hung his head and took so long to speak, I wanted to scream, “What do you want?”

His voice held an apology when he said, “I was pretty upset the last time we talked and might have said something to upset you.”

Might have? I wanted to tell him how much he hurt me, but I kept quiet and let him continue.

“After you mentioned Tom as a suspect for the fire, I worried about damage to the rest of my family. If he destroyed my brother’s boat, J.B. would be ruined. I decided if I stayed away from you, I’d be protecting everyone.”

Each word stung like antiseptic on a cut. Of course he’d worry about his family.

Heather huffed. “Are you serious?”

I spoke to Sam. “I understand how you felt. You’d been up all night, watching your business burn, and I added Tom to the mix.”

He stared at me with those beautiful aqua eyes and whispered, “I’m so sorry if I caused you pain.”

I stood there unable to speak as a leaden ache lifted from me. Sam’s dimple and grin surfaced as he lifted my chin. Then he rubbed his thumb across my lower lip and said, “I’ve missed you.”

When his head dipped toward mine, Heather interrupted us. “Hey, take it inside before Mrs. W has a stroke. She’s had enough excitement this week.”

I grinned up at the man whose dimpled smile sent my heart into a joyous dance. Arm around my shoulders, he steered me toward the door with Heather following.

In the hall, she hugged me, smiled, and whispered in my ear, “He looks like a hooked fish.”

Inside my apartment, a sudden shyness affected me. I was at a loss for words. Even though I’d been praying for this moment, I worried Tom or the ghost might ruin it.

My silence didn’t deter Sam, though. He captured me, seized my lips, and showed me how much he’d missed me. “I can’t believe I did that to you. I was afraid you’d never speak to me again, so I decided to show up in person and beg if I had to.”

I gave him a lopsided grin. “I don’t believe there’s been any begging yet.”

The kiss he gave me had me ready to beg.

He wrapped his arm around my shoulders and said, "Let's sit for a minute." He held me close while he talked. "I've been running around like crazy the past few days hoping to get the merchandise I need to keep my business alive. A friend of mine in Lynn has promised to lend me tools. I have to go there tonight. Thank God my credit is good. I've been able to purchase supplies. Bob and I can handle a couple of jobs this week."

I was about to launch a protest when he raised my hand to his lips. He took his time as he kissed the palm. Heat spread throughout my body. How could he do this to me when he was going to leave? I leaned in, and he claimed my lips once more.

"Don't go." The words came out in a whimper.

I wanted more, but all I got was a chaste kiss to my forehead. "I have to leave, but I'll be back. I owe you a dinner, and I have Wednesday night off. Does that work for you?'

"I believe I can clear my schedule."

His mouth tilted into a fresh grin. "I'll pick you up at 6:00 PM."

This time, when we walked together to the door, I got my goodbye kiss.

~ * ~

Despite the presence in the other room, I slept. I credited my new sleep ensemble—the sofa bed, my favorite nightie, and what I'd dubbed my *magical necklace*. I steered clear of the bedroom and any action which might aggravate Elias. From our last encounter, I'd learned not to poke the bear.

Wednesday night I hurried home from work and stripped off my clothes. I tore around the place like a cyclone, searching for the perfect outfit. My rejects lay piled on the bed. Sam had mentioned casual dress. What did that mean? I didn't want to be too casual. My bedroom resembled a war zone. Since I'd had no problems in there for a few days, I found it safe to move around in short spurts. However, I'd taken the precaution of keeping a few things in the living room closet.

I settled on a pair of black slacks, a green lacy blouse, and a comfortable pair of leather sandals. Dangling, copper-colored earrings completed the ensemble. The restaurant overlooked the waterfront in Marblehead, so I added my leather jacket. September evenings were cool.

Tonight I'd decided to trust him with my spectral secret. I hated to expose the whole haunted drama, but I wanted to ask him to go to Heather's psychic evening on Friday. I'd have to give him a reasonable explanation first.

From his frank appraisal and the upward curve of his lips, I gathered my choice met with his approval. My confidence expanded while excited flutters rippled in my chest. This would be a fantastic night.

We opted to eat outside on the deck, where the cool, sea-scented air made me glad I'd brought a jacket. Our cozy conversation was accompanied by the splash of waves as they washed ashore and the occasional nosy seagull. When I spoke to one of them, Sam laughed.

"Don't get too affectionate. He's lulling you into a false sense of security so he can steal your food when it arrives." He raised an eyebrow and tilted his head. "Never trust a gull."

The waitress brought our plates, wished us an enjoyable meal, and the bird headed in. With a wave of my hand and a loud "Shoo," I ended our budding relationship.

An impressive amount of golden fried clams claimed my interest. They were yummy. I couldn't help but make appreciative murmurs. I stopped when I noticed Sam's lips twitch. My face heated, and I focused on my plate. "The food's delicious."

He chuckled. "So I gathered. I'm glad you're enjoying your meal. This is one of my favorite places."

After dinner, he steered me to Fort Sewall or, as he called it, "The Fort." We strolled around the outside edge of the man-made fortification. Built on this rocky promontory to protect the mouth of the harbor, the land protruded enough to give an awesome view of the shoreline and the open ocean at the same time. Part of the area dipped to a space where soldiers camped; the rest formed what he called a hillock with barred windows and a door built into its side.

He gestured to the mound. "The original army base." I tipped my head in question.

"In one area they stored their munitions. In another they kept prisoners. The soldiers slept in tents."

"Prisoners?"

He laughed and pointed to the underground bunker. "They had to keep them somewhere."

The hillside dugout elicited eerie sensations in me. My imagination seized on the poor prisoners. How they survived, locked in a dank, dark hole under mounds of earth, wondering if they'd live another day. I shook off the morbid thoughts and concentrated on Sam.

Unaware of my discomfort, he continued, a note of pride in his voice. "Marblehead has always played a part in the safety of our country." Excitement colored his story about General Glover who, with his Marblehead crew, rowed General Washington across the Delaware. While I listened, my mind drifted—his sexy voice, the easy way we meshed, and how comfortable his arm was around my waist.

"We'll come back in the daytime when it's sunny. You'll enjoy the rolling waves splashing against the rocks and the salt in your face. There's nothing like it."

On the way back to the truck, he took my hand. Though I wanted to trust him with my spectral doubts, I wasn't quite ready to reveal the whole weird reality of my life, our new connection somehow too fragile for supernatural revelations.

On our way back to Salem, he pointed to a twisty side street. "My parents live there. Their house has an awesome widow's walk on top. You'll love the view from there."

The road didn't look big enough for one car to maneuver. "How do vehicles navigate these narrow lanes? It's like that in some areas of Gloucester."

"When these towns were settled in the seventeenth century, the streets were laid out for horse-and-cart traffic."

His brother also lived in Marblehead, not far from him on Front Street. "We're a close-knit family. I'd like you to meet them sometime."

He brushed my cheek with his fingertips, a gesture so sweet I could cry. "Why so quiet?"

Oh, rats. He'll think I don't want to meet his relatives. "A widow's walk sounds like fun, although some poor women spent their lives up there waiting for men who never returned."

"Hence the name." He squeezed my hand.

Now might be a good time to talk about Friday night. I drew in my courage and blurted, "Guess what?" Oh, damn, that was lame.

With a half-grin, he said, "What?"

"I need a friend for Friday night." Jeez, this wasn't coming out the way I'd wanted.

He raised his eyebrows. "Sounds a little ominous. What would this friend have to do?"

I'd been twining my hands together and stopped. With a deep breath, I plunged in. "Here's the deal. Heather has invited a psychic medium to her house Friday night. Her job is to act as a go-between for people who want to contact loved ones who've passed." There, I'd said it.

"I understand what a psychic medium is."

We'd arrived at my place. He twisted in his seat to face me. "Oh, good." Persuading him might not be so difficult. "I want to take Elias's diary to her and ask her about it." I hesitated before continuing, "I'm sort of afraid of this mystical stuff. That's where the friend comes in."

He gave a short laugh. "You want me along as muscle in case

anything happens?"

I leaned against the seat in relief. "Right."

In a sultry voice guaranteed to smooth rough edges and make my heart flutter, he said, "Okay sweetheart. I'll do it for you."

In that moment, with his easy acceptance of my awkward circumstances and his willingness to make me happy, a bubble of pleasure replaced my worry. Instead of minimizing my fears, Sam promised to face them with me.

Chapter Twenty-One

Sam opened the driver's-side door to get out. I touched his arm. "Wait a minute. Before we go in, I want to ask you a question."

He tilted his head, a glint in his eyes. "Yes?"

"Did you mean it when you said you didn't believe in ghosts the other night?"

"What?"

Damn, he was scowling. "Did you?"

"Yes." At his sharp answer, I studied my clasped hands. He lifted my chin and whispered, "Why?"

I blinked and said. "I might have one."

"Dani…" he said, his voice soft.

Before I realized what was happening, he reached across the console for an awkward hug and murmured, "It's okay."

With his soothing voice in my ear, I spilled out my woes, starting with the nightmares, the tobacco smell, and the cold, ending with Heather's pictures, Izzy's non-accident, and my own terrifying experiences. When I finished, I sat back and asked, "Do you believe me?"

He smoothed the hair from my brow and gave me the sweetest kiss I've ever experienced. Then he whispered into my mouth, "I believe you, honey."

With his next kiss, I forgot all about Elias and his lair. My thoughts and emotions fused together in increasing desire.

After a minute, he pulled back. "Let's move this inside."

"Great idea," I said as I tried to ease my breathing.

On the way to my apartment, he held me tight against his side. I didn't dare glance toward Mrs. W's. At least I was consistent. Sam was the only guy she'd seen with his arms around me since I'd moved here. My hero entered the hallway first, alert for unwanted surprises. Once inside the apartment, he asked for the diary. For those few wonderful minutes in the truck when we'd held each other, I'd been able to forget the book and its author. The abrupt switch to reality saddened me.

I plucked the journal off the table beside the sofa and handed it to him.

I left him to examine the diary, while I made coffee and threw some cookies on a plate. I brought the snack in and sat next to him. "Notice anything weird?"

He held me close. "It's pretty old."

"A few hundred years. Do you find anything else odd?"

"No. Unless you count the stains on some of the pages."

"Oh, my fault," I said. "I cut myself when I attempted to open it and dripped some blood."

For a minute, the temperature in the room cooled. I shivered. His eyebrows lowered. He didn't say anything, though.

He closed the diary. "You're cold?"

"A little. Maybe the hot coffee will help."

"Let's see if I can warm you up." He pulled me tight against him and stroked my back, his searching fingers creating erotic sparks. I loved the feel of his strong body and the increasing warmth radiating from my shoulders to my abdomen.

He released me, gazed into my eyes, and claimed my lips. His soft, seeking kisses stirred my blood. With his hands cradling my face, his mouth brushed my forehead, my eyes, and my lips on its slow downward journey—agonizing and delicious torture.

His caresses became more urgent, and I gave myself up to the sensations burning through my body. I massaged his neck and his shoulders then grabbed his arm, the muscles rock-hard beneath my fingers.

When he whispered, "Do you want to continue this in the other room?"

I forced out a ragged, "Please."

As liquid fire claimed me, I teetered on shaky legs. He smiled and scooped me up into his arms. His kisses deepened as he approached the bed. For a moment, the specter of Elias flared in my mind, but Sam's heated touch chased it away.

I arched into him and moaned. His lips ignited breathtaking sensations. Heat and desire built inside me until nothing else mattered. He took his time undressing me. My hands ached to explore him. My body screamed for release. I wanted him right now.

With his heart-stopping tutelage and expert manipulation, I learned in exquisite detail the difference between a selfish and caring lover. He enjoyed giving me pleasure. Again and again, I gasped his name.

Later, I lay there in the crook of his arm, as his fingers traced my skin in an intimate remembrance. I wanted him to hold me forever. My body was sated, and my heart sang. I'd never been this happy.

When, after a luscious, drawn-out kiss, he said he had to leave, I was crushed. "Can't you stay?"

He captured my face in his hands and kissed me. "I'd like nothing better, but Bob has my truck. I borrowed my brother's. I said I'd drop it off tonight." He inclined his head as his finger played with my mouth. "A lobsterman's day starts at 4:00 AM. and it's almost 2:00 AM now." He trailed sweet kisses from my nose, along my cheek to my neck, then back to my mouth.

I wanted more, but he said, "I hate leaving you. It goes against everything in my heart." He cupped my face in his hands, and I was lost in his blue eyes. "You're beautiful, Dani Trent." After a final kiss, he rolled off the bed then yelled, "Ow!"

I gaped in confusion at this beautiful, naked man hopping around my bedroom, roaring out expletives. "What's the matter?"

"The damn book broke my toe."

The journal, now on the floor, had fallen off the nightstand right onto Sam's little toe. I raced into the bathroom for a Band-Aid, wondering who moved the diary. By the time I'd gotten back, Sam had his pants on and was buttoning his shirt.

I went over to him. "I'm sorry."

"It's not your fault. The stupid book is dangerous." He pulled me into his arms for a deep, thorough kiss, said he'd call me on my lunchbreak, and left.

After he was gone, I lifted the journal to check the weight. Not that heavy. I didn't understand how a book did so much damage. It warmed as I held it. What? I clenched the book, ready to throw it against the wall, but stopped. It wasn't mine. I placed the diary on the table.

If I'd caught the scent of pipe tobacco then, I might have left. The moment passed, and I hugged myself, remembering Sam's lovemaking. I didn't want to leave our nest. Snuggling under the covers, I inhaled his spicy aroma. Then I played back the whole evening in my head and fell asleep dreaming of him.

He held me in front of him, running his hands all over my body and whispering his love for me. My response was immediate, hot, and ready. I breathed his name and turned to kiss him, but I couldn't reach his mouth. Then his voice changed. It became rough, demanding. I didn't understand. The warmth seeped out of me. I trembled.

When I stretched to find him, a blanket of cold wrapped around me. Fingers dug in, hurting me. "Sam?"

An angry roar answered, "You're mine."

The thunderous voice jolted me awake. Terrified, I cringed under the blanket and peered around the room. The freezing cold permeated my body, and the dark, empty room hid its secrets. Oh, God. Another nightmare? Why? I'd had a wonderful night with Sam. My dreams should be joyful. No way would I stay there.

When I pulled back the covers, a light touch brushed across my face. Before I could scream, a hint of tobacco mocked me. Terrified, I raced into the living room.

~ * ~

I answered phone calls, listened to tenant concerns, and checked up on the painters, all the while musing about Sam and his incredible lovemaking. Bouts of heat assailed me, and I'm sure the flush was noted by a few residents. Let them wonder. I wanted to hug myself.

True to his promise, he called me at lunchtime. The timbre of his voice evoked sensual memories. I sighed. "Keep it up. Sweet talk always makes a girl's day."

"If you remember, I did a pretty good job of making a girl's night." His low drawl made my mouth go dry.

I flashed back to last night. The erotic images had me wriggling in my seat. Heat seared my neck, and I peeked over my shoulder. No one was in my office, and even if they were, they couldn't hear Sam's side of the conversation.

When I didn't answer, his tone changed. "Are you alone? Should I call you later?"

"No. No one else is here. Hearing those words in this place, though, threw me for a second. If my little ladies had access to my mind right now, they'd be shocked."

His chuckle was X-rated. "Don't kid yourself, honey. I'll bet quite a few of those ladies have stories that would give you a permanent blush."

In an attempt to banish outrageous images from my mind, I changed the subject. "How's your foot?"

"Sore, but I'll live."

I was so engrossed in the conversation, the scrape of a clearing throat startled me. Fischer. He stood behind me with a nasty smirk on his face.

All pleasure gone, I told Sam I had to go. "I'll call you later." I gave my boss a defiant glare, but his cold gaze forced me to look away.

"When was the last time you policed the place?"

"This morning." Every day, the manager was supposed to prowl around the property checking for problems and removing any trash.

His lips twisted in a sneer, and he threw a filthy, squashed coffee cup onto my desk. "You missed this."

Having ruined my day, my own personal demon departed. I was almost ready to believe he was the man who invaded my dreams. He was nasty enough to star in nightmares.

Chapter Twenty-Two

Friday afternoon, claps of thunder heralded a violent downpour, the beginning of a stormy night. Heather called to tell me she'd invited three friends to her apartment for the evening's reading. "The weather might be a problem. Low-lying parts of Salem tend to flood in heavy rains. I hope everyone can get here without too much trouble."

The storm was a typical window-rattling Nor'easter with strong gusts and vicious spurts of driving rain. The roads would be dicey.

I told her Sam agreed to come then added, "I think he's okay with it."

"He's a man. They refuse to believe whatever isn't right in front of their eyes. My dad is uncomfortable if you even mention the supernatural. Don't worry—this woman is supposed to be excellent."

"I hope it's true. I'm desperate to learn more about the diary and how to get rid of my unwanted ship's captain. Either that or find a new apartment. What can I contribute to the party besides Sam? A bottle of wine? Cookies?"

"They both sound great. Why don't you come here before the guests arrive? It'll give you time to meet everyone before we begin."

"Okay. I'm so nervous. I still hate the idea the place is haunted. With the temperature changes and the smells… I mean, I don't want the source to be a ghost, but there's nothing else it can be."

"No problem. Tonight you'll meet someone who can answer all your questions."

Sam arrived around 6:30 PM. I opened the door as he was shaking out his rain gear in the hallway. He ambled in, a little off kilter from his toe. Boy, he looked good. He leaned in and gave me a kiss.

Then he ruffled my hair and grinned. "I can't believe you got me into this wacky spiritualist thing. What kind of dramatic revelations can we expect?"

I grumbled about him ruining my hair and used my fingers to

comb out the mess he'd made. "Stop it. I just fixed this."

His smile grew. "I love your hair when it's mussed. I'll bet it's adorable in the morning when you wake up."

"Stick around sometime and find out."

With a playful twinkle in his eyes, he reached for me. I spun away. "Oh, no. We've got to be at Heather's in five minutes. We don't have time to play."

He kept coming. "Five minutes is plenty of time."

I laughed and fell into his arms, then with great reluctance, squiggled away. "Later," I purred.

We arrived at Heather's in time to meet two of her friends. Frieda was a colleague of hers from work who moonlighted at a T-shirt shop in Salem for the summer. I'd guess she was my age, mid-twenties. Her short, curly red hair, freckles, and big round eyes gave her a sweet, innocent appearance. This wasn't her first time at psychic events, and she assured us Serena was one of the best mediums in town.

Ted, Frieda's boyfriend, stood next to her. Tall, skinny, and a few years older than her, he was an investment banker with an interest in mysticism. He bounced around the room, picked at the food, and replenished wine glasses. Even when he sat still, his gaze roamed. He checked the time once more and confided in me that, although he'd never met Serena, her reputation was excellent.

"She worked with the police on a missing person's case a few years back." He thrust out his chest and grinned. "Serena's input helped the police find important evidence."

Although Sam didn't say a whole lot, the glances he tossed my way said I'd never get him to one of these gatherings again.

Traci, another friend of Heather's, skated in a couple of minutes before the hour, tossing water off her short black hair like an annoyed cat. Her first time at one of these readings, she oozed skepticism. Although she didn't disbelieve, she expounded on the fact there were lots of charlatans in this business. Sam warmed to her ideas right away. They were similar to his.

When Heather announced Serena was at the door, Sam and Traci migrated toward each other as if they were ready to join in battle. I fought off a twinge of jealousy. Damn Traci anyway; I wanted Sam to have an open mind. Now he'd found a skeptic, he'd be less inclined to believe.

The conversation stopped, as everyone poised to meet the medium. Her voice carried into the room. "Sorry. The road was flooded. I had to turn around and come a different way."

Her voice had a familiar ring. No. She couldn't be the person I suspected. I whipped my head around and peered at her in disbelief. Serena acknowledged everyone with a nod, but I fancied she stared at me a bit longer before tipping her head in recognition. Heather hadn't told me the medium would be her friend from the shop, the woman who'd sold me the necklace I held in a death grip.

I tried deep breathing to keep my nerves under control. They threatened to explode. I kept rubbing the pendant in a vain attempt to project a semblance of calm. An encounter with a medium was scary enough—now we had a real-life witch.

Serena was pleasant and open. No mysterious looks or dire pronouncements. She told us she lived in Swampscott, owned a shop in Salem, and taught classes at the local college. She introduced herself to us as a medium, never mentioning the *W-word*. When she moved to me and took my hand, her eyebrows came together in a momentary frown, which increased my mounting anxiety. She never seemed comfortable with me.

Noisy chatter brought me back to the present. Sam gave me a glass of wine, steered me to a seat, and whispered in my ear, "If she whips out a crystal ball, I'm outta here."

Unable to suppress a grin, I nudged him and said, "Shush."

For those of us who were new to this scene, Serena explained how she worked. "When people give me pictures or objects related to those they wish to contact, I get a sense from the spirit who wants to establish a connection from the other side. Many souls want to communicate with their loved ones. I'm their channel. I don't go into a trance or speak through a familiar. Direct questions can't be answered. What I will do is tell you what I hear and hope what I say makes sense to you. Any questions?"

Ted raised his hand. "Do you ever have to deliver bad news? Would you tell a person if you feared they were in danger?"

She smiled. "I don't hear good or bad. If someone issued a warning, it would mean nothing to me. My role is to reveal words or impressions from the other side. This isn't meant to frighten anyone. My connection to those who've passed on serves as a vehicle for the living to remain close to their departed loved ones. Any more questions?"

When Ted asked if she did personal readings, Serena gave him one of her cards. Heather handed us each a pad of paper and a pen. "This is to document what Serena says. It's best to let the person listen to her while the rest of us detail her findings."

Serena smiled at Frieda. "Let's start with you. What do you have?"

Frieda gave her a photograph of an older man.

Serena held the photograph, closed her eyes, and appeared to concentrate. "I'm sensing he loves you very much. I hear the word… 'frisky'? No, no, it might be 'fitsy.'" She smiled. "Mean anything to you?"

Frieda sat there for a moment, eyes wide and mouth open. "Fritzy. He was saying Fritzy. That was Daddy's nickname for me."

The sound of indrawn breaths filled the room, and I experienced chills. Serena spoke for another ten minutes, giving Frieda various names and words imparted to her. A few had meaning; others didn't. There was one other "Aha!" moment for Frieda, when Serena described a tall man with a decided limp and a special cane.

"That's him! My father." Frieda beamed at the rest of us. "Daddy always used a shillelagh carved by his grandfather." She told Serena how accurate some of her messages were and thanked her.

We took a few minutes to regroup and give Frieda the notes we'd taken.

Ted was next. He frowned in disappointment when Serena didn't hit him as well as she had Frieda. He'd given her a ring that belonged to his mother. However, at the end, Serena said, "I'm going to say this because it's what I keep hearing. Okay?"

He nodded. Again, she said, "This is what I hear— 'Kisses and hugs, Teddy boy.'"

Ted almost fell off his chair. His face was a perfect picture of surprise, complete with open mouth.

"That's what she always said to me. That was my mother." Tears formed in his eyes, and he dug around for a tissue while repeating, "That was my mother."

She was amazing. What a gift. I wished I'd brought a treasured object from my grandmother to give her instead of this stupid diary. I'd love to hear from Grams. Maybe Serena would come again.

Sam's forehead wrinkled in confusion. I whispered, "Well?"

"I'm surprised how good she is. I could almost become a believer."

Traci also seemed less skeptical than before. Serena was the real deal.

She moved on to Heather, who had a beautiful gold locket.

Serena smiled. "I sense pulses of love. I hear a woman. She's telling me she's there for you, and she's not alone." She paused and closed her eyes. "The man beside her is throwing a kiss with his fingers." Her forehead wrinkled, and she paused before adding, "Something about a kitten."

Tears dampened Heather's cheeks. She wiped them away with

her sleeve and managed a snuffling, "Granddaddy's big joke. He called me 'Kitten,' from his favorite TV show, *Father Knows Best*."

There were quite a few names Heather recognized, and she appeared pleased with the results. Before moving on to Traci, Serena looked at Heather, tilted her head, and said, "You've had trouble here."

Heather blinked, and her voice became a little breathless. "Yeah, I have."

"Take care." Heather's eyes widened, and I caught her nervous stare. I glanced at Sam, who'd straightened in his seat. What she said sounded ominous.

Traci, who was next, passed Serena a picture of a man who might be in his thirties. Serena held the photo and seemed to be concentrating. After a minute, she said, "I'm sensing he's still in this world."

Traci's voice rose in surprise. "That's right."

Serena said she was picking up something about long distances. She described a kind of uniform.

Traci's sharp inhale told us Serena hit the mark. "He's a pilot." Serena nodded as if she'd already guessed that. Her whole countenance projected calm and reassurance. I wondered how anyone was able to stay sane with ghosts speaking to them. Yeesh!

"He misses you when he's away. Is there an important subject you need to discuss?"

Traci blushed and studied her hands. "Yes."

There were a couple more hits. A few misses. When she presented the big stuff, though, Serena was dead on. *Oops, I'm glad I didn't say that out loud.*

The next person was Sam, who explained to Serena he was there for moral support and took my hand. I sent a satisfied glance to Traci; he was mine. With a lift of her shoulders and a questioning look, Serena invited me to speak. My chest tightened. Maybe I shouldn't do this. The others had given her a special object from someone they loved. I had nothing in common with Elias. I despised him.

Before I turned the diary over to Serena, it warmed in my hands. Odd. "This isn't mine. Will it still work?"

"That's all right," but she hesitated before she touched it. "I'm sensing anger." She took the diary. Eyes closed, she held the book on her lap. Then she made a keening noise. Her head moved from side to side as if she disagreed with someone. She mumbled unintelligible words.

My breathing faltered. Panic clawed at my chest. Serena said she wouldn't go into a trance. If this wasn't a trance, it came darn close to one. Her voice grew louder, and she swayed. We all looked at one another in alarm. The temperature in the room dropped. I grasped Sam's hands. He put his arm around me.

Serena's shout terrified me. "Begone!" Moments later, her tone intensified, and her words became sharp and clipped. "Go. Away." By now, the room was freezing. Her hands shook, and her whole body twitched. "Leave. I command you. Depart." She shook her head, then she screamed, "No!"

When the book flew away from her and crashed to the floor, I leaned into Sam. Serena sank back in her chair, deflating like a leaky balloon. Heather moved to her side to help her. I froze in Sam's arms. The diary lay on the floor, open to the pages with Rebecca's name, the ones my blood had touched.

A liquid-like warmth settled around me. I was so tired. Whispers echoed in my head—whispers and laughter. "It's done. You're mine."

I sensed confusion in the room, but I didn't care. He'd found me. *No!* I fought the urge to give in; I didn't want to go with him. "Please leave me alone!" His voice faded.

Loud, sharp noises battered my senses. "Dani! Snap out of it." The voice was familiar. "Come on, honey. Wake up."

I forced my eyelids open. Sam peered at me, his face pale, his expression wild. What was he upset about? A persuasive force pulled me away. I relaxed into it, until frantic barking jarred me awake. As if from a distance, I came back to the room.

My mouth and brain worked in tandem. "Sam?" His arms tightened around me. I looked up at him. "Don't let him get me."

"Jesus." He crushed me into him.

Everyone clustered around Serena who fought to stand by herself. She'd changed. Her staunch personality faded to a pale replica. Dark eyes in a bloodless face stared into my own. For a moment, she held my gaze, then twisted away from concerned hands and grabbed her shawl. "I have to leave. Please let me go. I can't stay. I have to leave."

She rushed to the front door. In her hurry to get to her car, she'd forgotten her purse.

I needed to talk to her. My head cleared a bit. I slipped out of Sam's embrace. "I'm okay." I snatched Serena's purse and darted off to return it.

"Wait." He chased after me.

The wind drove spikes of rain into my face. Serena slid into her car. I was still kind of woozy, and it took all my strength to twist away from Sam to get to her. When I knocked on the window, she jumped and leaned away from me.

I yelled against the shrieking wind. "You forgot your purse." I showed it to her.

She blinked and rolled down the window. In a coarse whisper, she said, "It's you. He wants you. Get out while you can!" She seized her purse then sped off into the storm.

Sam covered me with Heather's coat before leading me back to her apartment. The scene was chaotic, everyone talking at once. What happened? What did it mean?

Heather was a mess. Her party had been a success one minute, shot to hell the next. She glared at me. "The book."

"I…I'm sorry."

Sam tucked me under his arm, thanked Heather for the use of her coat, then steered me toward the door. "Wait a minute." An odd compulsion seized me. I scooped up the diary. Sam mumbled something like "nothing but trouble" as he ushered me out.

In my kitchen, he placed his hands on either side of my face and whispered, "You need a hot shower. You're soaked and shivering."

He was right, but I was so tired. He asked me if I wanted him to stay the night.

I shook my head. "All I want is to warm up and go to sleep."

My answer wasn't what he wanted, but he didn't push. "I have a job in the morning. I won't be finished until late afternoon. If you have any problems at all, call my cell. I'll be in Salem. I can get here in five minutes."

I promised I'd call if I needed him. His goodnight kiss left me unaffected. No heart palpitations. No ache for more. I hated the disappointment on his face. My indifference to this gorgeous man confused me. Earlier I'd planned to skate out of Heather's as soon as possible for a repeat of last night on the sofa bed.

Too tired to let it bother me, I decided against the shower and fell into bed. I was asleep in minutes. A while later, I awoke aching for Sam. I searched for him, but he was gone. Where was he? He'd just had his hands all over me. As I floated into sleep, a whisper followed me. "Ah, Rebecca, my love. Soon."

Chapter Twenty-Three

I ducked under the covers, then shoved the pillow over my head. No matter what I did, the blaring noise continued to echo through my mind. Sleep. I needed sleep. When the noise ended, I relaxed and started to drift off. The clamor began again. I sat up and grabbed the hated phone. My hand squeezed, wanting to send the disruptive device flying, but I needed it for work.

I answered it. "What?"

Heather's voice, taut with fear, seized my attention. "Something awful has happened."

"Huh?" I was so comfortable. I hated to be awakened. "What time is it?"

"Ten AM. Are you still in bed?"

"Ten? It can't be. I never sleep that late. Wait a minute."

I forced myself to confirm the time. Oh, my God. How could I have slept so long? What was wrong?

"Dani, are you listening?"

I hadn't been paying attention. "Sorry. What did you say?"

"Serena was in an accident last night. She's at the hospital in serious condition."

"Serena?" I had a vague memory of the evening's events. We'd been at Heather's. Serena was awesome. I remembered her speaking to me. What was it she said?

Heather was talking again; I'd have to concentrate. I wondered if I was getting sick. "What's the matter with you? Are you okay?"

"I think I might have picked up a bug or a cold."

"I'll be right there. We have to talk."

"Let me get dressed, and I'll put the coffee on," I told her.

"Right. I'll be there in ten."

"Make it twenty."

After a quick shower, my mind was less fuzzy. In case I might have a bug, I took two Tylenol. It couldn't hurt; I'd gotten soaked last night. I'd better not get pneumonia. Fischer would have a fit if I missed work. I snagged a pair of jeans and a T-shirt while I searched my memory for the sequence of last night's events. I was having a good time until I handed Serena the diary.

I remembered her scream. The rest was a little hazy. Sam's arms comforted me. Oh, right. I gave Serena her purse. That's how I got soaked. What did she say to me? I lost the thread when Heather arrived. She started talking before I closed the door.

"I can't believe the insanity I witnessed in my living room: Serena in a trance, her crazy commands, and throwing the diary." Heather shook her head. "I wish she'd waited to recover before driving in the storm."

We sat at the table with our coffee. "Why was she upset?"

For a minute, Heather was speechless. When she found her voice, it sounded like a growl. "The diary! The minute Serena touched it, everything went crazy. You have to get rid of it."

"Come on. It's just a book. There must have been another reason."

She shook her head. "No." Her voice rose. "The problem is the diary. It sent Serena into a trance, and she lost it."

"What about her accident?"

"Oh, God. She missed the turn on Paradise Road. Around the curve by the river. The car crashed into the guard rail, flipped over, and landed in the water. Thank God the tide was low, otherwise she'd have drowned."

"That's terrible. How bad are her injuries?"

"A friend of mine at the hospital said she's still in the ICU, either in a coma or they induced one. I guess she has a bunch of broken bones. They'll have more information later."

"I hope she'll be okay."

"Me too. Did she speak to you when you gave her the purse?"

"Yeah. She acted strange. Almost like she was afraid of me. She said something like, 'He wants you.'"

"You mean Sam?"

I shrugged. "Beats me."

"Yeah, it's pretty clear he wants you."

"Is it?"

"Give me a break. The two of you are so obvious. Anyway, the diary started the trouble. Serena went nutso after she held it."

"That doesn't make sense," I said. "Why would the journal upset her?"

She lowered her voice to say, "Maybe it's the ghost? He might be part of the diary." She twisted her ponytail around her finger and bit her bottom lip. "Frieda and Ted told me they sensed evil in the room last night."

I couldn't help myself. I laughed. After a couple of seconds, she chuckled. I poured us another cup of coffee. "They're into this weird stuff, aren't they?"

"They were thrilled with the evening. They wanted to bring a Ouija board into my apartment before they left last night. I told them no way. I didn't want one of those in my house."

I agreed with Heather. Ouija boards were freaky. "Some people call them witch boards."

Heather lowered her cup. "Those two may be a bit intense, but you've got to admit last night was super weird."

"Yeah. Serena sounded like she was casting out the devil."

"Don't forget the room got wicked cold, and you were way out there."

I took a sip. It tasted good. "I was surprised to see Serena in full-blown psychic mode. Is that her shtick?"

"No. The word is she's the real deal. I guess because she's a witch."

I ran different scenarios through my head to explain what happened. Not much came to mind. "Maybe, she wasn't expecting whatever she found. You heard her yelling. With the strain I've been under, her actions might have sent me over the edge. Like mass hysteria?"

"Damn, Dani. It's the diary. All the trouble happened when you gave it to Serena."

"All I can think of is that she conjured the ghost. I hope she'll be okay."

"I hear you." She leaned back in her chair, crinkled her eyes, and grinned. "You and Sam are, like, super tight. He had a fit last night when you zoned out. You were saying crazy things, yourself."

I lifted an eyebrow. "Like what?"

"You told Sam not to let him get you. I was at a loss. Serena fainted, and you were talking ragtime. It got pretty intense for a while. Which reminds me, are you still having nightmares?"

"Not for a few nights now. I do remember a sexy dream about Sam last night, though."

"Yeah, I love those. Whoops. Look at the time. I've got to take JoJo for a walk. The rain's stopped. Want to go with us?"

"No, thanks. I want to get some housework done. Sam's coming later."

She pointed at me, winked, and said, "Lucky you," before she closed the door.

The bedroom was a mess. I walked in and glared at the diary on my nightstand. Was Heather right? Had that book caused all the trouble?

I sat on the bed and leaned my head in my hands. Part of last night was hazy. I was finding it more and more difficult to distinguish dreams from reality.

~ * ~

Sam arrived a little after five. His presence no longer spiked my blood pressure or my libido. I was tired and told him so. He ignored my complaints, overruled my excuses, and insisted I go out with him, carrying on about the benefits of fresh air. Humbug!

By the time we reached the stairs, all I wanted to do was sit. "Let me rest for a minute." I was furious when he wouldn't let me. He had to help me to the truck. When my foot wouldn't reach, his gentle hands guided me. Our first stop was the sandwich shop. From there we were headed to the beach.

Although I wasn't tired any more, I didn't like him treating me like a child. Pouting like a two-year-old, I said, "It's too cold to sit on the beach." After the storm, the temperature had dropped.

He kissed me and ruffled my hair. "Stop whining. I've got this." While he drove, I grumbled about him ruining my hair.

At the beach, he took two chaise lounges, two blankets, and a radio from the back of the truck. He placed the chairs on the sand and settled me into one. As he put the blanket around me, my body reacted, humming with desire. I remembered how talented those strong hands were. When he grinned, I wanted to seize his face and devour those fresh lips. Why hadn't I reacted like that earlier, though?

He turned the radio to a classical station, gave me a sandwich and soda, then sat next to me. Not too many people had braved the cool September day. We had the beach pretty much to ourselves. The last rays of the sun still provided some warmth. I sucked in a deep breath of invigorating salty air. The storm had aroused the ocean's fury, and the explosion of massive waves delighted me. Our biggest problems came from the thieving seagulls. Before long he had me laughing.

After we'd finished our sandwiches, he brought up the previous night's fiasco. "I'm worried about you. For a few minutes at Heather's, I couldn't get through to you at all. Then afterward and today, you didn't even want to be with me. It made me wonder if you'd found another guy."

"No. Don't say that," I cried. "You make me happy. It would

break my heart if you weren't around."

He squeezed my hand, one of the few parts not covered by a blanket. "I'd be devastated without you, too, but you've been so distant since the scene at Heather's. The lassitude is worse at your place. I can't figure it out. I'm halfway convinced there's a gas leak affecting you. Last night, you had to fight to keep your eyes open."

"I don't understand either. Maybe I picked up a bug. I slept until ten this morning, something I never do." I grinned. "I'm fine now."

"You need to have the gas company check your apartment."

"Okay. Monday I'll call the gas company, and I'll make sure to keep my windows open." His stern countenance reminded me why I didn't want to leave my windows open. "Okay," I said. "I'll call the gas company today."

With a little persistence and a lot of muscle, he managed to get me out of my chair and onto his lap, still wrapped in my blanket where his arms and lips took very good care of me.

~ * ~

Sam made the call to the gas company when we got back to my apartment. Thirty minutes later, I was in front of my building, in his truck, while he brought a serious young man with a buzz cut through the apartment and the cellar to search for leaks. The guy insisted on inspecting the other apartments, which ticked off my favorite couple upstairs. He finished and told me he hadn't found any leaks. I apologized, but he assured me he'd rather have an inspection without problems and make sure everything was safe.

Sam had been keeping an eye on me since the front door closed. When I leaned against the counter and yawned, he said, "Okay. Pack whatever you need. You're staying at my place tonight."

"Don't be so dramatic. The gas guy checked the whole building. No leaks."

My reasoning didn't faze him. He nudged me into the bedroom. I gathered a few things together, but the sight of my warm, comfortable bed distracted me. What could it hurt if I lay down for a few minutes? I was so tired.

Sam caught me before I hit the mattress. One arm held me against him, and he used the other to scoop up what I'd packed. Then he dragged my complaining butt to his truck, ignoring my whining rant on the way out.

When I stopped yawning a few minutes later, he said, "Over our tantrum, are we?"

I gave my head a shake to clear the last remnants of the sleepy fog. "I don't understand these bouts of exhaustion." His look of disbelief hurt me. "I'm telling the truth. I can't help it. I don't understand what comes over me."

"It's okay. You're not doing it on purpose. I'm concerned. The fatigue and indifference started last night with Serena and the book. I don't like what's happening."

I opened my mouth to deny his conclusion, but he put his finger against my lips. "You didn't see what I did. Once Serena touched the diary, the whole atmosphere changed. Whatever happened affected you both." His fingers caressed my neck, and he gave me a quick kiss. "You're the one I care about. When you're not half asleep, there's a terrifying distance about you. I'm sick with worry. You need to find a new apartment."

I hurried to assure him. "Heather and I have been checking the papers. Kirsten came up with a couple of possibilities, but they were in Beverly, and I like living in Salem. It shouldn't be too much longer."

"One more night is one too many."

"A tad melodramatic? A couple more weeks won't kill me."

A few minutes later, we arrived at his place. His apartment was in the back of an old house right on the harbor.

He held my shoulders. "Stay with me until you find a new place."

Whoa. I liked him. A whole lot. In fact, I might even love him—but move in? Living together was serious business. I hadn't forgotten how the same decision had ended with Tom, and I wasn't sure I was ready for that kind of commitment again.

I was glad Sam didn't push me to respond. Instead, he kissed me. "We'll talk about it later. Let's get you settled in for tonight."

We rounded the corner to his back door, and I came to a dead stop. A small patch of grass led to a rocky ledge overlooking blue-green waters. I lifted my face into the stiff breeze that blew my hair around and enjoyed the sound of waves crashing against the rocks. Entranced by the spectacle, I followed the course of each swell as it surged in to send white foam flying into the air. Even though the specks didn't reach us, their briny scent did.

"This is gorgeous."

He put his arms around me and squeezed. "You could enjoy it every day, if you lived here."

I snuggled against him. "Mm, the perks keep adding up."

We spent an incredible time at his apartment. He even rented a chick flick for me. To his credit, he never once complained. We popped popcorn in the microwave and toasted the salty result with wine. We made love on the couch and later in his room. The next morning, he served me breakfast in bed.

"You should get chick flicks more often, Mr. Gregory."

Serious for a minute, he gazed at me. "I don't care about the flicks. And you're the one chick I'm interested in."

Sometime after noon, we walked down the street to his favorite lunch place. I listened to his stories about townies, most of them bust-a-gut funny. Later, we ambled along the waterfront where he pointed to his brother's boat. "Right there. The white-and-green lobster boat. The *Rachael S.*"

There were at least fifty fishing vessels that color. "Which one?"

"Right there between the black sailboat and the blue-and-white cabin cruiser."

Again, not helpful. "There are too many boats in this harbor, and they're headed the wrong way to see the names."

He tucked me in his arms and helped me pick out his brother's vessel. When I discovered the right boat, I was rewarded with a kiss. If I'd gotten prizes like that in school, I'd have been an A student. I hated the day to end. We both had work the next day. I didn't have the right clothes with me or my car. I needed to go home. He tried romantic blackmail to talk me out of it, but even after a smoking kiss, I was adamant.

He escorted me into my apartment and stayed to gauge my reactions. While he was there, I pulled together an outfit for the next day to hang in the living room. Until I found another place, I planned to steer clear of the bedroom. After about twenty minutes, when I hadn't yawned once, he gave me a tantalizing kiss and left.

I made one last trip through the bedroom to retrieve the big square flashlight I kept beside the bed. I glanced at the nightstand and back again. What was different? The diary. I'd placed it there yesterday morning. Now the table was empty. My body shook, I rubbed the goosebumps on my skin, then peeked around the empty room.

I needed to track the diary down before it got dark. When I was unable to locate it in any of the rooms, unease stirred in my gut. One place left. I stared at the loft. It took all my courage and the help of the pendant to get me up those stairs. I hadn't set foot in my office since the awful day I discovered Izzy was pushed.

The last time the diary took off, I found it on my desk, and that was where it sat tonight. The journal's movements made me ill. I had trouble breathing and forced myself to look at it. Something was different. The book lay open to a page I'd never seen—the last one. Curious, I leaned in for a closer glimpse.

The words staring back at me twisted my insides. My shaking

limbs undermined my visual perception. I closed my eyes. I must have read it wrong. I forced myself to focus and glanced one more time. No matter how much I blinked or rubbed at my face, the writing remained.

The last page of the diary contained a new passage written in fresh ink. The old inkstand and quill pen I'd purchased at the antique store sat next to the book as if the writer had just finished his latest entry. A sharp pain sliced through my insides. I tried to deny the terrifying reality, praying I was having a hallucination. I wanted to run down those stairs and forget I'd ever seen it. Not happening. I clutched my queasy stomach. I examined the page again.

Nothing had changed. The writing matched the previous script, written in the same hand. Two words whose significance cut to my soul.

She's mine!

I have no idea how I got downstairs or what happened next. Hours later, I found myself in bed, crooning Sam's name. I twisted and moaned as his hands caressed my body. His words fanned my desire. "Your beauty is breathtaking." His touch made me moan with pleasure. "My Rebecca."

What did he call me? Who? I rolled over but found an empty space. I leaned on my elbow, rubbed my eyes, and searched for him. "Sam?" No one was there. I was alone. Dregs of sexual tension still clung to me. Wow, the whispers and caresses seemed so real. I yawned.

Fleeting memories from earlier skipped through my brain. The diary. A fresh entry. Had I dreamt it? I held my breath on the edge of panic when I was disoriented by a wave of exhaustion. *It's not that important.* I lay back in bed. A hand touched my forehead. A kiss claimed my lips. I smiled, closed my eyes, and fell back to sleep.

Chapter Twenty-Four

The next day on my way to work, I agonized over my unwarranted fatigue. When my alarm blared in the morning, I almost tossed the phone against the wall. If I weren't terrified of my boss, I wouldn't have gotten out of bed.

By the time I arrived at work, I was wide awake. The crisp air cleared away any lingering cobwebs. Sam was right. The exhaustion problems I had were in my apartment. It might be a good idea to stay with him until I found another place.

While I waited for my computer to boot, uncomfortable scenes from last night's sleep crowded my mind. I remembered the name Rebecca. Then I awakened to a kiss. That had to be wrong. Didn't matter. For the past few weeks, even my waking moments resembled hallucinations. I wondered if I needed to speak to an expert in paranormal affairs or a psychiatrist.

My life was no better at work. I found a message from Fischer. A managers' meeting was scheduled at his office after lunch. Attendance mandatory. I hated these sessions. Most of the time he expounded on his many talents, bragged about his accomplishments, and dumped on his managers.

Today his glare zeroed in on me as he said we needed to review our emergency policies. *Oh, hell.* I was the goat. "Dani, what's the first thing we do when there's a fire?"

A telltale flush heated my face. "Call the fire department." My insides quivered while he paused.

When he spoke, he gave me a superior smile. "Correct." Next, he itemized an emergency checklist and finished with a direct scowl at me. "I will not tolerate mistakes."

Although I hadn't done anything wrong, his insinuation made me want to crawl beneath the table.

I was grateful the other managers were aware of his attitude toward me. Most of them came by afterward to lend their support and relate their own Fischer horror stories. Encouraged by my colleagues, I ignored Fischer's jibes.

Chuck, who managed a large complex in Lynn, put his arm around my shoulders as we walked outside. "Hey, we're all human."

Another manager whispered in my ear, "Everyone knows Fischer's a jerk."

I was glad my peers stood by me. If I needed recommendations for a new job, I'd be able to count on them.

My car was parked down the street. The lot had been full when I'd arrived. My mind wrestled with the possibility of securing a job with another management company. Scratch that. I'd need a recommendation from my boss. Not likely to happen. Lost in thought I ignored my surroundings until I reached Minerva. I clicked the button to unlock the door, then reeled back at the sound of Tom's voice.

"Hi, Dani."

I swiveled my head around to find help. No one. We were alone. The smug jerk leaned against the fender with his legs crossed and arms folded on his chest, the nasty smile I hated pasted on his face.

"My, my, how low will you go?"

God, what was he talking about now? "Please get away from my car. I have to leave."

He ignored me. "First the loser in Salem and now you're cuddled up to a black guy."

His racist remark must have been for my colleague, Chuck. How dare he? I clenched my teeth. "Don't you talk about my friends, you prejudiced bastard. Leave them and me alone. If you don't get off my fender, I'll drive away with you on it."

He laughed at my attempt to gain control. I waved my arms and yelled, "Stay away from me."

When he headed toward me, I opened my mouth to scream. It worked.

He stopped, frowned, and squeezed an ultimatum between his teeth. "We'll discuss this later."

"Is everything all right here?"

"Eddie!" *Oh, thank God.*

He said no more and moved past me, right into Tom's face. Although his cheeks flushed a deep red, he didn't move. Not good. Tom towered over Eddie, but Eddie stood his ground.

"The lady asked you to leave, pal. I'd advise you to do it."

"Lady?" Tom croaked a forced laugh. "That's a good one. She's been screwing around with all kinds of trash. You must be her latest. Or is it you and the black guy together?"

The action sped up then, moving too fast for me to anticipate or stop. When Eddie moved forward, and Tom's head snapped back, I missed the arm and fist that caused the action.

Astonishment flitted across Tom's face. He touched his mouth, and his fingers came back bloodied. With a roar, he threw himself at Eddie. After that, I couldn't tell who was doing what. The sickening sound of fist against flesh held me pinned against my car. I covered my mouth, afraid I'd vomit.

The fight might have lasted five minutes or fifteen. Time ceased to mean anything. At some point I became aware we weren't alone. I spun around to find a red-faced Fischer standing behind me. His gaze cut into mine, promising trouble. Damn! This would have to happen outside his office.

Sirens blared in the distance. Their imminent arrival caused Tom and Eddie to break apart. As Eddie wiped blood from his face, Tom took off, and Fischer told Eddie to leave. By the time the officer arrived, both men had disappeared.

Fischer growled at me, "Let me handle this." He presented a benevolent façade to the policeman and, in a voice like an understanding parent, said, "A couple of boys fighting, but they got over it and left."

Oh, God. I can't let Tom get away with this. He doesn't care about the restraining order. I'm not safe anywhere. I hated to buck my boss. I didn't want to lose my job, but a quick glance at Fischer's furious countenance, and the disgust in his eyes told me he was going to fire me anyway.

The policeman questioned me. "Have you got anything to add?" After a peek at Fischer's red face, I spilled the whole story.

While the officer went to the car to call in his report, Fischer turned his glacial smile on me. "You're finished. I'll escort you to your office, and you can clean out your desk."

"But—"

"Now!" he bellowed.

I shook with anger and grief when he ushered me into my office and supervised everything I touched as if I were a felon. A few residents in the vicinity stood by, foreheads wrinkled in obvious confusion. I looked away from them and glared at Fischer. In a last act of dominance, the rotten creep stood in the parking lot, legs planted apart and arms crossed until I drove away.

I clenched my fingers around the wheel, wishing it was Fischer's neck. I'd been fired. After all his threats, he'd done it. Sacked me because of that no-good jerk. The punishment wasn't fair. I'd done nothing wrong. He should be protecting me. What about Beach Street? Who'd take care of my tenants? At the next red light, I scrounged in my purse for my phone. I wanted to call someone and rant.

With the appearance of Tom, the fight, and the embarrassment of being fired, I'd forgotten to switch the phone back on. Two messages from Sam. I punched in his number.

"Hi, he said. I've been trying to call you." My voice faltered as I said, "I got fired."

"What?" he said, his voice almost a yell.

"Tom showed up outside my manager's office, and Eddie punched him. They got into a big fight. The police came, and Fischer fired me."

"Did the police arrest Tom?" Sam asked.

I wished I could say yes. "No. They both left before the officer arrived."

"You told the police you had a restraining order, didn't you?"

I inhaled and blew out a long breath. "Yes. I can't talk anymore." I was too angry and upset. "I'm driving. I'll call you when I get home."

I disconnected and smacked the wheel. When I got home, he was there in the hall. I walked into his arms. "I can't believe it."

Sam held me. "It's okay honey. You did the right thing. You're going to be fine."

Heather came around the corner. "Hi, Sam. Dani, I have to talk to you." At the sight of my face, she gave Sam an ominous glare. "What's wrong?"

"Fischer fired me."

"That no-good...I'm sorry."

The three of us trooped into my apartment where she steered me to the sofa. "That bastard! What happened?"

I told her about the fight and how everyone took off before the police arrived. "Fischer told me not to say anything to the officer, but I had to."

"Of course you did," she said.

I looked up at Sam. "He wouldn't let me speak to my residents, and I forgot to take my plant."

He joined me on the sofa for a hug. "I'll buy you a new one." Heather cleared her throat. I sat back and waited for her to speak. "I hate to spring this on you after the day you've had, but it's important. I got a call today from a friend of Serena's. The good news is Serena's out of the coma and much better, but she insisted on giving her friend a message for you." Heather paused and bit her lip. "Serena called it a warning."

"For me?"

Her gaze slid from me toward the bedroom, and her finger zipped in circles worrying her ponytail. "Yup. Said the information was a matter of life and death."

"That's a little much."

"Listen. Serena said the spirit is very, very strong."

I wanted to brush off her claim with a laugh, but my breathing was too shallow.

"She said he claims you belong to him."

I managed an awkward chuckle. "Oh, please."

"This is serious. Serena's terrified to call here or have anything to do with us. The ghost or spirit held her foot on the gas pedal at the bend in the road. She couldn't hit the brake."

Cold fingers plucked at my spine. "Oh my God. Can ghosts do that? How much wine did Serena have to drink?"

"She didn't finish her glass. Did you forget what happened after she touched that book? She fought with the demon."

Sam put his arm around my waist as I said, "What am I supposed to do?"

"She said you have to leave here."

Fear crept through me. Yes, I had a problem in the apartment but… A huge yawn cut off the rest of my answer.

"Hey," she said. "I discovered an apartment yesterday. It'd be perfect for you. I can find something else. I don't have to leave this instant."

Sam squeezed me. "She's going to my apartment."

Heather ignored him. "Where's your laptop? I'll show it to you." I pointed toward the bedroom and another yawn overtook me.

Before he could reiterate his claim, she sprinted to the bedroom.

He held my shoulders and pushed his face close to mine. "Listen. You're coming home with me tonight."

I was too tired to argue. A shriek from Heather snapped me out of my lassitude. "What's this?"

He dragged me along to see what had upset her. "What's wrong?"

She stood next to my desk in the loft, a mask of horror on her face. Her finger pointed to something. An almost-memory played in my head—something about the diary.

She gripped the railing and peered at me. In a shaky voice, she said, "This looks like fresh ink."

Sam sped up there in seconds. "Let me see that."

Two accusatory stares bore down on me. He spoke first. "What's with the new writing?"

An uncomfortable memory surfaced. "I...I forgot. I was going to tell you about it."

He looked down at me and arched an eyebrow. "Who wrote it?"

I shook my head. "No idea."

He stared at me for so long, I blurted out, "Maybe Tom snuck in and wrote it to frighten me."

Sam's eyes widened into an incredulous stare. "That's your answer? Tom tried to scare you? This entry bears an uncanny resemblance to the rest of the writing in the diary. Is he a good forger?"

I was becoming perturbed and wanted them both to go. With a shrug, I glared at him. "No idea." Another mammoth yawn attacked me. "I'd like to go to bed now."

Heather's face lost all its color. "It's the ghost."

Sam banged his hands against the metal rail. "This has gone too far. We're getting out of here now."

I shivered as the room cooled off. I needed to rest for a bit. I ignored the noise in the loft and lay down on the bed.

I was snatched from my bed and shaken. The jarring motion scared me enough that I opened my eyes.

Sam's concerned face reassured me. "Come on, honey. Wake up."

I blinked. "What? I am awake."

I didn't understand the stormy expression in his eyes as he said, "Let's go."

"Where are you taking her?" Heather asked.

"To my apartment. This place is unhealthy."

I sidled around him and headed for my comfy bed. I ignored him when he yelled my name. Why wouldn't he let me rest?

He pulled me to my feet and turned to Heather. "Help her gather clothes for a couple of days."

"What kind of clothes?" she asked.

"Nothing fancy. She doesn't have to go to work."

Work? My foggy brain focused for a minute. *Oh, hell.* I didn't have a job anymore.

Sam hustled me to his truck. The last thing I remember is trying to sit on the steps and him urging me up or maybe carrying me.

When I came to, I noticed we'd passed the college. "Where are we going?"

"My place."

Most of the maple trees and a few bushes had begun to display colors. I rubbed my arms and grumbled, "It's cold."

"It's almost October." He might as well have said, "Where have you been for the past few weeks?"

We drove by a cemetery when he glanced at my hands. "What do you have there?" Before I could answer, he yelled, "Is that the diary?"

I cringed at his tone. "I don't remember taking it. Wasn't it in the loft?"

He snatched the diary and threw it to the floor.

We were on the downside of a steep hill. He ran his hand through his hair. "Jesus, we've got to get rid of that damn book."

A second later, he let out a roar and grabbed the wheel. The truck swerved across the road toward a tree. Sam's muscles bulged as he fought to regain control. He pushed back against the seat, jamming his foot on the brake.

I screamed. My gaze was drawn to the book. Pulses of fury rippled from it. The ghost was angry that we'd rejected his diary. He'd kill us. I reacted on impulse and picked it up. The truck came to a sudden stop. The view through the windshield made my heart hammer. Dark ribs of bark filled the glass. Another few feet, and we'd have been wrapped around it.

I bent over, fighting a bout of nausea. My hands, clutching the book, wouldn't stop shaking. Sam sat there, fingers glued around the wheel. The sound of strained breathing filled the silence. When he turned to me, the horror on his face twisted into anger. I leaned away from him, afraid he was upset with me, but his wrath was directed at the diary on my lap.

When he spoke, though, his voice held alarm. "What kind of demonic book do you have?"

We sat there for seconds…or was it minutes? The blast of a horn brought us back to the present. The truck sat at an angle to the side of the road and blocked part of the right lane. "You need help?" a guy yelled to us.

Sam waved at him. "Thanks. We're good." He switched gears and backed onto the road.

I forced myself to breathe. Sam still had a death grip on the wheel. My fingers ached from clutching the book. Then my insides cramped as if squeezed by a cold fist. He gained control of the truck the moment I'd retrieved the hellish tome. The diary wanted me. *Oh, God.*

He peeled one of his hands off the wheel to hold mine. His squeeze communicated his commitment to stick by me.

Chapter Twenty-Five

The terrible truth I'd refused to accept hit me. Elias was part of his diary, and they were both dangerous. "Sam?"

"Yeah?"

"That's what must have happened to Serena. Elias drove her off the road."

"Let's not talk about that now," he said with a meaningful glance at the book.

I stared at what looked like an innocent object in my lap. What could we do? I had to get rid of this source of evil, but how? A germ of an idea formed. I'd take the book back, deposit it in the loft, and we'd get away without it. Then we'd be able to discuss solutions or find a person who might be able to help.

With an effort, I managed to keep the fear from my voice. "Would you bring me back to the apartment?"

"What!"

"I forgot to pack my toothbrush."

He was ready to argue when I nudged him and darted my gaze back and forth to the book. He shot me a puzzled look but played along and reversed the truck.

The minute I walked through the door, the book warmed in my hands. I had a colossal urge to throw it out the window. The action would be pointless. Whatever spirit inhabited the book was powerful. I didn't dare anger the vindictive specter anymore. Since I'd found the book in the loft, I brought it back there. Halfway down the stairs, my vision blurred, and I thought I might faint. I clutched the rail and tottered to the bed.

Sam was beside me, ready to help. "Are you okay?"

"Sort of dizzy. Maybe I'll rest."

"Not a good idea." He helped me up, and we walked into the kitchen. "How about a cup of tea?"

Too tired to answer, I rested my head on his shoulder. Then, he took a right and guided me out the door to the hall.

I had trouble trying to walk. By the time we got outside, he was carrying me. I fought to stay awake as he put me into the truck and took off. Right before I lost consciousness, he uttered some pretty colorful swear words.

I awoke to the tiny glow from the dashboard and darkness on either side of the truck. Ahead twin beams of light gobbled up the road. I yawned. "Where are we?"

"On Route 128, headed to Gloucester. It's a good thing you're awake because I don't have your sister's address."

"My sister?"

"Yup."

I tried to understand. "We're going to Kir's?"

"Yup."

I shook my head in confusion. "Why there?"

"First, how are you doing?"

I shrugged. "I'm a little confused."

"Are you still tired?"

"No. Did I sleep all the way here?"

"Pretty much. You fell asleep when we left the house. I carried you to the truck. You've been out since."

"What is it with me?"

"You're sure you aren't tired?"

I faced him, emphasizing each of my words. "I…am…fine. Not…tired…at…all!"

He favored me with one of his exasperating grins. "Okay. I guess it's safe to tell you."

If he didn't hurry and explain, I'd smack him. "What do you mean, safe?"

"Do you remember when the truck headed for the tree?"

"Oh, God. I do remember. The diary." My insides churned, and I looked at the floor where I'd thrown it.

"It's okay, honey. The book is at your apartment. I made sure you didn't have it when we left. I'd rather not discuss anything until we're off this dark highway. I don't want to take a chance of anything happening here."

I sucked in a breath and whispered, "How can you be sure?"

"Judging by the fact you're conscious and alert, I'd say we're safe. I want to pull into town first to be certain. Which exit should I take?"

I scanned the dark highway to get my bearings. "Okay. Take the exit after the bridge at the rotary. Why did you choose my sister's?"

"I'll explain everything when we stop. Is there a place nearby where we can talk before we get there?"

I gave him directions to a restaurant where he parked the car. I'm sure he noticed my bewilderment, because he held out his arms. "Come here, sweetheart."

I scooted up, and he maneuvered me across the console onto his lap. He held me so tight, it made me nervous. When I pulled back, he said, "I've been so worried about you."

I loved the comfort of his warm embrace, his spicy scent, but I was ready to explode if I didn't get a few answers. I rested against his chest for another minute. "Okay, what's the story? Why are we going to Kir's?"

He released me after a very thorough kiss. "You remember going to your apartment after I lost control of the truck?"

"Yes, I wanted to get rid of the book and get away from there to talk. I didn't dare say anything in case the entity attacked again."

"After we got back to your place, your eyes kept closing. I'm pretty sure there's nothing wrong with the gas or anything else in that place. Your exhaustion is part of the ghost, entity, or whatever's plan to keep you under control. He puts you in a kind of trance. A way to keep you compliant. The night at Heather's, when I couldn't get through to you, scared the shit out of me." He placed another kiss on my lips. "After you fell asleep tonight, I wanted to get you far away from him. I prayed he wouldn't attack the truck again. I guess he can't hurt you the way he did Serena. I'm lucky you were in the truck with me. I'm sure he considers me a rival and hates my guts. Anyway, I remembered you said your sister lived in Gloucester and hoped it would be far enough away. It must be, because you're wide awake, released from his influence."

I'd begun to shiver, and he tucked me back into his warmth. His voice shook. "I was afraid I might lose you."

Our roles had shifted—I'd become the comforter. "I'm okay. We're okay." I melted into him as our lips met again.

I wished we could stay like this forever, pretending Elias didn't exist, but he did, and we needed to get to Kirsten's. "I'd better call my sister to tell her to expect us."

He kissed me and unwrapped his arms. I hated to leave his warmth.

"I know Kirsten won't mind if we arrive unannounced," I said. "She's been dying to meet you. Her husband, Rick, is a great guy, and Izzy should be in bed by now. It'll be a good time to talk. I'll give her a heads up."

He trailed the back of his hand along my cheek. I cupped his fingers in mine and planted a kiss on his palm.

I dug out my phone and directed Siri to call Kirsten. When she answered, I said, "Hi, sis. How are you?"

"I'm fine. How's everything in Salem?"

"Um, well, I need a favor," I said.

The sound of Kir's voice was comforting. "Sure. Something wrong?"

That was an understatement I thought. "Would you mind if Sam and I came over?" I twisted in my seat. "Right now?"

"What do you mean right now?" She sounded a little nervous when she said, "Where are you?"

"About a mile away."

I pulled the phone away from my ear when she yelled, "What! Has Tom done something?"

"No, no," I said. "Nothing to do with Tom. This time I'm running away from a ghost."

Sam was hungry. We'd missed dinner. "Let's stop at a pizza place. I'll order a couple of large pies."

While he ordered the food, I called Kirsten to explain why we'd be later than anticipated.

"Oh, no. Don't be foolish. I can fix you both dinner," she said.

"Sam would never impose. You'll like him. He's the best." Then I whispered, "I think I'm in love."

"I'm sure I'll love him too." In a more serious tone, she added, "As long as he treats you right."

I chuckled. "No worries. Thanks for always being there for me. I love you."

"Oh, honey, I love you too. Hurry up and get here."

Inside the pizza parlor, I inhaled the delicious smells, and my stomach gurgled. I was hungry.

When we got back in the car, he caressed my cheek. "You think you're in love?"

Heat scorched my face. He'd heard me.

He rubbed his thumb across my lower lip. "I guess I am too." His kiss erased all my doubts. We'd survive this together.

We arrived at Kirsten's house laden with food. The door opened before we knocked, and my sister crushed me in a bone-breaking hug. She did the same to Sam—which wasn't easy with the pizza boxes. Rick, behind her, said, "Come in, come in. It's cold out there."

We followed her into the kitchen, where Sam unloaded the food. Rick brought out plates and napkins, then my sister began her interrogation. "What did you mean by a ghost?"

"Wait a minute. Let me have a bite and get my head together. This story will take a while." I dragged a piece of hot, gooey pizza onto a plate and satisfied my angry tummy with a huge bite. Rick poured me a beer.

I took a big swig and sat back to begin the tale. "You remember the night I hurt my toe?"

"Oh, Lord. You carried on about it forever."

"Cuz it hurt," I said.

"Okay, okay. Moving on?"

"That's when I found the diary." I took another bite of pizza and wiped sauce from my mouth. "You remember how nosy I am."

Kirsten smirked at Sam. "She's terrible."

"I tried to pry open the lock and managed to cut myself." I looked at the fading scar. "Anyway, the diary belonged to the man who built the original house, which is my bedroom."

Rick peered at me as if I had two heads. "Your bedroom is a house?"

"No. Yes."

Sam described the renovation around the original cottage, and I continued, explaining about the nightmares, strange noises, and the fact Heather insisted Elias haunted the apartment. With that last, I pivoted to Kirsten. "At the time, I thought she was being dramatic."

She nodded and spun her hand in a circular motion for me to go on.

"Heather came up with the idea to have a psychic party at her place. Then I'd bring the diary and ask the medium for help." Sam rolled his eyes. "That worked out well."

I gave him my version of a quelling look. At the same time, I caught sight of one of Izzy's toys on the counter. I swallowed and sat back. I had to tell them. "The worst part is…I'm sure the ghost pushed Izzy the day she fell at my place."

My sister clutched her chest. Rick planted both hands on the table and leaped out of his seat. A piece of dark blond hair fell across his forehead as he said, "You let her go into a haunted bedroom?"

I didn't blame him for his anger. I'd want to kill anyone who placed Izzy in peril. "No. If I had any inkling my apartment harbored a dangerous entity, I never would have let her in."

Kirsten came to my defense with a ferocious glare at her husband. "Dani would never have let Izzy play there with a ghost."

He looked down and scooped another slice of pizza. "Sorry."

When Sam explained what happened at the psychic party, I

interrupted, "I don't remember it all."

"Because you were in some kind of trance." He turned to Kirsten. "When she was out of it, she said, 'Don't let him get me.'"

My sister let out a shriek. "Why didn't you tell me this?"

"Because you'd react like you are now, and I didn't want to believe anything supernatural was at work." I shrugged. "Even when Serena told me the spirit wanted me, I attributed her words to the night's drama."

"You never told me she said that." Sam's voice vibrated with anger.

I patted his hand. "At the time, I was too confused. Let me finish."

I described my fatigue, Serena's accident, and her belief the entity pushed her foot on the gas pedal.

Kirsten clasped my hands. "You're scaring me."

I went on to tell them what happened at my apartment and in the truck today.

After Sam filled in the fuzzy parts, he said, "I don't want her to go back to that apartment. I needed to find some place far enough away where the entity couldn't get to her." With a wry smile, he tilted his head. "Here we are."

Kirsten crushed me in an awkward bear hug, and Rick went for the whiskey.

Sam lifted his hands in a gesture of defeat and shrugged. "I'm out of options."

My sister took over. In a no-nonsense voice, she said, "You will both stay here tonight. I don't want either of you near that place."

When Sam and I spoke at the same time to say we had to get back, he glared at me. "You're staying. I'm the one who's leaving."

"What about Heather? It's dangerous for her to be there."

"We'll call her and tell her to leave."

Before I had time for an angry retort, Kirsten used her reasonable, if cajoling, voice. "Dani, you don't have to go back there. Stay here for a few days. Call work. Say you've got the flu or a migraine. It'll be fine. Or I'll call them and say I have to take care of you."

The look on my face must have been pathetic.

"What's the matter?" she asked. "Everyone gets the flu."

"You don't have to call anyone." I sucked in a breath. "I don't have a job anymore."

Sam put his arm around me. "You hated working for that jerk. This is your chance to start over."

When my sister asked for the gory details, I said, "Can I tell you later?"

She took pity on me and agreed.

Sam explained why he had to leave. "I have to get back to round up the inventory I need to keep my business viable."

Kirsten wasn't deterred. "You'll have to go to work tomorrow in the same clothes. You can't drive back tonight. I'm not up on all the habits of ghosts, but I'm positive they're more powerful at night, and he's already attacked you once today."

Oh, Lord. She was right. I reached out to Sam. "You can't go back until we're sure you'll be safe. He tried to get you earlier and might try again. I couldn't stand it if anything happened to you."

He stroked my face. "I love how much you care. Without the book in the car, I'll be okay. Besides, if he was able to hurt me, wouldn't he have done so when I drove you here?"

"What if Kir's right and he's stronger in the dark?"

He gave me a tight hug. "Okay, what if I stay tonight and leave in the morning like Kirsten suggested? I'll call Bob, tell him I'll be late. Then we can have breakfast together, and maybe our heads will be clear enough to find a better game plan."

"Good," Rick said. "Now let's drink."

~ * ~

I woke up to the sound of Sam's comforting voice as he spoke on the phone.

"Okay, Bob. I appreciate your help. Right. Talk to you later."

When he finished, he kissed me until I was breathless. I could get used to waking up to him every morning.

"Bob said he'd take care of the pick-ups today. That means I'm all yours until this afternoon."

"Words to warm a woman's heart." I gave him an amorous hug. "Oh, no. Breakfast will be ready in a few minutes. I've got to go finish explaining to Isobel who I am. Come out and help me."

His interest in Izzy delighted me. My niece was my favorite person in the world and the smartest six-year-old I'd ever met. I might be prejudiced since her blue eyes sparkle every time I come into the room.

Izzy sat at the table swinging her feet, tapping her fingers, and humming to herself. Her pink cast was filled with names and funny pictures. A rush of love surged through me. How could someone, even a dead someone, hurt such a sweet innocent? My heart ached that it happened in my home.

She turned around and yelled, "Auntie Dani!" jumped off the chair and threw her body into me.

"Oof! You're pretty strong for a girl." I hugged her. "You're the cutest lovebug in the world."

"I'm not a bug, Auntie Dani."

I laughed and tweaked her nose.

"I like Sam," she said. "He's fun to play with." She shook her blonde curls like a golden spaniel shaking off water. "Not like Tom."

Sam grinned. "Izzy's mom said we could make the pancakes. Want to help?"

I placed my hands on my hips and pursed my lips. "You bet I do. I don't trust you two."

Izzy giggled.

What a relief to stand in the kitchen and act silly with people I loved. For these few moments, the ghost didn't exist. Sam put a dab of pancake batter on my nose and asked Izzy if I looked cute. She screeched with laughter and put a dab on his nose. Of course he had to add a dab to Izzy's. When Kirsten came in, we were all laughing.

After breakfast, Rick drove Izzy to his mother's house, which gave Kirsten, Sam, and me time to plan. Rick took the day off from work and Kirsten switched office hours with one of her co-workers. I was grateful for his and my sister's help but didn't hold out much hope that we could solve the problem of Elias at this point.

We sat at the table while Kirsten poured the coffee. "I've been analyzing the problem, and I have a solution."

I jerked my head up. "You do? Great. What is it?"

"You should talk to one of those Catholic exorcists."

I slumped in my seat. "Oh, come on, that's the movies, not real life. Besides, their job is to get rid of demons who've taken over a human. No one is possessed here. They can't perform those rites on a book."

Sam chimed in. "Wait a minute. Maybe a priest might be able to steer us to the right individual for this type of situation. We might as well ask."

I didn't put much faith in the plan. Right now, though, the church was all we had. "Are either of you acquainted with a priest?"

From the disheartened frowns on their faces, the answer was no. Kirsten was undeterred. "There's a Catholic church downtown. Why don't we go there and ask?"

"What about the Boston Archdiocese?" Sam said. "They must field questions like this all the time."

Kirsten wanted to go to try the church in town first. I volunteered to go online and research paranormal events. In the meantime, I checked my phone for messages. There was one from

Heather asking me to call her ASAP.

I was ready to hit the "call back" button when I remembered Serena. She'd been afraid to speak to me because of the ghost's influence. I didn't want to take the chance Elias might get to my friend through me, so I asked my sister to call her.

Sam checked his watch. "I've got to get back to Salem."

"No," I said. "You told me Bob was all set until this afternoon. You don't have to go to work for hours."

He'd already decided. "I'll be fine. Without the damn book, he can't get to me. You, on the other hand, may be susceptible. You have to stay here."

"Did you forget Serena? She didn't have the book."

"Serena's a medium," he said. "Elias can get to her through her psychic powers. Although, I'm sure his power would have the same geographical limit we discovered."

"What if you're wrong?"

"I'm not."

I flounced into the bedroom but didn't want to miss any of the conversation, so I listened by the door. Kirsten asked him when he was leaving.

He sighed. "I guess I'll wait till this afternoon."

"Call us right away when you're safe."

"I'll call your number. It's too dangerous to contact Dani."

He didn't even plan to talk to me? I wanted to throw something until I remembered Serena and her worry about the phone connection. It would be foolish for us to ignore her theory. I swallowed my aggravation and decided to make the bed.

"Hey. Need any help?" Sam said, peering in.

I stopped what I was doing and turned to him. "Do you have to go this afternoon?"

He twirled me around, his face serious. "Listen to me. I have to go to work. If I wait an extra day, I'll get behind. Without you or the diary in my truck, there's no reason for Elias to bother me."

I knew he was right, but I wasn't happy.

He gave me a little shake. "I won't let anything happen to you. Do you understand? I care too much about you. Now stop pouting and give me a kiss."

Such an aggravating man, but when he brought his mouth so close to mine, I forgot my irritation. I couldn't help myself. I stood on my tiptoes and ran my tongue across his lips. He drew me in tight against him and crushed my mouth to his.

Chapter Twenty-Six

Kirsten, who had no luck contacting Heather, left her a message. Then she and Rick headed out to find a priest who could give them information on how to deal with ghosts and demons. I proceeded to the study to see what I could find on the Internet. Sam accompanied me.

"Oh, my God," I said. "Listen to this."

"Some outward manifestations of demonic activity: objects might disappear and be found in another location or seemingly move around by themselves; scratching sounds might be heard; dark shadows might be seen; animals might become spooked or growl at something they can sense, but you can't see; you might have a feeling of being watched or hear voices; and lights might go off or not come on when turned on. Finally, there might be apparent retaliation after an attempt to stop the activity."

He leaned over my shoulder to read with me. My voice came out in a whisper as I said, "That's what happened after we said we wanted to get rid of the book. Elias must have been threatened."

Sam raked his hands through his hair and paced. "I accepted there was a ghost. I didn't recognize the escalation until you explained the events to your sister. My rational mind rebels at the insanity. It's like being in a Stephen King novel."

I sat back and checked the time. "I'm worried about Heather."

"I'll go into the other room and try her," he said.

For the short time he was gone, I missed him.

"Heather's fine. I got her at work. There haven't been any problems. She can't wait to move and plans to investigate the new apartment on her way home. She said you can stay with her once she finds a new place." He planted a kiss on my head. "I told her you were taken."

When he sat down, I swung my chair around. "I wonder how Kir and Rick are doing at the church. I wish they'd call."

"A couple of hours isn't time enough to overcome the hurdles the church will be throwing at them." He gave me a quick kiss. "What do you say we take a break? My brain needs a breather."

"Sounds good to me." In the kitchen over coffee, I worried about his decision to drive back and gave voice to my concerns.

Sam gave me a crooked grin. "Bob doesn't understand why I'm not coming back until tonight. He thinks I'm acting like a lunatic, and that you've bewitched me." Sam chuckled and ruffled my hair. "I guess he's right."

"Quit it." I smoothed my hair. He was always messing with it. "Seriously, just the fact that I've been with you, in your truck, might give him access to you."

He leaned in and trailed his fingers across my cheek. "The ghost isn't that powerful. I'll be fine." He kissed my palm. "We'll get through this together."

~ * ~

When Kirsten and Rick arrived a while later, their expressions weren't hopeful.

"Well? What happened? Did you get any answers?" I asked.

Kirsten threw herself into the chair and heaved a big sigh. "I was certain we were getting the runaround at first, but it turns out there aren't too many requests for this kind of trouble nowadays. The priest we spoke to made a few calls to people who contacted others, etc. After a while, he got the name of a priest in Boston who might have some answers for us. He wasn't available at the time, so Father Drinker..." She giggled. "What if he really is a drinker?"

"What did Father Drinker"—more peals of laughter—"say?"

With a snicker, she pulled herself together. "He gave us Brother Manelli's address and phone number. We can try him later."

Frustration ate at me. I hoped we could contact the priest before Sam left. Rick headed for the liquor cabinet. I didn't blame my brother-in-law. If I could get drunk enough to forget all this, I'd have put a dent in his supply.

Kirsten heated the soup she'd prepared yesterday and made grilled cheese sandwiches. My stomach gurgled and my salivary glands worked overtime. I passed on the sandwiches in lieu of French bread slathered with butter. When I tucked into her hearty creation, I was in heaven. After lunch, Rick tried Brother Manelli's number again. This time he answered.

Rick gave the brother a brief outline of the situation and listened for a minute before he put his hand over the phone. "He says he can talk to you next week."

"We need to see him now," Sam said.

Rick asked if he could fit us in us sooner. "Wait a minute, Brother Manelli, let me put Dani's boyfriend on. He can give you more details."

Sam took the phone. "Hi, Brother Manelli. Sam Gregory here. I need to emphasize the danger. I brought Dani here from Salem for her safety. The entity has control over her when she's in her apartment with the diary."

I listened to Sam's side of the conversation. "Yes, the book. We presume it's haunted… Right… That might not be wise… Yes, the book has been in the hands of a psychic who encountered the presence of a powerful entity. The woman wanted no part of it and refuses to speak to us for fear of retribution. She claims she was in a serious accident caused by the entity… Okay, that would be great. Thanks."

Sam shook his head. "He can't make it here, but if we want to go to Boston tomorrow, he has an 8:00 AM time slot open. He needs to talk to Dani." He put his arms around me. "I wish I didn't have to leave you now. Maybe I don't. It depends on what happens with the job."

"What did he say about the ghost?" Rick asked.

"He didn't want to speculate until he talked to Dani. I gathered he didn't like the sound of what I told him."

For the rest of the day, we hung around and waited for Bob. He called after three to say he didn't need Sam for the next day's job. I was so relieved. Sam could stay without hurting his business.

"I need more food," Kirsten said. "Come on, Rick. Come to the store with me."

"While you two shop, Sam and I will get busy doing more research."

My sister sent a pointed look in my direction. "We'll be gone at least two hours."

I grinned, understanding her code and wink. Plenty of time for Sam and me to "rest."

The minute the front door closed, Sam and I were in the bedroom. My body craved his touch. I needed to be held, to become one with the man I loved. The future was so uncertain. Our sweet, desperate entanglement left me breathless and terrified.

I trailed my fingers across his chest. "I don't want to lose you."

When he whispered, "I love you," I planted kisses all over his face. In between each one, I pledged my love.

If I had my way, we'd lay there and savor what we'd experienced, but we didn't have time. Laughing, he led me from the bed to the shower. Well, we did have time for that.

Chapter Twenty-Seven

When Kirsten, Rick, and Isobel came home, we were in the den.

Isobel ran in, yelling, "Auntie Dani?" Sam laughed. "What about me?"

Izzy held on to my hand and peered through her thick lashes at him, her earlier bravado gone. "Hi, Sam."

Kirsten took over. "Come on, Izzy. Let's go into the kitchen. I'll get your dinner."

Later on, Sam and I went to help her with supper while Rick got Izzy ready for bed. I worked on the salad. Sam hunted for the plates and silverware. We discussed neutral topics—Sam's business and my sister's part-time job in a real estate office.

"Wait a minute," Kirsten said, "What did your friend, the owner of the apartment, say about the ghost?"

"Eddie? When I brought up the subject, he got upset. Said he didn't need rumors about hauntings on his property. 'There was nothing wrong with my apartment, and there was no such thing as ghosts.'"

"He's right about gossip regarding homes. Paranormal activity isn't a great draw in real estate. Sounds like he's one of those people who refuses to believe in anything supernatural."

"I feel sorry for him. If we can't get rid of the ghost, I don't see how he'll be able to rent the apartment."

"It's not as if this doesn't happen in homes," Kirsten said. "I mean not like this. You'd be amazed at the number of houses reported to have strange occurrences." She lifted a shoulder. "While we were out, I called a friend who has been in the real estate business for years. She said for the most part, any spirit activity is benign, but every now and then you come upon something else that lingers in a house. Those properties have a high turnover rate. The problem isn't that people see a manifestation, it's that they sense the adverse vibes. The negative atmosphere wears on the occupants, making them uncomfortable enough to leave."

"What about my place, the Gale house?"

She shook her head. "I asked, but Salem isn't on her radar, too far from Gloucester."

Izzy came in to say goodnight to everyone. I kissed her, gave her a big hug, and grinned as she skipped toward her room. I peeked at Sam and wondered what a child of ours would look like. When he caught my gaze, heat rushed to my cheeks.

While we sat around the dining room table eating dinner, Sam and Rick, big tough men, were deep in conversation debating possible solutions. They decided they'd run into the apartment, grab the diary, and burn it. Rick expounded on the theory. "We should perform an exorcism on the whole house afterward."

Kirsten shot down their ideas. Her face crinkled with worry. "What about the force that attacked you in the truck, Sam? Even strong guys like you two aren't any match against supernatural strength."

No matter how many times I ran the problem though my head, I couldn't figure out any options. Nothing but obstacles leaped out, one in particular.

"If you try to attack his journal, the demon will come after you," I said. "What then?" My voice became shrill. "Are you going to avoid Salem for the rest of your life?"

Instead of answering me, he turned to Kirsten. "This chicken is delicious. What did you put in it?"

When she ticked off a list of ingredients. I slapped my hands on the table, garnering everyone's attention. "This conversation is ludicrous. On the heels of discussing a dangerous demon, we're chatting about chicken recipes?"

My rant put a damper on the dinner conversation.

Sam threw his napkin onto the table. "It's so aggravating to have to sit here and do nothing."

He strode into the den, his forehead wrinkled in a frown. I ached to comfort him, but there were no words to brighten our situation. I left him alone.

I didn't sleep well that night. I was nervous about the next day. What if the priest or brother, whatever, couldn't help?

Sam didn't sleep much better. Around three in the morning, both awake, we talked. Worst-case scenario, I'd never be able to go anywhere near Salem again. I hugged myself against the ache of the perceived loss. *I love it there.*

His fingers caressed my cheek. "Why are you crying, honey?"

I leaned in, my arms around his chest. I sniffled a couple of times, then told him my qualms. "I'll never be able to see you again." Then I cried in earnest.

He brushed the hair from my forehead, and kissed my eyes, nose, and lips. "Not a problem, sweetheart. If you leave, I'll be right there beside you."

"B-but you love your hometown. Your parents and your brother live there. All your friends are there."

"Shush. I love you. We'll find another nice place to live. Our relatives can come visit. No way will I lose you."

I gave myself up to his embrace and prayed I could be with him forever.

The next morning, I didn't want to get up. I was exhausted. Opening my eyes required exerted effort.

He took both my hands. "Come on sleepyhead," he cooed. "Breakfast is ready."

I let myself fall back, hoping to stay in bed a little longer. A minute later he was in my face and shaking me. "Wake up!"

His harsh tone snapped me awake. Panic engulfed me. He sounded like Tom. "Stop. I'll get up."

When Sam recognized my fear, he enfolded me in his arms and held me tight. "I'm sorry, sweetheart. I didn't mean to scare you. I thought you were in another trance. You're okay?"

I let out a relieved breath. "Yes, I'm fine, but tired. I didn't get much sleep last night." I smirked. "You didn't help."

There was a twinkle in his eyes and the corners of his mouth twitched. "I don't remember you complaining."

Chapter Twenty-Eight

Kirsten wasn't working with any clients right now, so she was able to drive me and Sam to Boston. I wasn't about to meet Brother Manelli alone, so the three of us followed him into his office, a large clean space with a desk, file cabinets, and four padded chairs. A small table by the window held an unexpected bamboo plant. The man wasn't the older type of cleric I anticipated. Young, late thirties. A good six feet with sandy hair and a welcoming smile. From his physique, I'd say he made time for the gym.

Kirsten was the first to speak. "We're so grateful to you Brother Manelli for taking the time to see us."

"Please don't thank me, Mrs. Morrison; I'm here to listen. I'm not certain I can help. First, though, I have to hear the whole story." He reached across his desk, secured my hand in both of his and gave it a compassionate squeeze.

His smile reassured me. "Can you tell me everything, from the moment the problems began?"

I hated to reveal my personal relationships in front of a priest/brother, but I was desperate. My cheeks heated up, but I managed to squeak out a smile. "The whole thing started with a bad relationship." I filled him in on what I remembered, and Sam provided the rest.

Brother Manelli was interested in Heather's photographs. When I mentioned my dreams, he wanted more detail. I didn't mind revealing the scary parts. The erotic elements were another matter. My voice faded to a whisper, but Sam frowned. I'd forgotten he had excellent hearing. I hadn't mentioned the sensual aspects to him.

When Sam referred to the new writing, Brother Manelli stopped him. "Could Dani have written it?"

"Me?" I yipped.

"I can't imagine how," Sam said. "Those words mimicked the penmanship of the diary in every respect."

He nodded for me to continue. When I finished, Brother Manelli asked me to go over certain parts again. The name of the entity? I almost wished we didn't have it, but I relayed Mary's horrible story, then explained how the book opened to a certain page, the one with Rebecca's name on it. I told him those pages were difficult to read because of the bloodstain.

He signaled me to stop. "Your blood?"

"I cut myself, and a few drops fell on the diary. Unfortunately, they seeped into a couple of pages."

"That isn't good," he said, shaking his head.

A ball of dread formed in my gut. I looked at Sam and Kirsten before whispering, "Why?"

"The demon has drunk your blood. Before that, he haunted the apartment. After he tasted your blood, he wanted you. From what you told me, he made every effort to consummate his lust while you slept."

"Oh, dear God." The ghost's obsession made sense now. "He thinks I'm Rebecca."

"Perhaps he believes Rebecca can come back through you. I wish he didn't have your blood."

I hugged myself and wished he didn't either.

"You need to destroy his diary," he said.

"What else could happen?" The second the words were out of my mouth, I gave myself a mental kick. Way to tempt fate.

Sure enough, Brother Manelli wasn't finished. His steady gaze captured mine. "I'm concerned about the additional entry in the book. I don't believe you did it in a trance. Nor do I believe the demon could have written it himself without human intervention." He included everyone in the room when he said, "I hope I'm wrong." He wrinkled his brow and heaved a deep sigh. "I'm afraid the demon might already have possessed someone."

That did it. I promised myself I would never go back to my apartment again.

Before we left, Brother Manelli placed his fingers on my forehead and gave me his blessing. When he was finished, he smiled. "There is some good news. I find no sign of evil within you." Once again, he urged me to destroy the book.

After we were settled in Kirsten's car, Sam lit into me. "Why didn't you tell me about his nighttime assaults?"

His accusatory tone hurt. I protested my innocence. "I was sure they were about you." Heat seared my face as I peeked at my sister.

Kirsten interrupted the uncomfortable discussion. "Never mind the dreams; we have to find a way to destroy the book."

"I'm ready to do whatever is necessary to end this horror," I said.

We drove a short way before Sam spoke. "Maybe we should test the limit of his power. I'll bet he can't control you when you haven't been near the book. The diary, with your blood, is the catalyst for his influence over you."

"Okay," I said. "We need to head back to Salem."

"Wait a minute. I'll figure a way to get the damn book."

My breath hitched. I smacked him and cried, "The ghost is too powerful. He'll kill you." In a more even tone, I continued, "He'll let me handle the diary, so I'll grab it and transfer it to you."

"I don't like that idea, but," he rubbed his face, "what other choice do we have?" Defeat echoed in his voice. "We'll have to estimate how close you can get to Salem before he senses you."

"Wait a minute!" Kirsten yelled, almost swerving off the road. "I won't let you deliver her into that bastard's clutches."

"Of course not," he said. "I want to determine if he can reach her without the diary. If I sense she's in trouble, I'll bring her right back."

She scowled at me. "You're staying here."

Sam mumbled something about no alternative, and I gulped down a panicky scream. We were out of options. After a tense ride to Kirsten's in which she demanded I stay, then pleaded with me, she gave up. Sniffing back tears, she crushed me in a goodbye hug.

Sam and I drove toward Salem. For the next ten minutes, music covered the uncomfortable silence in the car. Unable to subdue my anxiety, I posed the question we both seemed to be avoiding. "What will we do when we get to the apartment?" We still hadn't devised a plan.

"Whatever we decide, you do not go in there."

We argued my part in the scheme. He wanted to retrieve the diary and set it on fire. I reminded him what had happened in the truck until I'd picked up the book.

"You're not going to have anything to do with that thing."

My phone interrupted our discussion. The ID read *Peter Gallagher*. "Who's Peter… Oh, Heather's Peter. Why would he call me?" I accepted the call. "Hi, Peter."

"Oh, thank God. Have you seen Heather?"

"No, not since yesterday. Why?"

"Could you go to her apartment and see if she's okay? She didn't come into work today, and she's not answering her phone. That's not like her."

"Peter, I'm not home. Are you sure she didn't call anyone at work?"

"Positive. I checked. I'm concerned."

Heather was the friend who'd been there for me through this whole horrid affair. I couldn't abandon her now. Since we were headed home anyway, I'd look in on her, while making sure to stay away from my apartment.

"Okay, Peter, I'll do what I can. I'll get back to you." I told Sam what Peter said. "I've got to find out what's wrong."

"Damn it." Sam slammed his hand against the steering wheel. "It's dangerous for you to be near that building, let alone inside."

When I pursed my lips and glared, he gave in, but said, "I bet Heather took a mental health day and decided to ignore the phone."

"No. She'd never jeopardize her job." With a twitch of my lips, I added, "And she'd never ignore a call from Peter."

"Maybe they had a fight?"

"Doesn't matter. She'd have called into work. No. Something's wrong. I have to find out."

I paused to consider the safety of Heather's apartment. There was the break-in. According to Heather, the items taken were supposed photos of the entity. Then the awful night with Serena. Elias was able to reach out to Heather's apartment.

A tightening coil squeezed my chest. *Dear Lord, please let Heather be all right. Please don't let that beast have hurt her.*

~ * ~

We were about ten miles outside of Salem. My pulse raced, and I couldn't suppress a shiver.

"Are you okay?" Sam asked. "Just nervous."

Five miles later, when he checked again, I wondered if my hyper-vigilance was masking my lassitude. I swallowed and looked at him. "I-I'm okay."

Before we hit Salem's city limits, he pulled over. "Are you tired yet?"

"No. I'm shaky, but wide awake."

"Tell me the second you get tired." "Trust me—you'll get the message."

Ten minutes later, he whispered, "It's the next street. How are you doing?"

"Fine."

We turned onto Cove Street.

The strain of waiting for an attack left my nerves raw, but no fatigue, not even a yawn. The house loomed close. I clutched my necklace and sent up another prayer for Heather.

We crawled along until we found a place to park. Someone yelled my name. What the heck? Goosebumps sprouted along my neck and arms. We both spun to see Mrs. W wave at us.

We got out of the truck, and she screeched, "Wait! It's not safe."

Her words slammed into me. I stared in alarm as she launched herself off the porch and came toward us with a rolling gait. The problem must be serious to draw her off her perch. Sam and I met her halfway.

"What's wrong?" I struggled to contain my mounting fear. "What's happened?"

She bent over in an effort to catch her breath, and Sam held her arm to steady her. "That man," she gasped. "Your boyfriend. The one who chased you. He's in there."

"Son of a bitch," Sam growled.

Mrs. W was right. Tom's black Buick was parked across the street. I'd forgotten to scout for trouble. Oh, God. He hated Heather. "We've got to hurry."

Sam told Mrs. W to call the police, and I broke into a run. We'd decided the front door would be the safest; that way, we wouldn't have to pass my apartment.

I tried the knob. Locked. I banged on Heather's door. No answer. JoJo barked. I knocked once more and yelled, "Heather. It's Dani. Open the door." The lone answer was the dog's frantic barking and the sound of his claws as they scraped against the door. I used soft words to calm him without success.

Sam tugged my arm. "Come on. No one's home."

"Something's wrong. We have to try the back door. If we can't get in, I'll call Eddie."

We were at the sidewalk by then. Sam wanted me to stay there. "I'll go in and try the back door. You stay here with Mrs. Wallace."

She'd followed us with her cellphone. "I just called the police."

"I'm not staying here," I said. "I need to check on her. I'm going in."

He clenched his jaw, and Mrs. W insisted I'd be safer staying with her. I stood firm. The last place on earth I wanted to be was in this building, but I owed my friend who'd stuck by me even after her disastrous party. We passed by her windows, but they were too high to see in.

At the bottom of the stairs leading to the back hall, I stopped. My whole body trembled. I flashed back to the night we found Tom there. Sam took the stairs two at a time and cracked the door open. I held on to the railing for support.

Before we entered, he gave it one more try. "Let me do this by myself. You stay outside."

I shook my head.

The corridor was empty. When we passed my apartment, my legs went weak, and I tripped. Without Sam's arm around me, I'd have fallen. He tried, once again, to send me outside. I refused and told him to hurry. When JoJo barked, goosebumps covered my arms. The sound was too loud. I discovered why when we rounded the corner.

Heather's door was ajar. I pushed it open and hurried through the kitchen into the living room, calling the dog's name. I found him next to a chair. He faced us. Back legs apart, front legs forward, and tail up straight, he growled a warning.

"What's the matter, boy? Come on, JoJo. It's Dani." He recognized my voice, but he stood his ground. All of a sudden, the reason was obvious. He was guarding his mistress. "Oh my God. Heather's on the floor behind the dog."

When Sam rushed over to her, JoJo, teeth flashing, lunged. While Sam veered to avoid a dog bite, I froze, my mind in chaos. Like snapshots from a horror show, flashes of my dream came back to me—blood, Heather's blonde hair, and a skeleton.

Sam's voice tore me back to the present. "It must have been that bastard."

"Who?"

"Tom."

"Why would he… The backyard. Tom looked ready to kill Heather when she'd told him to leave. The evidence was there. In my heart, I hadn't believed it. He was cruel, but a murderer? I should have warned her, insisted she leave. *It's my fault she was—*

"She's alive. Call 911." His words broke my inertia, and I rushed to her side while he backed away from JoJo. "Never mind. I'll call. Take care of the dog."

I knelt and crooned JoJo's name. The pup relented, and his growls eased into a whine.

My friend was in bad shape. The blood congealed in her hair, and her pale face terrified me. I ran my hands along the dog's back to calm him. In between scared little yips, he licked Heather's face. I leaned back on my heels to catch my breath. Then JoJo resumed his growls.

Behind me, Sam's voice. "What are you…" The sentence was cut off by a heavy thud.

I twisted around and screamed. He lay crumpled on the floor. "Sam!"

JoJo's grumbles became angry barks as I crawled to Sam's body.

There was blood in his hair. Please let him be alive. I touched his neck and found a pulse. I grasped his cell to call for an ambulance when I noticed a pair of jean-clad legs by the door.

Oh, no. He was still here. I couldn't believe Tom hurt Heather and Sam because I left him. I looked up, prepared to defend myself.

"Oh, thank God." Not Tom. "We need help. Sam's hurt, and Heather's in bad shape."

"Don't worry. I'll take care of everything."

Chapter Twenty-Nine

I exhaled in relief as Eddie helped me to my feet. He was a good friend. When he took my hand and pulled me out of the living room, I stopped. "Wait a minute. We have to help Sam and Heather."

"We have other work to do first."

"But..."

That's when I noticed the club in his fist. Blood dripped from it. I stopped speaking. He squeezed my arm so hard I cried out. He didn't pause but continued to drag me through the kitchen and into the hall.

I tried to reason with him. "Heather needs attention."

We kept going.

"She might die!" I screamed.

He grinned. "Wouldn't be the first."

As he unlocked my door, a numbing cold seized me, and I went limp. He jerked me up and threw me into the kitchen, where I fell over a large mound on the floor.

I struggled to get to my knees, to see what tripped me. A strangled scream tore from my lips. He grabbed my face. "Keep quiet or wear tape across that pretty mouth."

I gazed into dark, expressionless eyes that had once belonged to a friend.

He tipped his head, smiled, and said in an affable voice, "Quiet?" I nodded.

When he let me go, I slumped back to the floor. I squeezed my eyes shut and dragged myself away from the sightless stare of Tom's bloody face.

Nausea threatened. I covered my mouth with trembling hands. "What? No gratitude?" he said. "I did you a favor. He'd never have left you alone."

"You killed him?"

"Oh, for crying out loud, you can be so dense." He paused,

squatted to peer into my face, and caressed my cheek. In a gruesome whisper he said, "I killed them all." He poked Tom's body. "Too bad about him, though. He made the perfect patsy for Allison and the fire."

"Why, Eddie?"

His eyes blazed as he stood and slammed his foot into the corpse beside us. Ready to hurl, I looked away.

"You all tease and taunt until someone better comes along."

The normalcy of his voice, like the old Eddie discussing everyday work problems, made the situation even more terrifying. That's when I got it. This guy was crazy. There was no Eddie. He was a character in a play written by a madman.

I noticed dirt all over the floor, like the muck from the horrible room downstairs. "Were you in the cellar?"

He gave me a look as if I was brainless. "That's where I store my tools." He ignored me and fooled around with something on the kitchen counter. When he turned around, he wore a manic grin. He raised his hand to show me.

I choked. It looked like an enormous hunting knife.

He had a sick smile on his face. "I'd planned to go back and play with Heather. Then you and your boyfriend showed up." Twisting the knife in the air, he chuckled. "I guess you'll have to do."

Fire erupted in my gut. I almost wet myself. I should run, defend myself, scream. Instead, I sat on the floor of my bright little kitchen, all but paralyzed. I stared at the jagged blade and pictured what he'd do to my body. He talked about *playing* with Heather.

Tremors rolled through me. At that moment, I realized my death would be slow and painful. It broke my heart that, a little more than a month ago, this man, my friend, smiled and laughed as he'd shown me this apartment, even helped on the back stairs. What happened to that man?

This psychopath brandishing a knife was a stranger. When he put the weapon down, I puffed out a relieved breath. Maybe there was still hope. "Eddie…" That dream crashed when he spun around.

Nothing could save me now. Insanity glittered in his eyes, as he brandished duct tape and rope.

Out of time. Cold spikes clawed into my neck. Now! I had to save myself. I bunched up my muscles ready to push off and run. He stopped and looked toward the bedroom. My nose detected the acrid smell before the cold descended. Oh, God help me. Elias. I held my breath. Serial killer or ghost?

His essence swirled around us. Eddie paused. Did he sense him? I shivered. "Aren't you afraid of the ghost?"

He threw back his head and laughed. "You crack me up. Elias is the reason you're still alive. I would've killed you earlier, sent you off with the other ungrateful sluts." He kicked Tom's body again. "This jerk would have been blamed. But he wanted you."

I rubbed my hands along my arms as tobacco raked my nostrils. Eddie stilled. Moments later he reached for me. I screamed and drew back.

"No, no, do not fear. I shall not hurt you."

The voice. Not Eddie's. I recognized it, though. My dream visitor. The eyes also changed. They were almost black, and his hair had darkened. "My dear, he would have killed you had I not interfered."

He helped me to my feet. "Come."

I'd fallen into a nightmare world. I jerked away from him. What if Eddie returned to his body? Hard to believe I was more terrified of Eddie than Elias.

Elias, Eddie—or whoever—squeezed my hand then yanked me after him into the bedroom. My rug was tossed to the side. A large chalk star covered the floor. Oh, no. A pentagram.

With each new perception, my mind tilted. Murderer or specter from the past, or both. My abductor pushed me inside the chalk star. He removed candles and a well-worn book from the box he'd retrieved in the kitchen. "We have to hurry. That fool has left bodies everywhere."

"Eddie, please, stop this."

He touched my face. "My love, that man is gone. I've come back."

I backed away. He grabbed me. "Don't pretend you don't recognize me. You were willing enough to share your love when we lay together in your bed."

"No!" It made me sick that the man in my dreams had been Elias, not Sam. Shame coursed through me. I squirmed away from Elias's touch on my chin.

He scowled, then snatched me back and grabbed my face. He squeezed so hard, tears slipped out. "Be still or suffer the consequences."

A knife flashed in his hand. He held it to my throat. The sharp point pricked my neck. I did wet myself a little then. I waited for death. He lowered his head, as warmth dripped to my shoulder. His tongue laved my skin. I gagged.

"Aah," he said in a gruff, almost guttural voice. "This tastes far better than the drops you shed on my journal."

"What do you want from me?"

He roared in my face, "Sit."

No problem. My legs gave out, and I crashed to the floor. I was so terrified, I had trouble swallowing. A few minutes later, my mind began to work again. He'd mentioned the book. "What if I hadn't found your diary?"

He paused for a moment. A self-satisfied smile played on his lips then he said, "I made sure you would. He was supposed to unearth the tome and leave it by your bed. You came home too soon." He leaned in and ran his hand down my back. His touch made me sick.

"A very pretty sight you were flying naked through the air." His smile faded, and he quirked an eyebrow. "I do have to thank you for releasing me. Without the blood and the witch, I might still be in hell."

Oh my God. He meant Serena. I was so stupid. I'd done exactly what he'd wanted.

He placed the candles around the floor, then pointed to the old lantern, my sister's gift. "Bring it to me."

When I gave it to him, a loud bang on the door startled us. Sam called my name. He was okay.

"Sam." I lunged for the door. Elias stopped me. When he shoved me back into the circle, I tripped over the lantern and spilled oil on the floor. The scent of kerosene burned my nostrils.

Elias didn't seem to care. His voice softened. "Rebecca."

Was she there? I peered around, but he was looking at me. I wanted to roar out my identity, "I'm Dani!" but didn't dare. He bestowed a satisfied smile on me, then focused his attention back to the old, leather book.

While he was distracted, I worked up my courage to escape. This might be my last chance. I'd gotten to my knees. I leaned on the floor, ready to push off. I got no farther. He pointed at me and chanted. I held my hands in front of my face. Too late. My head spun. I slumped backward and closed my eyes.

When I opened them, my fear was gone. The circle held no more terror for me. I found the cadence of the incantations comforting—the familiar timbre of his voice, a balm for my senses. I gaped around me in confusion. Not my Elias. Though his eyes and tone were the same, he was younger. There was no scar, although, if I squinted, a faint outline of the face of my lover peeked through.

The room was familiar yet different. The hearth was the same as were the boards under my feet. Ah. The pentagram and his book of spells. He promised to teach me to use the magic for myself. My neighbors already called me a witch. I might as well make it true.

He intended to induct me into the coven at the next full moon. I must be ready. Why is there no fire in the fireplace? How will he light the candles? Oh, but I forget. My Elias has no need of outside fire. "Rebecca, come." He lifted his arms.

I rushed into his embrace.

"When I complete this, we will be together for all time. No one will ever tear us apart. Are you ready?"

"Oh, yes, my love. Proceed." I sat in the circle.

I welcomed the spell, but loud thuds in the background punctured the rhythm of his voice and made me nervous. I ignored the noise. Elias would keep me safe. A tremendous crash frightened me. A gust of wind attacked the candles, extinguishing them. He set them alight again and continued to read.

A soft, feathery sensation filled my soul. All would be well. I'd spend the rest of my life with my love.

From the corner of my eye, I sensed movement. Another joined us. The man paid no heed to Elias. He ran over and grabbed hold of me. I wrenched away and lashed out. "Leave me be. Elias, help me."

When the man let me go, I relaxed until Elias grunted in pain. I rushed to help him with the attacker, but he roared at me, "Stay in the circle!"

"Yes, my love."

When the man came at me again. I fought to stay put. I scratched and bit our enemy. I was no match for the large man with the strange-colored eyes. He yanked me from the safety of the circle.

I yelled, "No. Elias, help me."

The crazed intruder screamed at me. "Dani!"

Then the smell. Fire! Devil tongues raced across the oil-soaked floor, talons of flame seeking fuel—bedclothes, books. The sound of its greedy appetite all too familiar. Fiery tentacles streaked toward the wall. Fumes invaded my nose and caught in my throat as the blaze sped through the room.

Memories cut into me. Searing pain. Not again! The ominous crackling of fire consuming everything around me. I have to get out. No escape. My neighbors block the doors and windows. Their cries, "Burn, witch! Burn!" echo in the night. The heat, the smoke...suffocating.

I cannot breathe. Dear Lord, the agony. "Elias where are you? Save me!"

For a moment, I froze. I covered my ears and shut my eyes as I had done that day. This time, though, I wasn't alone. The thud of a falling body brought me back to the present. The intruder lay on the ground. A spark caught at my blouse. I batted at it and bent over in a fit of coughing. I fought to find Elias in the blinding smoke. His voice had quieted. Where was he?

"Rebecca."

"I'm here." I hurried to him. The fire growled around us. "We have to get out."

He swept me into his arms and carried me from the hungry flames. Outside, he put me down. Where were we? I looked around in bewilderment. We'd stepped into an alien land—no meadows, no towering elms. I drew back at the sight of stone paths and great metal contraptions. "Nay, what place is this?"

*A voice unlike Elias answered, "*Move, now.*"*

As he thrust me forward, I clung to his arm to avoid a fall. He shoved me inside one of the fearsome monsters. I held my breath. The beast exploded in movement. It jerked us one way then the next in an attempt to devour us. I screamed and slid into darkness.

Chapter Thirty

"Ow!" My head and shoulder slammed against an unyielding surface. I came to in a car, speeding along Derby Street, headed toward the Willows. I tugged my seat belt and snapped it into place. When I turned to tell Sam to slow down, I choked on the words.

Eddie regarded me. "Rebecca?"

The name set off a wave of confusion. Rebecca's thoughts wove through my head. I opened my mouth to speak, but another's voice answered, *"I am here, yet I am not."*

Her terror became mine. This wasn't her world. What had Elias done? I fought the woman for control of my body. I wanted it back. Her terror won out, and she ceded command; she wanted no knowledge of our time.

I held on to the door as we raced ahead. "Rebecca is shocked and scared. She doesn't belong in this century. Neither do you."

He gave me a malicious grin. "Would you rather have Eddie?"

Terror ripped through me. I remembered the knife. I looked away in defeat. The predicted storm had arrived. Water ponded on the road. I sucked in my breath as the car skidded.

"You'll kill us driving this fast. Where are you taking me?" My insides twisted in horror as we flew past the House of Seven Gables.

"I want to talk to Rebecca. I sense her in there." He mumbled some foreign words, a kind of invocation, and issued a sharp command, "Rebecca, speak to me."

My identity faded. *"My love, I fear for our lives. What will this beast do with us?"*

"Fear not. You are safe with me, dearest. I am taking you to a special place. Had you lived, it is where you would have become my consort in the coven."

The car swerved as he smacked his hands against the steering wheel. “Would that I could kill those bastards once again for you.”

Rebecca’s essence faded, and I focused on the neighborhood. We raced toward the Willows. Maybe Eddie had a house there. We didn’t get that far. The car veered into Winter Island.

He muttered, “All is changed. No matter. We will find a place.”

We stopped at Execution Hill. What had he said? His coven? No wonder he was so strong. What resistance could I pose? Then I spotted a building, and a spurt of hope blossomed. I might be able to save myself if I got inside.

“This will do. Eddie tells me the cottage is vacant, and this storm should keep people away.”

Oh God. Was that monster still in there?

An image appeared in my mind. Rebecca, with her beautiful, raven hair and soulful eyes. She smiled and spoke to me. *“I have no wish to live in this strange world. We don’t belong here. Run.”*

When Elias leaped out of the car, I whipped open my door and took off.

An animalistic roar from behind urged me even faster. I sped away from him, my thoughts in turmoil. Was I losing my mind? It didn’t matter. Escape was imperative.

Spurred by the instinct to survive, I raced down the road. I splashed through puddles and hoped they didn’t hide holes. Thunder rumbled above me, and rain spattered my face. Wind gusts slammed against my exhausted body and slowed my flight. My chest heaved, and I coughed. How much farther to the main road?

His footsteps pounded in my ears. Closer, ever closer. Don’t look. Ignore them. I couldn’t. I twisted my head around. The lightning flashed and gave me a terrifying glimpse of his crazed features. Wet hair clung to his scalp and madness gleamed in his eyes. I gasped. My body shuddered, and I tripped. Propelled forward, I spread my arms to save myself, hit hard, and slid along the ground. Dirt and stones dug into my hands and knees. Blood seeped from my palms. I winced as I pushed myself up. Too late.

His howl of victory immobilized me, and I lost all strength to resist. I accepted my fate. He closed his hand around my hair and yanked me backward. I yelped as pain tore through my scalp.

“You cannot get away from me. You are mine. We will finish the spell, and I will have my Rebecca back.”

His fingers dug into my skin as he lifted me to my feet. No more chance of escape. He bent over, pressed his shoulder into my stomach, and tossed me up like a sack of grain. We lurched toward a grassy area, my head bouncing against his back. The sweet sound of sirens gave me hope. He paused then changed direction.

Stinging rain peppered my face. Lightning flashed and thunder roared above us. A heavy rumble, different from the ominous bolts in the sky, caught my attention—the crash of waves beating against the shore. Oh, no! The cliffs.

Strength fueled by desperation restored my courage. I fought to pull away from him. I pounded his back and yelled, "There's nowhere to go." Shouts from behind us gave me hope. I screamed, "Help!"

Elias never paused.

"Let me down. I'm not Rebecca."

He ignored me. We reached the bluff at the end of the road. Waves exploded. Clouds of spray filled the air. Salt stung my eyes and coated my lips. The wind roared around us.

Before us were mounds of stone, the outer rim like the jagged teeth of a salivating monster. He advanced to the closest precipice.

From my head down position, I had an intimate view of slimy, wet rocks.

When he slipped, I was terrified we'd crash together into the maelstrom below. He lost his balance and let go of me. I flung my arms out in time to save my head from slamming against the ground. I was close to the brink and sliding backward. My bottom half drifted toward the edge.

I scrabbled around for a crack or bulge in the cliff to hold on to. Pain erupted from my bloody palms. I scraped my feet along the rock face. Cold water splashed against me. When my sneaker found a crevice, I dug my foot into it and prayed. Icy rain beat against my fingers, numbing them. I clutched at clumps of grass. I couldn't hold on much longer. A few blades slid from my fist as my grip weakened. I screamed. I didn't want to die like this.

Strong hands encircled my wrists, and I relaxed my grip. Relief washed through me. I didn't know who my savior was. I prayed it was Sam.

Chapter Thirty-One

"Come," Elias commanded.

He dragged me after him, his eyes wild. The entity, like Eddie, was insane. Elias struggled forward, one fist clutching mine and the other grabbing at the rocks.

My breath came in spurts. I could only scream in my mind. To keep moving was certain death.

I slipped and caught myself. When I tripped and fell, he growled and jerked my arm. I expected to hear it pop out of its socket. In the distance Sam's voice called to me. I hoped he'd get to me in time.

When Elias stopped, I sat down, happy to rest. Until I looked around. We were at the end. Nothing left but angry ocean. My insides churned.

The crazed lunatic's gaze softened as he looked at me. Yearning evident in his voice, he said, "Ah, Rebecca. Speak to me."

I shook my head. "No. I'm Dani."

He shrieked. "We shall be together, if not in this life, then in death. This time you will not die alone, my love." He pulled me up and crushed me to him.

I thrashed my head from side to side. "I'm not Rebecca," I roared. "She's gone."

As I struggled, I gaped at the drama unfolding beneath us. I pictured my body tossed about as the waves smashed against the granite barrier. How long would I survive after the fall? Time enough to feel the water invade my mouth and slide into my lungs? How painful would it be when my body connected with the sharp, unforgiving spikes? Or would the waves be merciful and fling me hard enough into the ledge to crush my brain, allowing me to escape any more agony?

A sweet voice interrupted my misery. "Elias?"

He looked at me. "Rebecca?"

I tossed my head back and forth.

"Here," she said.

We both turned to see her, her raven hair streaming in the wind. Her beauty was awesome in the midst of the storm.

"Rebecca, my love."

In a second, Elias dropped me. I lost my balance but managed to fall forward. There were no handholds on the smooth surface. I slid toward the edge. My feet hung in the air. I screeched and clutched at some weeds on the side. I kicked my feet frantically trying for purchase. Each boom of the surf resounded in my chest. The rock shuddered beneath me.

I was too weary to call for help. My foot snagged on a slight bulge. I jammed my toe against it, prayed, and shoved. The leverage was enough to boost me up. I scrounged around until I found a jagged projection in the cliff. I grabbed onto it.

The temporary security of my perch gave me the courage to look at my abductor. What I witnessed will haunt me forever.

Rebecca, suspended above the churning violence, held her arms wide. "Come to me, Elias. Come to your lover."

The man, ghost, or demon wore a look of sheer joy on his face. He reached for his love. With Rebecca's name on his lips, he stepped off the ledge into her waiting embrace.

In that instant, she met my gaze, and I believe she smiled. Rebecca held him all the way down to the watery deathtrap below.

Bit by bit, I dragged myself forward until I could rest in safety. Sam found me there. He helped me to my feet and squeezed me to him. I became aware of big, gasping sobs. Mine. The image of Eddie's body slamming against the rocks below seared my brain.

People swarmed us. Questions came from all directions. I clung to Sam. Someone bandaged my hands. Then warm blankets and a siren.

Voices penetrated my foggy mind. "She's delirious, talking about ghosts."

I remember struggling. "He was a witch."

Gentle hands held me down. "Okay, lady. We believe you."

Someone held my arm. A pinch, then nothing.

~ * ~

I struggled to wake. Rebecca's terror clawed at my insides as she cried, "Help me."

"Easy, sweetheart. It's all right. Wake up." Sam's voice.

Tears dripped from my cheeks while Rebecca's memories played in my head. "She was in her twenties. Just a kid. They burned her, but she was under his spell."

The doctor found us like that. "What's going on here?" he said to Sam. "Who are you?"

"Her fiancé."

The doctor rolled his eyes and peered at me. "Would you like him to leave?"

I wiped my cheeks and hiccupped. "Fiancé?"

I attempted to sit up, but the doctor wouldn't let me. He was poking around to see if my heart was working, I guess. That happy little organ was doing fine. As a matter of fact, it swelled in my chest.

Sam walked around the doctor and brought my wrist to his lips, avoiding my bandaged hands. "I love you, Dani Trent, and I want to marry you."

My mind cleared fast. Love and excitement will do that. "You do?"

"I do."

"Oh, Sam. I love you too. I want nothing more than to spend my life with you."

The doctor was gracious enough to move over, so Sam could give me a proper kiss. I met his lips, eager to show him how much I loved him. When I moved my hands to his head, we both yelled, "Ow!"

The doctor clucked his tongue. "Better wait a while for that." He shook his head as he left. "I'll leave prescriptions for you at the desk. Oh…" He turned back, smiling. "Congratulations!"

I waved goodbye and focused on my fiancé. I took a good look at him—black eye, cuts on his face and arms, and a massive bandage on his head. "Eddie did this to you?"

"Most of it." He grinned. "I also had trouble with Rebecca."

"Rebecca?" Then I understood. "You mean me? I'm sorry. I couldn't help it."

A noise from the door interrupted us. Detective Lavoie. "How are you, Ms. Trent?"

"Much better, thank you." My mother would be so proud of my manners.

Lavoie acknowledged Sam before focusing his attention on me. "I hate to be the bearer of bad news, but the fire gutted your apartment. Everything in it gone—a total loss. The whole building is uninhabitable."

For a minute I mourned the destruction of everything I owned, then I remembered and tapped Sam's hand with my bandages. "The diary was in there. It's gone." The realization that I no longer had to fear that bastard and he would never be able to hurt anyone else eased the horror of the past few hours.

When Sam rubbed the back of his fingers across my cheek, I saw the relief on his face. I knew my terror was over.

"Sorry. I hope the book wasn't important," Lavoie said.

I smiled. "No. Not important at all."

"I'm glad," he said. "Now I need to ask you a few questions."

I didn't wish to answer them but nodded anyway.

Holding his pen above his notebook, he asked, "What did Eddie say about the murder?"

"Which one?" I hugged myself and bit my lip. "He killed Tom and the other woman, Allison. He wanted to add me and Heather to his list."

Detective Lavoie's pen sped across the paper, as I explained how Eddie had access to all the apartments. "He told me he stored his tools in the basement room under the apartment."

"Thanks. We'll check it out." He explained they'd found Eddie's knife and were confident it would prove to be the weapon that killed Allison. "I guess that's all for now." He clicked his notepad shut. "I'll want to talk to both of you again."

Before he left, I stopped him to ask about Heather and JoJo. "She's in serious condition, but I'm told she'll survive. Oh yeah. The little dog. Some woman from across the street took him. I think it was the same lady who told us about Westin chasing you."

"Mrs. W?" Once again, the woman had surprised me.

Sam chuckled. "I told you. She's something else."

"I may have to talk to you again, Ms. Trent. Glad to see you're okay."

After he left, I leaned back on my pillow, grateful we were alive. Sam sat next to me on the bed. "Heather can't have visitors yet. I'll take you there the minute she can."

"Thank you." I moved to rest my head in my hands. The bandages protecting my palms stopped me. "I can't believe how much trouble I've caused everyone."

"No, honey." He took me into his arms. "You didn't cause any of the problems. The chaos and insanity came from Eddie and the damned ghost."

"I'm sorry I believed Tom was behind it all."

"Wait a minute. I wouldn't wish him dead, but he put you through hell and would have hurt you given the chance. Don't make him out to be a saint, and remember, Eddie was a killer way before he met Elias."

A nurse poked her head into the room to tell me I was free to go home any time.

I scooted off the bed before Sam could help me. My head spun, and I panicked, afraid Rebecca was back. When he held me, my mind cleared. "I need a minute to get my bearings."

"Take whatever you need. I'll be here."

Warmth fluttered through me. Though I'd rather focus my attention on Sam, there was one more thing I needed to do. "Do you mind if we make a stop before we leave?"

"No problem."

"I'd like to talk to Serena. I introduced her to Elias, the reason she's in here."

"That might not be a wise move." he frowned. "Remember she didn't want to have anything to do with you?"

"Please. I need to talk to her."

When we reached Serena's room, I peeked inside. Machines hummed. Lights blinked. I wondered if I should come back later. I'd decided to leave when her head snapped in my direction. Her dark eyes widened for a minute. Her hand made a "stop" gesture. I backpedaled, until she relaxed and smiled. "It's okay. Come in. Both of you."

"I…I hate to disturb you."

"No. You're fine. I perceive a distinct change in your essence. Tell me what happened."

I explained all that had gone on after the party followed by the horror of the last few hours. When I finished, she nodded.

"I sensed a release of power." She paused and shuddered. "The entity had a substantial hold on this world. I can guess what must have happened. At the end, he used up most of his strength trying to control the strong personality he'd possessed. That diminished his hold on you and Rebecca. Then he lost his power base and had to deal with a strange world. In the end, though, the final emergence of his lost love gave him what he'd always longed for, and he was happy to join her."

She took a deep breath and closed her eyes. When she opened them, she smiled. "You're safe now. Elias died with Eddie. I've opened myself to the psychic ether. I can discern no sign of trouble. Not even a trace of evil."

Although Serena's pronouncement eased most of the terror and pain of the recent past, my anxiety reemerged when we arrived at Sam's apartment. The storm had passed, but the gusting wind caused an explosion of waves against the rocky shore. Stinging prickles of fear erupted across my skin. Saliva jammed in my throat. I skidded to a stop, pulling back from Sam.

The panic from the cliffs was still with me. As the surf pounded the coast, he recognized my terror and hurried us inside. He held me tight, captured my lips, then whispered against my face, "We can always move if the noise bothers you."

A surge of love for this man who'd stayed with me despite the supernatural danger threatened to overwhelm me. I leaned my head against his chest and wrapped my arms around him, being careful not to use my injured hands. "I'm okay. I'll get used to the sound. It might take a while."

"Okay sweetheart." He ruffled my hair.

"Ow! Damn it. Stop. Elias tried to pull the hair out of my head."

"Son of a bitch! I'm not sorry he's dead." He hugged me for a minute before dipping his head for another kiss.

My body responded.

He caressed my face. "I promise not to touch your hair again." Then he flashed me a devilish grin and whispered, "How's the rest of your body?"

Looking into those incredible blue eyes, I knew everything—absolutely everything—would work out.

Acknowledgements

So many people have contributed to the completion of this book. My husband, Paul, who believed in me when I didn't. My son, Paul, who sat up with me for ghostly discussions. My daughter-in-law, Dawn, my grandchildren, Tyler, and Vada. Patsy Peach, who walked with me all over the Salem neighborhoods. All the friends and family who have given me crucial feedback. Sisters in Crime and all the authors and writers, especially Dianne Herlihy, from Crime Bake conferences and Seascape who introduced me to a literary world of possibilities. I'm grateful to Cassie Knight, Kelli Keith, and Kat Hall at Champagne Book Group for all their help.

A special thanks goes out to my writing groups. The very first one online with Melissa Rader and Jayne Vasarhelyi. My Friday night friends from Peabody, Massachusetts who still cheer me on: Andrew Coyle, Liz DiFiore, Marc Feldman, Dianne Herlihy, Rachel Jylkka-Tesler, Lisa Pais, and Bryce Rammler-Young. Finally, the awesome group of writers I met when I moved to Florida: Michelle Caffrey, Robert Erickson, Beverly Jackson, Glenn Erik Miller, and Doug Williams. Without their painfully honest critiques and loving encouragement, this book would be nothing but a literary ghost.

About the Author

Margo Carey grew up near Salem, Massachusetts where tales of hauntings abound. She's a believer. Her childhood home had a benign nighttime walker and something darker that frightened her dog.

Trace of Evil combines her interest in all things ghostly, Salem's witch trials, and her memories of managing a senior living facility. Although Dani's narrative springs solely from Margo's own twisted imaginings, she loves to hear personal stories about encounters with the supernatural.

Margo's first writing attempt as a child was a murder mystery with her brother as victim and herself as sleuth. As she continued to write, something strange happened. Despite her plans, the supernatural slipped in. Finally, rather than fight her muse, she gave in to her pen's inclination, changed her genre to paranormal, and titled her website, My Haunted Pen.

Although this is her debut novel, she published a short horror piece, *Micah's Gift*, in Black Petals magazine. She is currently at work on her urban fantasy *Watcher* series introducing members of an ancient Templar Clan.

Today, she resides in Florida with her husband, an easily spooked black cat, a Maine Coon cat who talks a lot but keeps a low profile, and happily, no ghosts—yet!

Margo loves to hear from her readers. You can find and connect with her at the links below.

Website/Blog: https://www.margocarey.com
Facebook: https://www.facebook.com/margo.carey7
Linked In: https://www.linkedin.com/in/margocarey
Twitter: https://www.twitter.com/authmargocarey

Thank you for taking the time to read *Trace of Evil.* If you enjoyed the story, please tell your friends, and leave a review. Reviews support authors and ensure they continue to bring readers books to love.

And now for a look inside *A Taste of Evil*, a ghost story where a murdered woman is determined to find out who killed her and why by Christina Carlisle.

Julia Raymond doesn't know who murdered her, but she plans to stay around and find out.

Famous novelist Julia Raymond is found brutally murdered in the grounds of her estate in the English Lake District. Her death throws suspicion on her husband and sister, both of whom have reasons to want Julia dead.

The discovery of another vicious murder of a woman in nearby woods terrifies the close-knit community and police suspect the work of a serial killer who appears to be obsessed with Julia.

Unable to leave the scene of her crime, Julia's spirit watches as the police investigation gradually reveals her family's terrible secrets.

Chapter One

I didn't see who murdered me.

The impact was so sudden I failed to take a last gasp of air as a violent pressure around my neck forced my head back. I clawed at my throat and felt a thin wire cut into the tips of my fingers.

Staring at the trees above me, I kicked my legs aimlessly against the bench where I sat. The killer was quiet. I felt his bony wrists as I scratched frantically, then the softness of leather gloves. Gripping them, I could smell the pungent odor of good quality leather. He had come prepared to kill.

Making strange, guttural noises as I struggled for breath, vivid flashes of fun-fairs and laughing people danced before my eyes. They wore funny hats with Kiss-Me-Quick written across the brim.

~ * ~

Today was no different from my usual routine. I walked to the lake as I did most afternoons now that I had returned to my home in the English Lake District. The weather was warm with a breeze coming from the water causing small waves to slap arrogantly against the rocks at the bottom of the long, sloping lawns.

Placed at the edge of the lake were my comfortable chair and small iron table ready for me to begin work. I settled into place, my notebook and pen resting on the table. The sounds and smells of spring in full bloom enveloped me. This is where I write and dream with no one to disturb me. It is my sanctuary. Mind you, I put up with the occasional tourist boat loaded with sightseers that cruised by a few hundred yards from the shore making their way to the far end of Lake Windermere on their regular trips. The crackling of the tour leader's public address system echoes as a boat draws level, and his voice floats across the water toward me.

"On your left, ladies and gentlemen, is the beautiful home of the famous crime writer, Julia Raymond."

His voice vibrated as I withstood the scrutiny of a hundred pairs of curious, searching eyes. Some of the people waved, and I grinned and waved back.

The wind was stronger now, tearing at the pages in my notebook. I felt its strength on my face and my eyes began to water behind my sunglasses. Time to move. The wind would irritate and, besides, I would get sunburn here. Work would be impossible. I decided to go to my second favorite place.

The woods, a significant part of the estate, stretched along both sides of the huge lawn leading up to my house. Small pathways threaded their way through the undergrowth to open to glades covered with moss and clumps of primroses and bluebells. Every now and then, there was a tantalizing glimpse of the lake through the trees and here it was sheltered and cool.

The bench sat on the edge of one of the paths surrounded on three sides by flowering rhododendrons. Removing my shades, I settled again, notebook open on my knee. I was plotting my next novel, and the familiar bubble of excitement surged through me as I wrote notes at random.

To have this power to create was awesome. The fact that I had written five international best sellers and would be paid an advance of a million pounds for this next novel astounded me. But I never let on how unbelievable this seemed, not even to my family. I accepted my celebrity status and all of the trappings that went with it, as if it was my God-given right. No one knew that beneath my cool, sophisticated exterior was a vulnerable and insecure creature. That was my secret.

I didn't hear my killer and later puzzled over this, as did the detectives who worked on my case. Had I been so engrossed in my thoughts that I hadn't heard the footsteps of someone creeping through the trees? Did I miss the snapping of twigs and the sound of heavy breathing? The breeze was rustling the bushes around me but surely, I should have sensed that someone was there—felt their presence.

How could I be dead? I could see and hear and yes, smell. I was bewildered. Perhaps I was in the middle of a bad dream, a terrible nightmare. *Please, let me wake up.* I saw again the path through the woods and the bench where I'd sat. I stared with growing horror at my body sprawled across the seat, my face turned toward the sky.

I looked the same. Almost. I wore the same white sandals and flared green skirt which, in the struggle with my killer, had ridden up over my thighs. I hated that. It appeared promiscuous, as if offering an invitation to have sex. I wanted to pull it down and cover my legs. On my top, I wore a cream colored T-shirt.

I'd always been slim, perhaps even a little on the thin side and nothing had changed in these extraordinary last few seconds, or minutes, I didn't know which. Steeling myself, I looked at my face. It was grotesque. My eyes bulged, staring up, a strange milkiness tainting the blue.

Disgusted, I studied my gaping mouth. My tongue protruded to one side, fat and ugly like an over ripe plum. Around my throat, embedded into my skin, was the wire the murderer had used to strangle me.

So, this is how they will find me. The great Julia Raymond. What a story. What a joke! The media would have a field day and my book sales would shoot through the roof. What a pity I wouldn't be around to enjoy it.

Hesitating, I hovered over my dead body as the realization of what had happened set in. I'm sure that if I'd had a physical form in this new world, my legs would tremble with shock. I looked down and there was nothing. No hands to feel if I had a face. I was an entity who could hear, see, and smell. So this was what it was like to be dead. Now I know.

Was I visible in a mirror? Was I a wisp of smoke? Could other people see me? I could now sympathize with Patrick Swayze in the film *Ghost* when he was killed but lived on as a spirit. I looked around. There was no sign of my murderer and certainly no other ghosts. Only me, waiting—and for what? Why was my spirit still here? So many questions and no one to answer.

I checked the time on my watch, which was still on the left arm of my dead body. It was 3:00 PM. Only a few minutes had passed since my death. It was then I realized my spirit could move. I had been able to go forward to see my watch. I decided to test this new skill and eyeing the back of the bench, willed myself there. It worked. I hovered behind the bench looking at my corpse from a different angle. This is where the murderer had stood to commit his crime.

Again, I stared at my poor, contorted face. My skin had paled and taken on a fragility which was not unpleasant. If only my eyes weren't bulging and my tongue protruding. I wished I could physically adjust this horrible sight, but I was trapped in this strange spirit world. No one would worry about me for a couple of hours and then around 5:00 PM, Laura would stroll across the lawns carrying my usual gin and tonic. When she couldn't find me, she would walk into the woods heading for this place. She knew my routine so well.

I had an unhealthy desire to see her reaction to my body. Would she throw my drink into the air in shock and then yell and scream? Or was it only in my books that these sorts of reactions occurred? At least, I'd be able to tell whether she was the killer or not.

Who had murdered me? And why? The person was strong but he'd had the element of surprise when he attacked me. Also, I was at a disadvantage in a sitting position allowing him precious seconds to wind the wire around my throat and exert savage pressure on my windpipe.

I'd been garroted. I hate that word. It sounds so guttural and gruesome. I had used it as a form of death in a couple of my books, always with a sense of uneasiness. In my research and the plotting of novels, I had a lot to do with the police, forensic scientists, and pathologists. Their expertise was essential to the credibility of my writing and now I thought about some of the things they had taught me during the past seven years.

The killer had carried the piece of wire with him, the wire that was still buried in my neck with the ends tangled in my blonde hair. He knew my afternoon routine and I had walked into my death.

Leaving the analysis of how he had murdered me, I considered who would want me dead and whether the killer was male or female. I'm only too aware that I can be very difficult, and that I'm known for my eccentric sense of humor. I prefer to call it quirky, perhaps a little too offbeat at times. Also, I have often been told by my husband that I can be insensitive to peoples' feelings but surely, I wasn't wicked enough for someone to kill me?

I thought about the people in the house. My family, my agent, Laura, and our housekeeper, Shirley. Could one of them have murdered me? No. It wasn't possible. They needed me.

They loved me.

Chapter Two

I waited and waited hoping I would wake and end this hideous nightmare, or for someone to discover my body. After all, I owed it to myself to be there when it happened.

A fly hovered around my face—my dead face, that is, and I wished I had hands to shoo it away. Pesky thing. I knew something about forensic entomology and those ten minutes after a body dies and is left in the open air, the flies arrive and lay thousands of eggs in the mouth, nose, and eyes of the corpse. Yikes!

I waited some more. Glancing at my watch, I could see it was almost 5:00 PM. Not long before Laura, or someone, brought my usual drink and they would discover my body. My skin had taken on a waxy, almost translucent look and my lips and nails had paled. Rigor mortis would set in after three or four hours, but until then my poor, useless limbs would feel warm to the unlucky person who first examined me.

What were the others doing? Were they all in the house? That's where I had left them when I had walked across the front lawns three hours ago. Laura had been working in the study on an edit for her other client. She only has two of us as I'm pretty much a full-time job. My husband, Mike, had been practicing his golf swings on the backyard.

I shifted to the other side of the bench and continued to stare at my body. There was something fascinating about seeing yourself in death, although I had to admit to feeling rather protective. I hoped they would be gentle when they found me. A thought occurred to me. I'll be able to attend my own post mortem. Awesome. My thoughts inside my spirit brain were becoming more bizarre by the moment.

Deciding to leave my corpse for the time being, I successfully floated along the path through the woods and on to the lawns with a clear view of the lake. Another tourist boat was passing, and I could hear the tour leader telling the passengers about the famous Julia Raymond who lived in that big mansion.

"Yoo hoo. I'm here," I tried to yell but, unfortunately, this spirit doesn't possess a voice. I was avidly curious as to whether they could see me, even as a ghostly presence, but the boat chugged on by and there were no pointing fingers or terrified screams from its human cargo.

Turning, I looked over the grass to the marble steps leading to the house. The main door was open so if my thought transfer process worked, I should be able to go in. I moved across the yard a few feet above it, up the steps and into the entrance hall. This method of travel was working well. My next feat was to turn so I could see myself in the large mirror which hung above the dresser on the left of the hallway. If I had a body, my heart would be racing with expectation.

I faced the mirror expecting to see at least a misty, feminine shape. But nothing. Nada. I couldn't quite believe it and not sure whether I was disappointed or not, I moved as close as I could to the mirror. Still nothing. Thinking from side to side, I did a little dance in front of it, a rather mean rumba, if I do say so. Uh, uh. I was invisible.

Still, this had advantages. I could spy on people and find out who had murdered me and hopefully why. It was the ultimate in voyeurism and certainly beat those awful reality shows on television. So far, I knew I could see and hear and smell…and I could move around. Not bad for a dead woman. All I needed was the sky to open and a white light to shine and guide me upward, accompanied by a choir of heavenly angels. Then I could piss off out of here. Isn't that what was supposed to happen?

Cruising along the passage, I floated to the kitchen door, which was shut. What now? Could I go through closed doors and walls? Patrick Swayze could in Ghost, but then that was a movie. This was real life, or rather, real death. I could hear voices on the other side of the door and closing my eyes, thought hard and found myself in the kitchen looking at Laura and Shirley. It worked. Fantastic.

Laura was pouring herself a cup of coffee while Shirley swirled a dark mixture around in a cooking basin which she balanced on the kitchen bench. I sniffed the air. Hmm, chocolate cake, my favorite. That was another point. When and how did I get to eat and drink and perform other bodily functions? The message was becoming pretty clear. No body—no bodily functions. No eating Shirley's chocolate cake and sipping a G & T and certainly no doing the crossword in the toilet. Crap!

I rested on a chair at eye level with Laura as she sat at the kitchen table and dunked a biscuit into her coffee.

"Did you enjoy your walk?" Shirley asked as she poured the cake mix into a greased tin, smoothing the top with a large, flat knife.

"Yes, it was lovely. I went into Branfield but it was very

crowded so I walked back through the lanes instead of the main road. That's the trouble with holiday weekends, there are so many visitors." Laura sipped her coffee, and I studied her. Early fifties, short,

blonde hair graying at the temples, a pleasant face with hazel eyes, light make-up…and as butch as they come.

~ * ~

She was very much a closet lesbian and, as far as I knew, had only one love—me. I'm heterosexual although I have no problem with people who prefer same sex relationships. Didn't make me any less shocked when Laura declared her love for me about a year ago. She had been my agent for two years prior to that and had hidden her sexual preferences very well. I knew she was divorced from her husband, Jimmy, and there hadn't been any kids from the marriage.

At the time of her declaration, I had been frantically working on a deadline to finish the final edit of *Death Comes Softly*. Hmm, always thought that was a good title. It could certainly apply to my own murder.

Anyway, Laura had traveled north for the weekend to see if I needed any help. She lives in London but spent a lot of her time with me in the Lake District and had become part of my small, loyal family. I *didn't* need help. I *rarely* needed help when it came to writing my books. She had been annoying the hell out of me, twitching and fidgeting as she stood at my elbow, and I tried to study the words on my computer screen.

Exasperated, I turned to her. "Oh, for Christ's sake, Laura. You are driving me mad. Piss off."

I glared furiously at her and then hesitated at the strange look in her eyes. How can I explain it? Lovesick, I guess. Huge cow-like, lovesick eyes gazing back at me. Her chin shook and tears began to well.

I hesitated but decided to keep up my tough attitude. Laura was very much a drama queen. "Look, what is your problem? I need you to give me some space."

Then she said it, stumbling slightly over the words. "I…love you, Julia." Her face softened, and her hand stroked my hair. "I've loved you for a long time, *really* loved you, and I can't keep it to myself any longer. I even left Jimmy because of you."

I was astonished as I saw the sudden passion flare in her eyes as she moved to hold me. I pushed my chair back in a state of panic and stared at her as everything she'd said registered in my befuddled brain which, moments ago, had been grappling with a fictional, bloody murder.

Suddenly I was very nervous and didn't know what to say. To cover up, I made the mistake of giggling. I knew I shouldn't have. I couldn't help it and instantly regretted my lack of skill in handling the awkward situation. This poor, lonely woman had just declared her undying love for me—*me*, who couldn't even cope with her own love life.

Then I'd made matters worse. "Honestly, this is silly, Laura. You need to live your life, not hang around me," I'd said, holding my hands up as if to defend myself.

She had stood there, stiff with outrage at my perceived lack of sensitivity. "I suppose you'll want me to resign as your agent now." Then she seemed to crumble, her eyes downcast and more tears on her lashes.

I was mortified for the dear woman in her obvious distress and gave her a quick hug, rubbing her upper arms in what I hoped was a comforting gesture. "No, of course, I don't want you to resign, Laura. But really, I love you as a friend. I'm sorry I can't reciprocate your feelings but you should know that I like men, and I'm very happy with Mike. I'm not into lesbian relationships."

She looked up then, her expression sad. "I understand and I'm sorry to embarrass you. Please don't tell anyone about this."

Of course, I did but only Mike. I told him that night. Only he didn't think it was sad or funny. In fact, he was bitterly jealous.

"Get rid of her," he demanded. "She's sick."

I didn't get rid of her. She was a great agent and it suited me to keep her on. I never told anyone else about Laura's secret and whether Mike did or not, I don't know. He was very cool toward her but pleasant enough. As the weeks went by, things returned to normal, except for the odd times when I would catch her staring at me with a strange, indefinable longing on her face. Other times, her expression was full of hatred. I did my best to ignore both looks.

~ * ~

Laura finished her coffee and replaced the cup in the saucer with a clatter. "Well, I've had my fresh air and caffeine shot. I'd better get back to this edit."

Shirley wiped her hands on the cloth she always wore attached to her apron. "Are you going to take Julia's drink to her?" She loaded a piece of wood into the Aga's furnace. "It's gotten cold in here all of a sudden," she added.

Laura shivered. "Yes, it has. The sun will be going down before long. I'll let you do the honors for Julia today. I need to catch up on my work."

I registered two points. They had both felt cold suddenly. Did that mean it was true what I had read about the air temperature dropping in the presence of ghosts? If so, that was good. I quite liked the idea of having that power. Secondly, Laura had opted out of delivering my evening G & T. Was that because she knew what was waiting to be discovered in the woods?

"You've got mud on your shoes."

Another clue. I looked down at Laura's black sneakers. Sure enough there was mud around their edges. Could that be from walking in the woods? They had left several dirty smudges on Shirley's pristine floor.

"Oh, sorry. It's reasonably dry outside, but I stepped in a couple of puddles."

"Give them here and I'll clean them for you."

Laura obediently removed her shoes and handed them to Shirley. "Where's Mike?" she asked.

Shirley rolled her eyes expressively. "Do you need to ask?"

Nodding her head in some kind of acknowledgement, Laura opened the kitchen door and left. I was puzzled. What had that look between them meant? Had Mike's reputation as a rotten golfer become the talk of the house now?

I watched as Shirley busied herself in her favorite room, checking the temperature of the Aga, washing up the cooking utensils she had used to mix the cake and then...cleaning Laura's shoes. *You are destroying possible vital evidence, old girl.*

Deciding I had time to hunt Mike down before Shirley made the big discovery of my body, I willed myself through the back door and onto the lawn. There was no sign of him, although two of his clubs lay in the grass along with a dozen or so golf balls.

I returned to the house, pleased that I was negotiating my travel technique so well. As I wandered from room to room, there was still no sign of Mike. Laura was seated in the study engrossed in a manuscript. She looked up as I passed. I thought for a moment she could see me but she reached for her jumper on the back of the chair and pulled it on. It must be true—this cold phenomena.

Mike wasn't in our bedroom either. Everything looked normal and tidy. Shirley had changed the linen today, and I sat on the huge, king size bed enjoying the smell of the lemon-scented sheets. I couldn't resist peering into the large cheval mirror opposite the bed. Perhaps, by some sort of miracle, I was now visible. Once again, I was disappointed. Not even as much as an aura to cheer me up.

Well, I would see what my big sister, Cathie, was up to, I decided as I moved along the passage to the west wing which was her domain. She never let anyone in there normally, even preferring to clean it herself. I stopped and looked around her pleasant, but stark, sitting room.

Where the hell was she? Cathie rarely went out at weekends, except to take long walks and commune with nature. For the rest of the time she kept to herself and, when she wasn't working in her role as a nurse in nearby Kendal, she hid away in this room, reading romances or watching soaps on television.

I could hear her voice coming from the bedroom. I listened at the door, nervous about going in. Cathie was always so particular about her privacy. Then I realized she couldn't see me. Great. I listened again.

"Come on, big boy. Really give it to me."

Big boy? Give it to me? What was going on? I thought my way into the bedroom landing at the side of Cathie's bed. She lay there naked, her mouth open as she yelled in the throes of an orgasm. On top of her, heaving and thrusting his 'big boy' into my sister, was my missing husband.

I would have known that ass anywhere.

What's next on your reading list?

Champagne Book Group promises to bring to readers fiction at its finest.

Discover your next fine read!
http://www.champagnebooks.com/

We are delighted to invite you to receive exclusive rewards. Join our Facebook group for VIP savings, bonus content, early access to new ideas we've cooked up, learn about special events for our readers, and sneak peeks at our fabulous titles.

Join now.
https://www.facebook.com/groups/ChampagneBookClub/

Made in the USA
Middletown, DE
09 August 2023